▲▲▲▲▲▲▲▲▲▲

PICKIN' GROUND

▲▲▲▲▲▲▲▲▲▲

JEANETTA BRITT

TWELVE STONES
▲▲▲▲▲▲▲▲▲▲
PUBLISHING
DALLAS • TEXAS

This is a work of fiction. The events described here are imaginary; the settings and characters are fictitious and not intended to represent specific places or persons.

Copyright © 2003 by Jeanetta Britt

All rights reserved. No part of this book may be reproduced or utilized in any form by any means, electronic or mechanical, including photocopying, recording, or by any information storage or retrieval system, without permission in writing from the Publisher.
Inquiries should be addressed to J Britt Davis
(jbrittdavis@hotmail.com)
Twelve Stones Publishing
P. O. Box 763066, Dallas, TX 75376-3066
www.poemsfromthefast.com

Library of Congress Control Number: 2002094320
ISBN 0-9712363-3-X

Printed in the United States
First Edition

Cover Design: Larry Powell & Associates, Inc.
Acknowledgements: Barry Davis; Naomi Dixon; Tommie Emery Davis Glorias Dixon; Fairrene Carter-Frost; Carol Allen, PhD; Ethel Morgan Smith, PhD; Diane Morton Moorman, PhD

UNRAVELING—Part II

…But I have comfort in knowing
   Death is but a door
     To the mansions up in heaven
     My Father has in store.
                Lottie

CHAPTER 1.
▲▲▲▲▲▲▲▲▲▲▲▲

Lottie pulled the drapes to block out the skyline her office shared with the other penthouses in downtown Manhattan. Usually she liked the view--it was a far cry from her humble beginnings--but not tonight. Tonight, she just wanted to hear from Raymond.

Earlier in the day he had left her a hastily scribbled note, "Urgent! Don't leave here until we discuss the Sinclair file!" But that was hours ago. Now it was nearly midnight. *This is not like Raymond. He never writes notes. He eats and sleeps E-mail. And where is he? He's a calendar slave. No way he'd miss an appointment. I don't get it, and I'm not leaving this spot until I do.*

As she waited, Lottie floated fluidly between the past and the present. Here she was a country girl from the South having the privilege to do what she had always wanted, and in New York City, too. She smiled contentedly as the thought fluttered by, but the telephone rang and startled her back to reality. It reminded her of Raymond and the tension rose in her neck again. Deftly, she scrambled for the phone in the dark.

"Hello!" she nearly shouted, attempting to beat the answering machine. "Beck and Associate."

"Hi, yourself. Catch you napping?"

"Raymond? No! Where are you?"

"Little testy, are we? Having to stay a little later than usual?"

"No. No. I just didn't know where you were; that's all. Where are you?"

"That's not important right now, Lottie. I need your help. Just listen!" he said, stifling her budding questions with the sharp edge in his voice. "Look in the file room and pull all the 'CL' files. Then get out of there. Get out of there as fast as you can. And Lottie. . . watch your back, Sweets."

"Wha--" she questioned, simultaneously with the click on the other end. She glared at the phone as though it had betrayed her. Bewildered,

she shook her head to summon her wits. She flicked on the overhead lights and checked her watch--11:58 p.m. *Raymond, you're scaring me. I'm outta here--and fast.*
 Lottie's movements were swift and methodical. Her efficient nature seemed to surface under pressure. She located the soft brown leather briefcase she adored. It had been her first purchase after landing this job. Since the job made her feel like a big city executive, she wanted to look the part, too. She knew her files intimately. She stuffed them into her briefcase and quickly shut the drawer. She locked the cabinet along with all the others, wheeled out of the file room, and locked the door behind her.
 She quickly scanned the office and caught a glimpse of something she hadn't noticed before--a piece of white paper poking from under the sofa near the glass-topped coffee table. She spun across the room and collected what was a business card. *Hmm. . . Clayburn & Clayburn Investments? That sneaky Raymond. Doing business with the competition behind my back. Wonder what else he's holding out on? This is all too bizarre!*
 Stuffing the card into her tailored jacket, Lottie resumed her speedy exit. She grabbed her

leather coat from the brass rack and tightened the belt around her waist to ward off the icy chill stealing into her bones. The rich mink collar felt good against the knot growing in her neck.

As she finished her preparations for departure, Lottie's eyes swept the room, almost as though she'd never see it again. It wore a signature quality of elegance, assuring clients that their needs would be catered to and their interests well served. Two desks of sturdy whitewashed pine, one large and one small on opposite ends of the room, expressed the dichotomy that existed there. Lottie and Raymond--Raymond and Lottie--one with broad-based public appeal, the other more suited to the details, but like opposite ends of a weighted scale, both indispensable to the equilibrium of this highly successful investment firm.

Prompted to meet her deadline, she hurriedly switched on the soft glow of the brass lamp on her desk and flicked off the overhead lights, a nightly ritual signaling her departure. At the door, she whispered a silent prayer and edged cautiously into the hallway. It occurred to her that prayer had once been very important in her life; although, she hadn't seen the inside of a church since she arrived in the city over ten years before. And oddly enough, at that improbable moment, a childhood memory flashed across her mind. It was of her mother, Miss Charity, praying for her family at their old kitchen table.

Lottie shrugged off the vivid image that threatened to throw her off schedule. She closed the office door firmly behind her and listened for the click of the lock. She scurried to the elevator, which responded promptly to her signal, jumped inside its mirrored walls and jabbed the *P2* and *Close Door* buttons. Relief flooded her when the gleaming doors closed and she was left to plunge into the bowels of the skyscraper to her car.

As she descended, Lottie opened the side flap of her briefcase to check for the small blade knife she kept hidden there. She touched the sheath in which it nested and patted the pocket approvingly. Carrying a knife was a precaution she had adopted as a teen. The terrors of urban school life are widely touted, but it had been her experience that attending high school in rural Alabama was even tougher. Her knife had been her equalizer.

The elevator doors opened on P2 in the underground garage. Lottie checked her watch--12:08 a.m. She strode toward her custom Lexus, the color of old money; her gait steady and deliberate. She kept her eyes moving--back, front, side to side, her senses on full alert.

Drawing closer, she double clicked the remote clutched in her clammy left hand and engaged the engine. As it idled, she picked up the pace of her cat-like surveillance. She inspected underneath the car before popping the locks. In a single motion, she hopped in, pitched her briefcase to one side, and snapped the locks shut. Gunning the engine, she squealed out of the garage, laying a trail of tire rubber behind her.

Above ground, Lottie's head was spinning dizzily and her brain felt like mush. She cracked her window and inhaled deeply. The night air cooled her sweaty brow and felt liberating to her nostrils. She was grateful to be on her way home. Raymond's warning was still ringing in her ears. "Watch your back, Sweets," he said. *'Sweets,' indeed? He only calls me that when he's frustrated or short-tempered and trying to camouflage it.* Her face surrendered to an involuntary smile when she recalled the first occasion he tagged her with the label.

▲▲▲▲

The first time Lottie laid eyes on Raymond was when he graced Max's Diner where she worked part-time as a waitress. She didn't know his name, but he bore the clean-cut, well-dressed marks of a successful executive in his budding thirties. Given his distinguished-looking six-foot-plus frame and athletic build, she marveled that he hadn't picked one of the more trendy eateries, which boasted of bottled spring water and organic sprouts, to *do* lunch. Instead, he traded the aroma of filet mignon for the odor of chicken fried steak. She assumed he either was humoring himself by patronizing the only retro diner in Manhattan's financial district, or he was ensuring his anonymity by mingling with folk who were far more impressed by a steaming plate of meatloaf than his net worth.

After her first sighting, Lottie noticed he came into the diner several times a week, around the ebb of the noon rush, and mounted a stool at the far end of the chrome-plated counter. He kept to himself and spoke to no one, save Max the owner, who he signaled for his usual fried chicken-caesar salad. He hovered over handwritten charts and graphs until his coffee grew stale; oftentimes crumpling in frustration the ideas he scribbled on napkins and scraps of paper.

His hieroglyphics were hardly intelligible to the untrained eye, but as Lottie passed back and forth to the kitchen, she recognized he was struggling to develop investment profiles. With her God-given talent for the computer, she could picture splashy color graphics for his disjointed data in much the same way as a gifted musician visualizes fine lyrics for a catchy tune. Her summers at the community college back home had paid off.

▲ ▲ ▲ ▲

Lottie's hometown was a sleepy, little agricultural community in rural Alabama, tucked away where the state's southeastern crease borders Florida and Georgia, and where license plates proudly sport the *Heart of Dixie*. Union City was a town where King Cotton had once ruled and where the privileged offspring of that heyday had struggled ever since to define their existence without it. Words like mansion, plantation, and ante-bellum were loosely strung together to conjure up images of money and respectability, when in fact only a few of the remaining founding families possessed it.

Lottie's love for computers dated back to her high school days. From the very first time she touched a keyboard, she was a natural. She had a ravenous appetite to learn more and worked odd jobs after school her sophomore year to purchase her own computer. She poured over books and manuals to learn on her own and spent her summers at the local community college pursuing her passion.

She attended Lurleen B. Wallace Community College, one of the many named for the former governor of the State of Alabama during her brief tenure. She became governor in 1966 when her husband, George C., was no longer eligible to seek office after his first term. "Shucks," some townsfolk would say, "Lurleen only started them schools just to prove George wasn't no monster when he stood in the doorway of the University of Alabama and faced down Federally-mandated desegregation in 1963."

But despite the twenty-year interval since the Wallace era, a remnant of the die-heart separate-but-equal faction remained in tact in Union City, tying up the social and political fabric and stripping away the economic vitality of the community. By 1986, the summer before Lottie's senior year in high school, it was to the point that skilled, high-paying jobs for young people her age were all but non-existent.

It was also the summer Lottie's daddy was killed in a freak sawmill accident. Her older sister, Rose, had been so devastated by their father's tragic death she found it impossible to remain in the family home. With their mother's consent, Rose moved away right after the funeral and found a job four hours away in Macon, Georgia, leaving Lottie to fend alone.

"But Mamma!" Lottie had objected strenuously. "It's my senior year. I can't leave Lincoln and transfer 'cross-town to Jim Folsom High just 'cause you work at the Poteet Mansion. I'll have to leave all my friends. I'd miss my senior trip! Rose got to go on her senior trip. But you and daddy always did love her best—"

"Gal, don't speak ill of yo' daddy. He dead."

"But why can't I just come home alone--"

"You'll do no such thing, Lottie Mae," Miss Charity bellowed. "You'll do what I say. You'll come to the mansion every day after school. And that's that."

"But I'm nearly eighteen--"

"That's that!"

During those incredibly lonely days without her daddy or Rose around, the computer became Lottie's escape hatch from the sadness that threatened to overtake her. Its cold companionship and her fervent prayers were her only solace. She couldn't unload her burdens on her mother; she was tending to her own grief. So that summer while other girls her age were dating, in hopes of finding a husband to care for them after graduation, Lottie hid away in her room for hours, melding with her computer and perfecting her skills.

▲▲▲▲

"Don't you like computers, sir?" Lottie inquired of the man on the first occasion Max had signaled her to serve his fried chicken-caesar salad.

"What's it to you, *Sweets*," he said, obviously having a particularly difficult time collecting his data.

"My name is Lottie."

"Hmph." He fumbled with his notes.

"Lottie Garrett."

Raymond looked up from his work and glared at her. "And what do you want of me, *Ms. Lottie Garrett?*" he said in such a way as to emphasize that besides being at least ten years his junior, she was neither his social nor intellectual equal. Motioning to the mass of scraps on the counter, he said, "As you can see, I am *quite* busy." He lowered his crown of jet-black hair and returned to work.

"*Quite.* Have it your way." Having been in the city only a few months, Lottie was easily put-off by what she termed, *legends in their own minds*--people with high-minded ways, puffed-up egos, and little regard for the feelings of others. *That's what I get for trying to help him.* Her hands twitched with anger, and she jammed them into her apron pockets. *Wait 'til I see Mr. Big-Shot again, I'll show him a thing or two.*

CHAPTER 2.
▲▲▲▲▲▲▲▲▲▲▲

"Whew! Thank God for anti-lock brakes." Lottie's heart pounded as she skidded through the intersection at William Street. A light drizzle had begun to fall. *I don't know what Raymond's been up to, but I do want to get home in one piece.* When the traffic light turned green, she ducked onto the side street, checking for suspicious vehicles that might follow her.

Never before had a Manhattan street seemed so deserted. It was a mass of dark shadows and parked cars. The sound of leaves crunching under her tire treads gave her the *willies*, like the opening scene of a horror movie. She tore out of there for the Washington Bridge like she was the next victim of a chainsaw murderer.

Lottie anted-up at the tollbooth and headed home to Stamford, Connecticut. As she settled down into her routine drive, her mind drifted back to her early beginnings with Raymond.

▲ ▲ ▲ ▲

Several weeks after her first encounter with *Mr. Big-Shot*, he came into the diner and sat in his usual spot. When he signaled Max for his order, Lottie responded and poured his black coffee while he reviewed his notes with deep concentration. Alongside his cup she positioned a transparent folder and strolled nonchalantly to the kitchen.

The folder caught Raymond's eye and he paged through it. It contained a simulated investment portfolio with typeset-quality text, a flashy layout and color graphics. From her concealed vantage point, Lottie watched as he scrawled something on the first page and slapped the folder shut. He gulped his coffee, dropped coins on the counter, and made a hasty retreat.

A few minutes later, Lottie casually sauntered back to the counter to retrieve the coins and her work. She could hardly contain her curiosity. "What?" she nearly screamed. "A+! Who does he think he is? Grading me? That's it Mr. Big-Shot. You win! Give me a predictable Pentium processor and a weirded-out computer jock over an uncivilized, pompous *suit* any day of the week." She stabbed her portfolio into her apron pocket and stalked off to the kitchen.

▲▲▲▲

Lottie turned aside from her musings at Chapman Lake, the halfway mark to her subdivision in Stamford. She tuned her radio to an easy listening station and looked forward to getting into her flannel pajamas under her warm fuzzy blanket. She sang along with, *Love, Lust, and Lies*, a ballad that had been a hit on the diner's jukebox. When she thought about it, her *Diner Days* hadn't been so bad. Max had been a fair boss, and the work had given her the opportunity to pursue her college degree.

▲▲▲▲

When her daddy died the summer before her senior year, Lottie had consoled herself with the thought of getting her associates degree in computer science from Wallace Community College. But, *the incident*, which occurred one bright spring day three weeks before her graduation from Folsom High, changed all that; stripping her faith to the bone, like the debarker machine at the sawmill that had killed her daddy.

She stood up her date, Chaney Masters, who had waited over two years to take her to the senior prom. She shunned her friends at Lincoln High who were trying to work her into their senior plans. She couldn't tell Miss Charity about *the incident*, nor could she bear lying to her mother by not telling her the truth. By graduation day, the strain was too much. The very next day, Lottie packed her bags, counted her cash--the $557 she'd stashed under her mattress for the senior trip--and traded it in for a bus ticket to New York City.

She didn't tell Miss Charity good-bye. She couldn't face her. *After all, ain't it Mamma who's always saying, "Prayer without action is a pity party that don't give God his due?"* Her good friend, Ruth Ann Wade, had also taken off for New York right after high school the year before. Lottie counted on bunking in with her until she got on her feet.

Ruth Ann's big-city ways annoyed Lottie from the moment she set foot in her messy apartment in The Bronx in the summer of 1987. She feasted on a constant diet of rap, hip-hop, and men. Lottie muzzled her disapproval, though, because she was highly appreciative of Ruth Ann's freehanded way and her open-ended hospitality. Realizing she was short on cash, Ruth Ann didn't ask her to pay rent, nor did she set a time limit for her stay. Out of her immense gratitude, Lottie rationalized that Ruth Ann was basically the same sweet girl she'd always known, so what was a little bump-didee-bump-and-grind between friends? But living with Ruth Ann had fanned the flame under her job hunt. Lottie longed for the day she could move out on her own and enroll in college for the fall semester. Nearby Columbia University was her choice, if only they would pick her, too. She wasn't content, however, to live, study, and work within a stone's throw of Harlem. She wanted to expand her borders downtown so she'd have the proper exposure when her *BIG* career break came along.

On her way to barrage the heart of Manhattan's financial district for the third day in a row, Lottie stopped off at a classic little diner on Church Street. She wanted to load up on cheap carbs to bolster her job-hunting frenzy to follow. She was beginning to get a little antsy about her prospects. It seemed every firm wanted local references and college certificates for their entry-level computer programmer jobs.

When it came her turn to be seated, Lottie picked the only remaining booth and sat there for a long time before a bountiful woman in her fifties, with *big hair* and a Texas drawl, came over to take her order. It was the noon rush and the place was a madhouse. Plates and hash were slinging in every direction with only the guy behind the cash register and the lone waitress to fend off the masses.

"This is not my order," Lottie said to the guy behind the register. "And it's not my order for the third time in a row! I'm in a real big hurry, Mister. I've got to get back to . . . my name is Lottie Garrett." She sputtered, eyes flashing. "You need help, and I need a job. I'm no waitress . . . but I'm sure-footed, organized, and honest."

"I'm Max. Max Hampton," the beefy guy at the register said, halting his counting. Her final word had won the hard fought battle for his attention. The lack of honest help was what had left him shorthanded. "If you help us out today and your price is fair, you've got yourself a deal."

The customers loved Lottie right off because she was pleasant, straightforward, and quick. Unlike the other waitress, Marcie, who was temperamental at times, Lottie provided the haggard mid-level managers a predictable, cookie-cutter lunch experience and they tipped her approvingly. Their hefty tips went a long way toward funding her college dreams.

Despite their personality differences, Lottie and Marcie got along famously from the start. On the first day Max brought her into the fold, Lottie gave Marcie her tips as a goodwill gesture. And Marcie, though hardened by years of big city life, "took kindly to that." As it turned out, she was Max's first cousin from Dallas, and the three of them made a pretty good team. Marcie encouraged Lottie's college dreams, and Lottie covered her slack.

"When do you break for fun, Sugar?" Marcie teased.

"School. . . diner. . . if I'm going to get it all in, not much time left."

"Well, you've always gotta make time for fun, Little Lady. Come by my house any night of the week and me and my friends we'll show you a real good time. All work and no play . . . you know what they say 'bout that?" Marcie added an extra dash of hot sauce to her strut. "Bet nobody ever accused us o' being dull. Y'all come on by any time, now; you hear."

CHAPTER 3.
▲▲▲▲▲▲▲▲▲▲▲▲

Headlights on I-95 closed in behind Lottie and the back of her neck bristled. She swung into the right lane and snapped around in the driver's seat for a better look. Bright lights blinded her as they zoomed pass. She smiled a sleepy smile, content with reviving pleasant memories. Exit 514.

She read her street sign aloud, "Golden Trophy," rolling it off her tongue. Although she had been taken with the entire neighborhood when she first discovered it, she had chosen this particular street for its regal name. She pulled into her front circular driveway and parked between her prized pom-pom cedars. No rear entry three-car garage for her tonight. The lights were dim back there and Raymond's weird phone call had left her a little too spooked.

Lottie killed the engine and stepped onto the driveway, briefcase in tow. Its weight confirmed Raymond's files were inside. She engaged her alarm and palmed the remote, digging her hands deep into her pockets to bundle against the cold rainy drizzle. Her flannel pajamas awaited.

Something wasn't right. She wasn't sure if it was the unfamiliar shadows that fell across the front door, or merely the cold uneasiness stealing back into her gut, but she sensed something was out of place. Her front door was slightly ajar. She hesitated, resisting the impulse to run. Slowly, reluctantly, she pushed against the front door, her wobbly legs protesting at her insistence. The door creaked open enough for her to peek into the room, and the soft light from the lamp in the foyer confirmed her worst fears. Her heart melted at the sight.

The white leather sofa she had found on her trip to Italy was violently slashed and flipped onto its side. Picture frames were stripped from their places and smashed to the floor. The black lacquered doors to her study swung limply on their hinges, and spikes of broken stained glass littered the art deco rug that covered the gleaming hardwood floors. Books and papers were strewn from their places like discarded

confetti, and her cherished crystal angel collection was lying in a grotesque heap.
 Just as her better judgment kicked in, Lottie bolted from the door, but a massive, hairy arm grabbed her from behind. She willed herself to scream, but her parched throat was paralyzed with fear. The masked man towered over her; his hot, pungent breath showering down on her like a smelly smoke stack. The stench of his sweat stung her nostrils and sickened her stomach. "Hee, hee, hee, hee." He whinnied like a wild stallion; his high-pitched laughter swelling an octave each time he increased the chokehold around her slender neck. Tighter and tighter he squeezed until her eyes bugged out.
 As she felt herself slipping into unconsciousness, Lottie's inner voice exhorted her to action. She kicked and squirmed, fighting like a woman possessed, but her strength was no match for his. Repeatedly, she aimed her knee for his groin, until at last she landed a grazing blow. For a split second he loosened his grip. One-handedly, she groped in her briefcase and located her short blade knife. In that horrible moment her mind went blank, until she felt a trickle of warm blood on her cheek and heard a man howling like a wounded animal.

She felt herself running to her car as though it were an out-of-body experience--hands glued to briefcase and knife. Her feet slipped on the crushed stone that paved the driveway, but somehow she managed to steady her bolting stride beneath her. She unlocked the car, jumped in, and gunned the engine. She peeled out of the driveway, leaving a stream of white rocks flying in her wake.

When Lottie came to herself, she flung her bloody knife to the floor on the passenger side and pried her fingers loose from the handle of her briefcase. Despite her besieging tremors, she managed to reposition the rear-view mirror toward her face to verify her existence. Her blood-streaked countenance stared back at her, but she was unable to locate the source of the bleeding. As best she could recall, she had stabbed her assailant in his shoulder with her knife, and his blood splattered her. She scrubbed her face to remove the alien stains with a napkin leftover from her hastily eaten fast-food lunch. It was moistened by her salty tears.

Lottie's mind was spinning. She needed help. But despite her decade in the city, no one came readily to mind. She checked her rear-view mirror, hoping her attacker was licking his wounds instead of chasing after her in hot pursuit. She streaked along the subdivision, weaving a crooked trail. Her breath was short and choppy, not from exertion, but from fear.

Calm down, Girl! Calm down. Think! Think! In that moment she would have traded all the stuff for which she had worked so long and hard, for a single, solitary friend. Contacting the police never entered her mind. From her earliest childhood, family members, like Uncle Bubba, had influenced her to handle her own problems.

▲▲▲▲

The summer Lottie turned ten her Uncle Bubba was slashed repeatedly across his face and neck with a switchblade one night outside a local juke joint in the Dunston Quarter of Union City. He stumbled home alone to tend to his wounds, dragging himself past her house and the sheriff's office along the way. Although the stabbing was nearly fatal, Uncle Bubba "kept his business to hisself until he was out the woods."

He never divulged the culprit, not even to her daddy--his only brother--and no one was taken into custody for the crime. To this day, the topic is hotly debated among the domino players who gather under the mammoth pecan tree outside the Piggly Wiggly on Saturday mornings, as to whether it had been Uncle Bubba's common law wife or her boyfriend, "what had wielded the knife that messed Bubba up."

▲ ▲ ▲ ▲

"Beck!" Lottie shouted into her voice-activated car phone for Raymond's home number, even though her feelings toward him were running the gamut from mild displeasure to seething disdain. On the first ring, she aborted the call. It occurred to her he probably had good reason not to go home, too.

Passing her neighborhood Quick Mart for the third time, Lottie realized she was driving in circles. Going back to the city to spend the night at a hotel was an option, but she didn't want to be alone. Then in a split second, the neon sign on the corner pub triggered an idea. "Barnett!" She shrilled, anxiously awaiting a response.

"How-dy," a voice greeted, barely discernible over the bellowing chorus of *Gimme a Back Door Love.*

"Marcie!"

"Yes, Sugar. Who's this?"

"Marcie, I need your help," she said, betraying the wealth of emotion she was desperately trying to conceal.

"Lottie? Honey? That you?"

"Uh-huh." She forced back the tears.

"Calm down, Baby, and tell Marcie."

"Marcie," she whimpered. "I can't talk over the phone... and I can't go home."

"Sugar, I said come--anytime. I don't say nothing I don't mean. Now shake your little tail over here; right this minute, you hear."

"Thanks, Marcie. Thanks. See you soon." Lottie had never considered Marcie a friend, but she knew she could count on her word. *Raymond Beck! What have you gotten me into?* She loathed the very remembrance of the first time she heard his name.

▲▲▲▲

"This is Raymond Beck of The Beck Company," he had said, with arrogant corporate pride over the phone that day.

"Who?" Lottie balanced her heavy serving tray and the receiver from the diner's pay phone. *Who'd call me during the noon rush?*

"You're a very efficient waitress, Lottie," he said, trading flattery for his wheeler-dealer approach. "But I'm even more impressed with your computer savvy."

Computer savvy? Who in the world is Raymond Beck?

"And I'd like the opportunity to meet with you in my offices at your earliest convenience. I have a business proposition to put before you."

Oh? This must be Mr. Big-Shot. Back to eat a little crow, I bet.

"Lottie, you with me?"

"Well, uh, Mr. Beck, is it," she said, electing not to use his given name. "I must agree with you. I am very good at what I do, and at the moment I am *quite* busy doing it," she said, reminding him of their previous encounter. "But since you've got me standing here . . . state your business."

Resisting the temptation to get knotted in a duel of wits with a seemingly worthy adversary, Raymond issued a straightforward appeal. "Miss Garrett," he said. "Please. May we meet at your earliest convenience?"

"Well, since you put it that way, Mr. Beck, I accept. I've got a few irons in the fire just now." She referred to her college enrollment and apartment search. "But I'll contact you as soon as I get some free time."

"Fair enough."

"What's your address, sir?"

"Max has my card, Miss Garrett," he said, rattling off his pre-planned closer. "Give me a call when you're prepared to talk business. Good-bye."

CHAPTER 4.
▲▲▲▲▲▲▲▲▲▲▲▲

Lottie fought against the painful thumping in her temples to find her bearings to Marcie's place in Brooklyn. Even in the best of times she wasn't gifted with a keen sense of direction, a trait she'd inherited from her mother, and this night ranked right up there with the very worst of times.

She cruised along; clumsily dodging parked cars and careless pedestrians, until she happened upon a narrow street packed with aging row houses. She fumbled with the map light and rechecked her log. *Longview Street. This is it.* She heard the dull thump of music coming from halfway down the block. Latching onto her briefcase with one hand, she straightened her mussed appearance with the other and trailed the alluring downbeat to Marcie's house.

To her surprise, Marcie was sitting alone on her front stoop clutching two cups of beer. Without a word, she shoved one at her. Lottie wasn't an experienced drinker, but she accepted and took a seat beside her. Silently, the two of them sat in the starlit blackness, sipping beer to the beat of honky-tonk music. The mellow foam gradually soothed Lottie's parched throat and unraveled her jangled nerves.

When she was finally able to face Marcie, her pained expression was warmed by Marcie's Cheshire-cat grin. It broke the tension between them like a giant hole in a hot air balloon. Smiles turned to giggles, and giggles to laughter, until tears rolled down their cheeks. Their howls lured several of the partygoers out onto the stoop.

"Hee, hee, hee." One of the regulars staggered outside with his date. "What y'all grinning 'bout? Hee, hee, hee. We like a good laugh. Let us in on it."

Their privacy invaded, Marcie and Lottie retreated inside, giggling arm-in-arm. The heavily gated front door heralded their entrance with a loud clang. They didn't notice when the noise level dropped a full decibel in the front room. The paying customers halted their frolicking and eyed them surreptitiously. "Look what the cat dragged in." One tobacco-chewing patron nudged another, pointing to Lottie.

Marcie led her to the long buffet table draped with a red gingham oilcloth and returned happily to her duties behind the bar. Lottie reached for a paper plate, but halted when she spotted a woman in a blonde poof wig, seated on a high stool by the bingo table, blowing smoke rings and staring at her indignantly.

Lottie held her ground. The adrenaline left over from her earlier combat readied her for all comers. She stood tall; arms folded tightly across her chest, and locked stares with the blonde. The room froze like it had been placed on pause. After a moment that seemed longer, a man in a weathered vest and kerchief, who was sniffing around the fried okra, sheepishly slipped a plate into Lottie's hand.

"Thanks," she said, releasing the menacing woman from her fiery gaze and the room from its inertia. The gentleman cowboy rejoined his date, the woman in the blonde poof wig, and enthusiastic gambling resumed.

"Had enough, Sugar?" Marcie smiled sweetly. "You look wore out."

"Um-hmm." Lottie sagged.

Marcie led her upstairs to the spare bedroom, clearing away fringed jackets and cowboy hats strewn across the bed. She offered Lottie clean towels with the scent of lilac and lingered at the doorway to give her an opportunity to bare her soul. Lottie smiled at the invitation, but lowered her eyes in refusal. Marcie didn't press. She closed the door softly behind her.

Behind closed doors, Lottie squeezed her briefcase between the wall and the bed for safekeeping. She felt soiled. She lingered in the hot shower, trying to wash away the fear and exhaustion that twisted her every sinew. She dried off her taut frame with one of the fluffy towels Marcie provided. With the other she wrapped her gentle curves to ward off the chill of the fragrant sheets when she finally climbed under the covers.

The sensation was marvelous. She couldn't remember when she had appreciated a bed more. *Except maybe . . . maybe back in Union City . . . after the incident.* But certainly she didn't want to dredge up those painful memories. Weighing them onto her present predicament would be self-destructive.

She fluffed her borrowed pillow under the hollow of her neck, trying to relieve the spasms that persisted despite her soothing shower. It was an annoying reminder of the horrible masked man and his brutal hands around her throat. Too wired to sleep, she channeled her thoughts to more pleasant waters and prayed for sleep to overtake her. *Now, let's see...*

▲ ▲ ▲ ▲

When Lottie moved in with Ruth Ann in The Bronx, she had noticed her friend's precarious financial condition right off and determined not to weigh too heavily on her straining budget. She made her bed on the lumpy sofa that Ruth Ann had redeemed from Goodwill, and that was the sum total of her intrusion. She worked and ate at the diner during the day, and at night she hung out in the deep basement at Columbia University with geeky Mouse McCollough and his band of computer junkies.

Lottie had met Mouse quite by accident when she tripped over a carelessly mislaid bag at the campus bookstore and crashed headlong into him. In the collision, their purchases took flight and skidded across the floor. Lottie's unwitting victim picked up her book while she scrambled on hands and knees to collect his six assorted candy bars to the amusement of passersby.

"I am so sorry," she said to the scrawny-looking kid who appeared to be stunned. His drooped shoulders and slack jaws provoked a wordy explanation on her part. "Here I am spending my hard earned money on this book," Lottie said, gently extracting it from his grasp, "and I just about take your head off." She smiled shamefacedly. "Please forgive me."

"Cutting edge stuff." The youngster nodded toward her book after an awkward pause. His raspy voice sounded as though it had been dredged up from the deep where he was contemplating more meaningful matters. "Like computers?"

"Sure do," she said, grateful to make contact with him on an earthly plane; she rattled on so as not to break the fragile link. "This guy comes in the diner, where I only work part-time, and he leaves behind skads of wadded paper, but he doesn't seem to be making much progress. I like solving problems with the computer so I thought this book might help him--"

"Helper type?"

"Pretty impulsive, huh?" Lottie flushed.

"Student type?"

"No. Not yet. But I really want to come to Columbia in the fall."

"Computers?" He twirled the smallish earring in his right lobe, shifting as though his boredom was returning.

"Something like that. What's up with the candy bars?"

"Sweet tooth." He shrugged and stuffed his gooey treasures into his grungy jeans, accentuated by prominent holes and exposed flesh. He grabbed her book and wrote on the jacket cover: "Mouse--Maxwell Hall--Deep Basement, B10--8pm SHARP." Beady eyes shifting cagily, he said, "Come tonight. Come alone. We've got stuff you won't find in books." He scooted away. An empty candy wrapper worked its way through a hole in his pocket and fell to the floor.

As it turned out, Mouse McCollough was a 16-year old computer genius whose squinty eyes and sub-par people skills were attributable to his soaring IQ and the non-stop hours he logged in front of a computer screen. Since Mouse was a Ph.D. candidate at the university, the Dean had entrusted him with a key to the lab's state-of-the-art equipment so he could have unimpeded access for his research. Unbeknownst to the professor, however, Mouse had assembled an elite underground think-tank to push the envelope on global high-tech communication solutions.

Every night Mouse smuggled his five handpicked mavericks into the basement of Maxwell Hall. Mouse respected their genius, and they respected him as their undisputed leader. They were tops, but admittedly, he was better. They called themselves Zero-One, or Z1 for short, in recognition of the binary computer language that united their diverse group.

"Who is this?" Jamaal's dreadlocks flapped in his eyes.

"I-I thought we didn't trust girls," Hyram Morgenstein stammered in his halting monotone, while the others mumbled their discontent.

"Enough!" Mouse raised his hand. "Get back to work fellas. This is Lottie. She's not a girl; she's a geek." He pulled her out of earshot of the rabble.

"I'll just go--"

"Stay." Mouse snapped. "I invited you. I invited them." He folded his arms and sagged to his usual posture. "Look see, Lottie. Society calls us anal-retentive rejects. Misfits. And no matter how radical our research, it means nothing if we can't put it to good use. We need . . . a regular person . . . who understands the work and understands us . . . to keep us balanced. That's you. Helper type."

"But they don't want me."

"This lab is the only place they feel free. They guard their territory. Can you blame 'em? But give 'em time. They'll come 'round."

"But—"

"And Lottie. Don't sweat the enrollment stuff. I'll talk to the Dean myself."

"Okay, Mouse. You've got yourself a deal," she said, happy for any place to escape Ruth Ann's grungy apartment and her assorted cold-nosed boyfriends who came sniffing around nightly.

After a four-month stint on Ruth Ann's couch, Lottie was happy when the day finally arrived to move into her own apartment. She had found an efficiency in Harlem, a stone's throw from Columbia. That was the day Ruth Ann came home in tears and frantically flung herself across the couch that had posed as Lottie's bed.

"What's the matter, Ruth Ann? What's wrong?"

"I can't stand it! They fired me and I didn't do nothing!" It was the second job she'd lost in as many days. Her body heaved with bitter sobs until finally she lay spent like a broken doll.

"Ruth Ann," Lottie cooed sympathetically, edging her way onto the couch to comfort her friend and to have the talk that was overdue. "Have you ever compared your struggles . . . and your revolving-door boyfriends . . . to the love and stability you once had back home in Union City?" She gave pause for the idea to sink in on her friend before delving deeper. "Have you ever considered," Lottie whispered, "giving up your uncertain life here, and going back home where people care about you, and where your next meal won't be so unpredictable? Your brother's the sheriff; he'd love to--"

"What? What that you saying, Lottie?" Ruth Ann croaked, her voice barely recognizable. She sniffed and raised herself to one elbow, wiping her tears with the backs of her hands. "You right. There was lots of love in our big ole family. But we was dirt po', Miss Lottie." She swaggered. "And love don't pay no bills."

"You got *that* right!" Lottie blasted. "But what will life be like when you're forced to *sell* your love to pay your bills?"

"What? What's that you saying?"

"My Mamma drilled it into me. When a woman puts her body with a man who won't marry her, she's disrespecting herself; it's dangerous; and it ain't the Lord's way. I'm pretty sure your Mamma preached it, too. But it looks like you've forgot everything you ever knew."

Lottie waved her hand at the clutter. "You never lived like this back home. And nothing good can come of you sleeping around with all these men, Girl. They don't care about you, and you don't care about them. Y'all are just using each other. And if you ask me, you're getting the short end of the stick--"

"That's right, Miss High-and-Mighty Lottie Garrett? Who asked you? Who asked you anything?"

"Don't get me wrong, Ruth Ann." Lottie slowly exhaled. "I appreciate everything you've done for me. I'll never forget how you helped me. But I'm concerned about you--"

"Who're you to be concerned about me?" Ruth Ann jumped up from the couch and glared at her as though she were appraising a lunatic. "Up to now, *Missy*, you've been too broke to even pay rent. And now that you can, you're moving out. I'm doing just fine here by myself; and my boyfriends, for your information, are my business. I don't have to answer to nobody, and that includes you! Besides, there's lots of work I can do. It's the North, right? Land of milk and honey, right?"

"But—"

"But, nothing!" Ruth Ann added her hands to her thick hips. "You sho' can't say that about Union City. You, for one, ought to know how lonely it gets back there." Her eyes darted about like double-barreled cannons preparing for a strike. "Anyhow, Lottie, at least I told my Mamma good-bye. You didn't have the nerve to do that!"

The words found their intended mark in Lottie's soft underbelly. It pained her deeply that her loyal friend had pulled out all the stops to protect her failing lifestyle, like a she-wolf defending her cubs. Lottie let the matter drop, and they parted cordially. To close the book on her nagging concerns about Ruth Ann's welfare, she borrowed one of her daddy's time-worn quips. "Well," he'd say, "at least the Gal's got indoor toilets and running water."

CHAPTER 5.
▲▲▲▲▲▲▲▲▲▲▲▲

"Where on earth am I?" Lottie snapped to attention the next morning, alarmed by the unfamiliar fragrance of lilac. *Oh, yeah! Oh, yeah!* She quieted her pounding heart. *Marcie's spare bedroom. Raymond's stupid files. My bloody knife.* She slipped into her clothes that felt foreign the second time around and cross-examined herself in the bathroom mirror. "What are you doing here, Girl?" She frowned. "And what has that lying Raymond Beck done to put you here?" If she were to be totally honest, Lottie had to admit that Raymond's proclivity for half-truths and lies dated as far back as their first meeting.

▲▲▲▲

Shortly after being accepted to Columbia, Lottie had taken Raymond up on his invitation to discuss *business* at his office. Max supplied her with his card, and she nervously fingered it in her apron pocket for days. She recognized his downtown address, a couple of blocks over from Wall Street. When she finally got the nerve to call, his secretary was very receptive. She made an appointment for her to meet him the very next day.

Sensing the significance of their first meeting, Lottie wanted ample time to prepare and arrive at his offices at 10 o'clock, sharp. Raymond appeared to be the sort that appreciated promptness, and try as she might to be nonchalant about their appointment, she wanted to please this man she hardly knew. He had that affect on people.

"But my future's at stake!" she pleaded with Max for the day off, not divulging Raymond's role in her untimely request.

"Well, okay," Max said, knowing that her short notice would leave him and Marcie in a bind. "Take the time if you must, but don't make this a habit." He was undeniably the boss, but it was plain to anyone who knew him that Max, who had no children of his own, had a fatherly affection for Lottie and he discreetly coveted her success.

When she arrived for her appointment with Raymond, a highly decorated, uniformed guard was on post in the lobby of 1000 Liberty Place. He was stationed behind a polished brass console that reflected the gleaming terrazzo floors. As she approached him for directions, he swept his braided hat from his head and tipped it. *My, my, my . . . a leg man's delight.* He stepped sprightly from behind the console. "Good morning, Miss. How may I help you?" In strict violation of regulations, he used his passkey to grant Lottie direct access to the penthouse on the 150th floor, all the while disrobing her with his eyes.

What had turned his head was a stately young woman, barely twenty and 5' 8" with shortly cropped raven curls that framed her lovely face. She was wearing her best and only tailored interview suit, steel gray, at-the-knee and sensible, with pumps to match. Yet, when paired with the crisp white blouse and bold sterling jewelry she chose to accent it, it set off her noticeable curves and her deep-set mahogany eyes in ways that demanded attention.

On the penthouse floor, the towering moniker announced, *The Beck Company*. The incestuous corporate label validated Lottie's notion that Raymond was thoroughly self-absorbed--Beck, and Beck alone. No associations; no needs; no help. She had half imagined dark mahogany, heavy paneling, and studded leather, with a myriad of tiny offices chopping up the space; a fitting match for Raymond's somber moods and close introspection. What she found, however, was entirely opposite. The openness of the room was breathtaking. Raymond's desk was in a far corner of a room so large that only his silhouette was discernible from her vantage point. No doors.

"Good morning, Miss Garrett." A gentle woman with tastefully coiffured gray hair rose from behind the front desk to greet her. Her presence lent an air of dignity and charm that completed the room. "Thank you for being so prompt," she said. "I'm Mary. Mr. Beck's private secretary. He's expecting you." She pointed to the rear of the room. "Go back and join him."

"Aah, there you are, Miss Garrett," Raymond said, turning to find her standing at his desk. He had been gazing over the penthouse view like a grabby land baron plotting his next coup. "I hardly recognized you out of uniform," he said, ". . . but you look as lovely as ever.

Welcome to The Beck Company!" He spread his arms proudly apart. He was dressed in the most fabulous navy wool gabardine suit Lottie had ever seen. His suede loafers and silk accouterments completed his look of dominance.

Raymond rounded the desk with a firm handshake and a glossy smile. "Come with me," he said, and strutted mid-way the room to an inviting seating area. "Make yourself comfortable." He offered her the nubby jewel-toned couch and sat beside her in a jade leather armchair. She smiled politely and set her portfolio gingerly on the thick glass top of a table artfully crafted from the trunk of a petrified tree.

Pleasantries aside, he launched into the business at hand. "Ms. Garrett," he said with a mischievous glint, obviously smarting from their previous encounter. "May I call you Lottie?"

"Certainly."

"Lottie, I'm a busy man so I'll get right to it. We're a small company in comparison to the financial giants in this town, like Dirk and Saxony, or Clayburn and Clayburn. But I make it clear to all of my clients. We're not on Wall Street, but we *are* Wall Street, just a few blocks removed." He carefully dusted his lapel for invisible lint. "What I don't offer in the way of walnut and mahogany and costly gimmicks, I more than make up for in personalized service. I tailor client's investments to their individual goals, and I don't dilute their asset growth by tacking on unnecessary fees."

He knitted his hands behind his head and slouched back cockily, making his pitch to the ceiling. "I have a burgeoning client list, built by word-of-mouth, not pricey advertising budgets. But I want my clients to know we're on the cutting edge. By tailoring technology to meet their specific needs, equal to or better than what they can find at one of the larger brokerage houses, I'll corner my niche in the market."

He gave her a side-glance. "Are you with me, Lottie?" Her rapt attention was sufficient inducement for him to continue his spiel. "Most of my transactions are conducted over the phone, and since my clients are focused on the bottom line, they've been satisfied with this practice. But I want to give them more. I want to provide them with slick prospectuses and profile sheets on potential investments. I want to bring them on-line with Internet access, up-to-the-minute stock quotes, and real-time portfolio information. Of course I have that capability right now," he said, fingering the crease in his pant leg. "But I'm not getting my money's worth out of my tech consultants."

He leaned toward Lottie and lowered his voice as though he were about to unburden his soul. "And also I've been itching to get on the lecture circuit. But I don't have a glitzy dog-and-pony show that'll make me click with this emerging *www.generation*. I know I've got to keep current or else I'll lose ground, and in this business, territory lost is territory never to be regained."

He reset himself, and Lottie nodded her continuing interest. "For me, the greatest inventions of the last century were the cell phone and the fax machine, not the computer; hence, this meeting. Rather than going the consultant route any longer, I'm interested in bringing aboard a computer aficionado, such as yourself ... and I was very much impressed with your work. Plus, Max tells me you're a *good Kid*." He eyed her squarely. "So there you have it, Lottie. The big picture." He exhaled with gust, suggesting he had come clean and was relieved.

"Raymond?" Lottie said with an impish twinkle. "May I call you, Raymond?" They exchanged a cheeky bonding glance. "I do see the big picture," she said, "and your drive appeals to my own personal work ethic. You're right. I do have a love affair with computers, but I have a confession to make. I'm not very experienced in the finer points of investing. I'll encounter the subject in my college curriculum, but it'll be two years before I complete my degree. Is that a problem?"

"Let's get this straight, Lottie." He poised himself on the edge of his chair. "I'm not looking for a partner. The investment business is my side of the house. I simply need you to wrap computer technology around what I do. That's all."

"Then take a look at these," she said, and spread her portfolio on the table to display samples of her work. Mouse had been right about Lottie and Z1. She had won them over with her easy manner and eagerness to learn. Before long they adopted her as their very own *groupie* and loved her for the privilege. Hyram loaned her his prized, yet-unpublished software to impress *Mr. Big-Shot*. With his genius and her knack for reducing complex concepts into their simplest terms, they had netted splendid results.

"Wow!"

"I can create concise account profiles and prospectuses for the sophisticated or the first time investor," she said. "I can develop a Webpage and bring them on-line. You and your clients can point-and-click over the Internet.

You'll be able to manage your business from anywhere in the world."

"Whoa! This is powerful stuff, Lottie! The market potential is staggering. Join me right now! I can make it worth your while financially." He raised his right hand. "And I pledge to pay your college tuition from this point forward." He smiled craftily. "And who knows? You might want to upgrade to a Masters or even a Ph.D. at Columbia some day."

"What? How do you know about Columbia?"

"I told you. Max tells me everything," he said, satisfied he'd outmaneuvered her. It more than made up for being bested in their first outing.

"Then I guess he told you I'm nobody's *Kid*."

"We're talking six figures here, Miss Garrett," he said, banking on having the last word.

"Six figures! In that case, all is forgiven. I accept!" Much later she learned from Mary that the salary had been a mere penitence compared to the millions Raymond grossed each year. Nonetheless, Lottie had been satisfied with her good fortune. Her *Diner Days* were over, and she had found freedom on Liberty Street.

But it was pretty tough going for Lottie during her early months at The Beck Company. She attended Columbia, nights and weekends, and wrestled with Raymond's temperament and his client's expectations during the day. She pursued her success to the abandonment of all else, persevering with tremendous results, but not without the help of Z1.

"You like it?" Mouse chatted on-line.

"It's perfect!" Lottie pounded back on her keyboard. "C'mon Mouse. Let me pay you. Come to the office. Meet Raymond. See your state-of-the-art system at work."

"No need. Built a hologram in the lab."

"The laptop Jamaal built is extraordinary. Amazing!

"Look see, Lottie. Don't you get it? You're one of us. Z1 takes care of its own."

Raymond was equally impressed. "This is wonderful, Lottie!" he said, removing the red bow that crowned his new laptop. "This thing's so fast it sizzles. I'll be able to scour the world for new business with this baby. Sure you can teach a klutz like me to use it?"

"Even a klutz like you," she said, eyes glowing with pride. "The world is at your fingertips."

"A powerful tool deserves a powerful name. I dub thee . . ." he said with a wave of his hand, "my very own . . . *Beck-mobile*."

"*Beck-mobile?*"

"*Beck-mobile*. I'll design a leather carrying case for it, and we'll hit the road. Have Beck-mobile will travel."

By the end of her second year at Beck, the rewards for Lottie's tireless pursuits had reached fruition. She completed her bachelor's degree in Business Systems and mastered her side of the business at Beck. Raymond's clients were singing the praises of the new on-line access to their portfolios on BECK.com. Moreover, Lottie had developed his *glitzy dog-and-pony show*, which added vitality to his lectures. Before long, his speaking engagements were taking him coast to coast and around the world, and the firm's market share had increased ten fold.

On the night Lottie accepted her diploma at Columbia, Raymond hosted a sit-down dinner party at a private Midtown dining room in her honor. Twenty-five of his special clients prized their invitation to the festivities. Well-heeled brokers, bankers, financial commentators, and mink-laden widows rung the elegant table, which was adorned in its center by a towering ice sculpture of an angel. The illustrious group had gathered to take advantage of their host's hospitality and to be introduced to the computer wizard that had revolutionized his company and strengthened their personal accounts.

"Hear! Hear!" Raymond blared, bringing his guests to a restless hush. He stood at the head of the table with the three-tiered chandelier casting a warm glow on his well-fitting white dinner jacket. He tingled the golden tines of his fork against his raised crystal goblet and proposed a toast. "Lottie," he said, voice booming. "My confidence in you has been fully justified. In recognition of your rapid progress and major contribution to this firm, I have officially renamed my company." His guests hung on his every word. "The Beck Company shall henceforth be known as, Beck and Associate."

He silenced the applause with a raised hand and continued to stoke the fires of the emotion-charged evening. "And because I have the highest confidence in your work, I predict that our company stock will go public in the not too distant future." He lofted his glass toward the ceiling. "To Lottie!" he proclaimed. "To Lottie!" the guests echoed jubilantly. The table was a-buzz with whispers of surprise and praise as Raymond took his seat.

Seated at the opposite end of the table, Lottie fought back happy tears. She was a long way from Union City. The gathering hushed when she rose to her feet. Her flowing gown was encrusted with golden threads that competed for the light with the gleam in her eyes. She bowed gracefully from her waist and tipped an imaginary top hat in Raymond's direction. She didn't trust herself to speak. Raymond stood again and faced her in a fairy-tale moment that floated on the excitement. Returning her gesture with a gallant salute, they took their bows. The guests applauded wildly.

Mary whispered to her as she took to her seat. "Really, Dear," she said, her words slurring from a little too much wine. "You do know there's never been anyone in our organization to hold a candle to you; don't you? This is well-deserved recognition and long overdue if you ask me." She nudged her playfully. "There never was a computer consulting firm, or anybody else before you came on board. Surely you recognized Raymond's ego talking?"

"Yes . . . yes, of course," Lottie said. But the truth was she was astonished to learn that Raymond had lied from their very first meeting. She vowed to redouble her efforts to earn his trust.

CHAPTER 6.
▲▲▲▲▲▲▲▲▲▲▲

Marooned in Marcie's bathroom, trying to discover a way to clean her teeth, Lottie wasn't the least bit amused with Raymond's lies. Neither did she regard his penchant for secrecy a quality to be admired. *Aside from his shrewdness in business, what do I really know about this man? We've certainly hit some high notes together, but he has yet to accept me as an equal. We share the same office, but not the same world. Come to think of it, the little I know about his background I could fit into a pea-sized thimble.*

▲▲▲▲

"Mary, is Raymond coming back tonight?"

"Still here, Lottie? Thought you were gone," she said, checking his calendar. Nope. Dinner at Manfred's with that long-legged blonde he dates off and on--Brooke . . . something or the other. Tell me she's an up-and-coming Madison Avenue lawyer."

"Manfred's? Oo-la-la. She must be special."

"It's odd how he gives me his dinner plans, but never lunch."

Lottie clamped shut, figuring he didn't want Mary to know he frequented a place like Max's.

"Football." Raymond had offered in tight-lipped response the time Lottie had asked about the prominent scar on his chin. "Arizona State. Put there by the helmet of an enraged middle lineman, if you must know."

Then there was the time Russ Chisholm, one of his football alum, had called the office. Lottie grabbed the phone while Mary was attending a political rally over her lunch hour.

"Where is the ole Scamp, anyhow?" the husky-voiced man said. "Tell him to call his friends sometime. Guess he thinks he's a big shot now, but I remember when the Boy was eating chicken feathers."

" I'll tell him--"

"He outta be in the NFL right about now, tossing some passes on my big screen."

"Football?"

"Quarterback. Didn't he tell you he was a Heisman Trophy candidate our senior year? Yeah, before his knee blew out in the last game of the regular season. Shame, too. Nothing worse than a jock chained to a desk. I oughta know. You tell him to call his friends. It's been too long."

▲▲▲▲

Lumbering downstairs to Marcie's kitchen, Lottie found a note waiting for her on the counter. "Hi Sugar," it read. "Off to work. Late as usual! Make yourself to home. Come by the diner later. Marcie."

The kitchen was a perky little pink-and-black number that resembled a 1950's malt shop. The only feature missing was a poodle skirt. It wasn't Lottie's style, but the playful ambiance was refreshing despite her abbreviated sleep. Like Marcie, it was cute and it grew on you.

Lottie checked the clock over the stove-- 9:35 a.m. Time for answers. She called Raymond's house. His phone emitted a strange busy signal the operator couldn't identify. No one answered the office phone and the answering machine didn't pick up. *That's right. Mary's out today. Notary class. Just like her to procrastinate until the last minute. But Raymond's usually in the office by 7 a.m. sharp. If I don't hear from him soon, I'll go out to his place.* Although she didn't relish the trip. He lived in a beachfront condo in a gated-community in Southampton, and she had no hope of getting in if he wasn't at home.

Sipping her second cup of decaf, Lottie turned the dial on the pink radio in the windowsill to an all news channel. She listened intently to the litany of murder and mayhem being reported from the previous night: "Coy Travis, age 30, apprehended in the act of blah, blah, blah; Terrance Long, prominent Midtown attorney, found murdered blah, blah, blah; bombing suspect, Willis Murphy, captured in the act of blah, blah, blah." But no Beck. "Good!" She breathed a sigh of relief. "At least his name didn't make the horrible hit parade." She built herself a *slum-gully* omelet from eggs and leftovers from the fridge and pondered over her next move.

▲▲▲▲

Meanwhile, at that moment, Raymond Beck was pacing the floor of his hotel room like a caged animal. He had slept fitfully in his

Lower East Side hideaway and now he wanted answers. He called Lottie at her home off and on through the night, only to receive a busy signal that the local operator identified as "trouble on the line."

He had attempted countless times to retrieve his messages from the office with his remote code, but no success. The greeting message was garbled and a strange hissing sound played back instead of his waiting messages. He desperately wanted to rush over and check the phones. They were his lifeline, his breadline. He had deals to make, clients to see, but first he desperately needed to find Lottie.

He slumped on the edge of his rented bed and listened to the report on the all news channel. After a moment, he shot straight up. "What? No! It can't be! It can't be!" He glued himself to the next TV news broadcast.

"There are no new leads in the apparent brutal beating death of attorney Terrance W. Long, managing partner of Stalworth, Dixon & Long, a Midtown Manhattan law firm," the reporter chronicled. "Long's body," she droned, "was found at 5 a.m. in his office by members of the early morning cleaning crew. The official cause of death is pending an autopsy."

"For Pete's sake!" Raymond mussed his slick black hair. "She had the same stupid grin on her face when she talked about the weather as she did when she reported a man's brutal murder. She summed up the totality of a man's life in a stupid sound bite. It's ridiculous! Ridiculous!"

He bounded onto the bed and dropped his head in his hands. "What have I done?" He groaned. His stomach flip-flopped violently. "People depended on me. And I've let them down--my buddy, Terry--and maybe Lottie, too. It's my fault. All my fault."

▲▲▲▲

As Lottie contemplated her options in Marcie's kitchen, she half-imagined Raymond reaching out to her in his distress. She stabbed his number into the phone again. Strange noise. No Raymond. Two-by-two, she rushed the stairs to the guest bedroom, retrieved her briefcase from its hiding place, and dashed off to the diner. Marcie's invitation, notwithstanding, she hoped that Raymond would have the good sense to show up there. After all, no one in his circles would expect to find him at Max's.

Lottie had visited Max on a number of occasions since her departure--birthdays, anniversaries--but on each of those happy occasions she had blown back to Church Street as an enviable hero who had made the *bigs*. This time, she was returning as a lost lamb. Regardless of her changing fortunes, however, Max had always remained the same--steady, unflappable--Max. Now, more than ever, she counted on his strength and his understanding.

"Hey." Lottie waved at Marcie as she squeezed through the door of the diner. She shoved her way through the mid-day queue and claimed the last stool at the counter.

"Hi yourself," Max said, after cashing out the last customer in line. "Good to see you, Kid." He reached across the counter and gave her a familiar squeeze. "How's the world treating ya?"

"Hey, Max. Been better," she said, not expecting her eyes to brim with tears.

"See my new Girl over there?" he said, pointing to the waitress handling the ten perimeter booths that once had been Lottie's assignment. "That's Claudia. Just got her last week. I think she's gonna work out just fine. She's got skills, that one. Take a close look and tell me what you see."

"Huh?" Lottie turned obediently and evaluated the tall, sway-backed woman who wore a visible hair net and glasses that were Coke-bottle thick.

"Well? What ya think?"

"O.K. Yes. I see your point." Lottie rated. "She's agile, pleasant, and quick. She's good, all right. You've got yourself a winner."

"So you can see all that simply by looking at her?" he said, eyes following Claudia's every move. "And while you were focused in on her, did your troubles kind o' give you the slip?"

"Max, you Sly Fox. Is this a lesson?"

"I learned a long time ago," he said like a professor, "a problem is a mere facet of the diamond of our lives."

"Another Max-ism? What's the meaning of this one, *Oh-Sage-One?*"

"Sounds like a bunch o' hooey, I know. But it's true. No facet of our life can shine any brighter than the light we give it. We can choose to focus on our problems and wallow around in self-pity, or we can major on the good stuff that keeps cropping up all the time. It's up to us. We can let our little light shine wherever we want," he said. "It's our light. It's our choice."

"You lost me."

"Take me, for example." He pointed to his packed house. "It's noisy. It's messy. It's hard. I could complain, but I don't. I just keep focusing on giving the kind of service that keeps 'em coming back for more; that's where I shine my light." He moved over to the register and checked out a customer who was fidgeting with his watch. "Thank you, sir," he said. "Sorry to keep you waiting. Come back and see us real soon."

"Think on things that are pure, and lovely, and of good report." Lottie's inner voice consoled. It wasn't a *Max-ism*, but it stirred her soul and kick-started her courage. *I am confused. But I'm alive, and I'm with people who care about me. And that's where I choose to shine my little light.* From her seat at Max's familiar counter, Lottie counted her blessings.

"Here you go."

"Thank you." Lottie smiled when Max brought her a small plate of meatloaf, mashed potatoes, and iced tea; her favorites from the menu. "Thanks for everything." Her cheeks flushed. "Seen Raymond lately?"

"No. Why? He your problem?"

"Not exactly. I've just got the feeling he's in some kind of trouble."

"Don't worry, Little One," Max said, returning to the register. "We'll find him. We'll find him together."

CHAPTER 7.
▲▲▲▲▲▲▲▲▲▲▲

    The bell jingled over the front door, and Max tapped on the counter to get Lottie's attention. It was Raymond. She leapt from her stool and rushed him at the door. Her heart was racing like a terrified mother being reunited with her lost child. She wanted to smother him with kisses, and at the same time, beat him to within an inch of his life for giving her such a terrible scare.
    Raymond looked haggard and unkempt, but still in one piece. His white shirt was rumpled. The jacket she recognized from the day before hung limply on his drooping frame, and his face was creased with concern. The Beckmobile was strapped carelessly across his shoulder, and without his usual swagger, he didn't strike quite as tall or commanding a figure as before.

Lottie pushed her way upstream against the people entering the diner, but Raymond reached her first. He steered her toward Max who was motioning in his direction.

"Hi," Raymond said sheepishly.

"Hi, yourself," Max thundered. "I hear some of your trouble's been rubbing off on this Girl, here. Straighten it up, Guy," he said. "Before this day is out. You got that?"

Max snapped his fingers and Claudia ushered Raymond and Lottie to booth number one for some semblance of privacy. She brought him a cup of steaming black coffee, and he ordered his usual fried chicken-caesar salad. Lottie wasn't interested in food. They were finally alone.

"What's up with you, Raymond?" she said. "You nearly got me killed!"

"Killed?" He'd been ready for her disapproval, but not this. "Killed?"

"Last night when I got home with those stupid files of yours, someone had trashed my house and he grabbed me from behind." She gave him the details, and he listened intently.

"Then they did kill him," he said with quiet conviction. "They killed Long."

"Long? Who the devil is Long? And who is *they*? You're losing me, Raymond." Her teeth chattered. The cold was stealing back into her bones. "And you're scaring me, too."

"Terry Long, my attorney friend. You remember him. You met him at my conference in Brussels last month. Remember? The nerdy little guy with the toothy grin. He kept saying, 'Wow! What a coincidence.' Remember--"

Claudia returned with Raymond's order, but her warm smile was lost on the stony-faced pair in booth number one. She made a speedy retreat, and Raymond continued. "I don't understand it all, but something weird is definitely going on. We've got to get to the bottom of it, Lottie . . . fast . . . our lives are at stake."

"*We*? What do you mean, *we*?" She rubbed her hands together to warm them. "How did I get in this mess?"

Raymond hadn't eaten in 24 hours and for the next few minutes Lottie witnessed his frenzied carnage. After completing his second cup of coffee, he signaled Max that he was leaving money on the table for the check. She failed to notice the two of them lock eyes like horns on a pair of battering rams, but Raymond received Max's guarded permission to leave with her.

"Let's get out of here," he said, guiding Lottie to the sidewalk. "I can't hear myself think in that place. Let's ride and talk. We'll have to take your car."

"My car?" she said, knowing his love for driving was matched only by his love for his new Corvette. "Where's your 'Vette?"

"My car? That's part of the story. It makes me sure they killed Long."

"Here, then." She pitched him her keys. "You drive. You've got my undivided attention."

"Yesterday . . . it's hard to believe it was only yesterday," Raymond said, as he tossed his Beck-mobile on the back seat and climbed behind the wheel. "I made a pit stop by the office at around 4 o'clock in the afternoon. You weren't there, and I was in a big hurry for my 4:30 appointment. So I dropped that note in your chair about the Sinclair file. Remember?"

"Yeah. I waited around for you."

"But when I went back to the garage, I found an awful mess. Someone had broken into my 'Vette just that quick--slashed the seats and rummaged through my things."

"What--"

"I can't figure out how they did it so fast without setting off the alarm. It had to be a pro.

The garage attendant didn't see anybody suspicious come in or out."

"What did they steal?"

"That's the odd part." He pinched his brow. "There was nothing there. I had the Beckmobile with me, and they didn't rip off my new sound system."

"But you said your friend, Long, was killed. "What's he got to do with your 'Vette?"

"I've gone over it in my mind a thousand times." Raymond drummed the steering wheel with his fists. "My first appointment yesterday morning was with Long in his Midtown offices at 9 o'clock. Terry had asked me to stop by and pick up some legal documents pertaining to Beck's common stock--"

Lottie's crestfallen expression stopped him short. "And you didn't tell me?"

"Ahem... surely you remember me saying I'd take Beck public some day. Anyhow, as I was leaving the meeting I grabbed Terry's hand like always. It was a joke between us. We would pretend to do a secret fraternal handshake. Terry's hand was cold as ice, and that wasn't like him. His handshake was usually solid as a rock. But I figured he had a lot on his mind. He just made partner in the firm last year and the pressures are enormous. But it just wasn't like Terry to be so shaky."

"I knew him from the old days. From the days when we had more energy than money, but we both had enormous drive. Back then, we frequented J-J's Pub in the East Village and slugged down a few beers at the end of the day, and exchanged war stories with some of the regulars."

"You? In the East Village with the *green-spiked-hair* set? Why is it I can't picture that?"

"J-J's is close enough to the action to be interesting, but far enough away to be sane. The few spike-haired creatures that accidentally wandered through over the years have usually been turned off by the *gray-hairs-in-suits* set."

"Anyway, after my meeting with Terry yesterday morning, I had a 10 o'clock speaking engagement, and returned to the office around noon. You had already left for lunch, and Mary was off to one of her political rallies for the 'gubernatorial candidate of her choice,'" he said, mimicking her matronly tone. "And the temp was there."

"This was at noon?"

"Yeah. Keep up. As I went through my mail, I had an unexpected visit from a guy who presented a business card from Clayburn & Clayburn."

"So that's the card I found--"

He scowled at her interruption. "The guy's name was Jonathan Lowe. Pompous sort. He said he was there to retrieve a client file he suspected I'd inadvertently picked up when I visited Long's office earlier in the day. I denied it, of course. And I wondered at the time why Terry hadn't called me himself. But it was immaterial. I didn't have the file, and I told that guy, Lowe, as much. He apologized and left."

"Go on. Go on."

Raymond rolled his neck. "Then only a few minutes later, Terry calls me with the same question. He was excited, and I kidded him. 'Heh, Long,' I said, 'slow down; remember your heart.' He had a mild heart attack a few years back. Then I made some stupid joke about not stealing his clients. If I had paid more attention, I would've noticed my pal was far too agitated for a minor thing like a missing file. Shortly after that, though, I left the office and didn't return until my 4 o'clock pit stop.

"When your 'Vette got trashed."

"Yeah. I had the garage attendant write up a report and tow it in for repairs." He patted his shirt pocket for the report. "By that time I was so disgusted with the whole situation, I didn't want to deal with it anymore. I just wanted to go home. I called my 4:30 appointment from the garage and canceled. I had planned to call the cops and my insurance company this morning."

"But I was there waiting for you."

"I forgot. All right. The temp had left for the day, and I thought you were long gone, too. I forgot the stupid note I left you. I swear. Otherwise, I'd have come back to get you. But instead I went to J-J's to have a few beers and figure out how to get home."

"So when did you remember me, huh?"

"As I sat there at the bar and retraced the day, it occurred to me that I had thrown a couple of loose files from my meeting with Long into Mary's filing box. Habit. I didn't recall. But I got to thinking how Terry and the guy from Clayburn seemed a bit too anxious about a misplaced file. And when I put their odd behavior together with the vandalism on my 'Vette, it started to fall into place. Somebody broke into my car looking for that file."

"What?"

"When I realized it, I called you at home to ask if you'd seen a Clayburn file. When I got your machine, that's when I remembered the note

I left you. Honestly, Lottie, I never thought for one minute this had anything to do with you."

"I stopped by the office to pick up my briefcase," she said breathlessly. "I saw the note in my chair and decided to get a jump start on the project, expecting you'd be back soon. I had no real reason to rush home--" She halted. Her lonely nights were her private business.

"That's why I called you at the office when I remembered the note." Raymond's temples pounded visibly. "I wanted you to get those stupid files and get out of there before anything else happened."

"So that's why you wanted me to get the 'CL' files. Clayburn & Clayburn Investments?"

"Bingo!" He banged the steering wheel.

"But there's no Clayburn file, here," she said, checking her briefcase.

"It's gotta be there. Look again!"

"No. No Clayburn file."

"What?"

He swerved the Lexus sharply around Columbus Circle and onto Broadway to the angry tune of blaring horns. He picked his way through the tight traffic in Times Square, dodging cars and yellow taxis, until they reached Liberty Place.

He decided against using the garage entry. Lottie's car would be too easy to spot. He pulled around to Rector Street and parked illegally behind Trinity Church's cemetery. Crusty tombstones, dating back to the 1700s, leered at him through the wrought iron fence. They gave him the creeps.

"I'm going, too, Raymond."

"Absolutely not! Stay here in the car, Lottie, in case the cops come by."

"I'm going."

"No time to argue with a stubborn person," he said. He grabbed her hand, and they sent pigeons flying as they raced through the plaza at Liberty Place.

"What's this?" He looked at her accusingly. The penthouse door was ajar.

"I locked it. I'm sure," she whispered. "I waited to hear the click."

"Stay here." He edged cautiously through the doorway, while Lottie made a mental map of an escape route.

"We're alone," he said, after scouting out the office. "But somebody's been here."

The office was a mess. Chairs overturned. Drawers flung open. Contents splattered. Shards of glass from the massive sofa table turned the floor into an obstacle course. The petrified wood base had been used to smash open the door to the file room. Locks on the cabinets were mangled and files tossed into heaps. "We need to get outta here fast." Raymond seethed. "But first, we've got to find that missing Clayburn file. We must."

"If *they* haven't found it already."

They tiptoed across the jagged glass. Lottie searched the file room while Raymond checked the piles of debris. Both of them came up empty. Raymond up-righted the telephone, and hastily replaced the outgoing message, explaining that the offices would be closed for repairs for two weeks. While he was at it, he retrieved nine messages and changed their remote access codes. He also telephoned Mary.

"Raymond, this is the most delightful surprise." Mary emoted in her prim manner. "A paid vacation could not have come at a more opportune time. What with the November election just around the corner, I can throw my energies behind my gubernatorial candidate, Chad Dunlevy."

"Who?"

"Dunlevy, Raymond. Remember? Our lieutenant governor was tapped to take over in the race when Governor Patrick dropped out for health--"

"But nobody knows Dunlevy, Mary. He's a ditz."

"Momentarily he is running a distant second to John R. Clayburn, but he has tremendous name recognition. His father is a former governor, you know. He will be our governor in '98--"

"Whatever. They're all a bunch of benign crooks if you ask me; just so long as they don't screw up the market too much with their shenanigans," he said. "Got to go, now, Mary. Have a great time with your campaign, and *do not* . . . I repeat, *do not* under any circumstance return to the office until I call you. I'm having some work done over the next several weeks and I don't want you in the way. If you need me, call me on my private line. Good-bye--"

Lottie and Raymond bolted from the tumbled offices with his packed bags in tow. She was the first to breach the silence as they sped along Amsterdam Avenue. "Raymond, what are we going to do?"

"We need to find somewhere to lay low for a while." He sputtered. "With Long dead and someone very intent on finding something we apparently don't have, it could get very unhealthy around here."

"But where can we go?" In her ten years in the city, Lottie had been too busy being successful to nurture friendships; she was pretty sure that went double for Raymond.

"Don't know. How should I know? We take risks for people every day, but I don't know anybody who'd take a risk for us. We could go to my house, but if the bad guys haven't made it there already, they're on their way. And I don't want us to be there when they show up."

"What about . . . the police?" Lottie bit her lip. "Can they help?"

"Police? Help us do what? What can we tell them? That my friend Long was killed because he misplaced a stupid file? They'll think we're nut cases; or worse yet, we had something to do with the killing and we're trying to cover it up."

"I'm not wild about the idea, either, Raymond."

He patted his brow with his shirtsleeve. "Don't you get it? I might have been the last person to see Terry alive. I'm not putting myself in the position to respond to questions I don't have the answers to. Anyway, the cops would try to keep us in the city, and it's not a healthy place for us right now." He shook his head rigidly. "No. No cops. Out of the question. Too many loose ends."

Raymond crossed the Trans Manhattan Expressway over to the George Washington Bridge. "Tell you what," he said, "we'll go back to your place, Lottie. They won't come looking for us there, at least not right away. From what you tell me, they've done all the damage they can do." He positioned the car into the exit lane for I-95 North. "You can pick up a few things while we decide where to go. We'll get out of town and this trouble will blow over us like a mean dust devil."

The blood stains on Lottie's front porch brought the violent attack on her life into full focus for Raymond. "It's all my fault," he said, surveying the wanton destruction.

"Don't say that, Raymond. It's not your fault. We're caught up in somebody else's nightmare. That's all. I'll grab some things and meet you at the car."

"It's about time." Raymond pouted as he slammed her bags into the trunk. He climbed behind the wheel and peeled off to I-95. "North or South?"

"South."

They rode in silence until they were on the other side of Midtown. "Lottie, you still here?"

"Hmm . . . yeah, just thinking."

"Well, we can't drive around forever. We need somewhere to lay low."

"I was just thinking . . . since we're headed south anyway . . . why not go to Alabama?"

"Alabama? Isn't that a bit extreme?"

"Extreme circumstances call for extreme measures, right? Alabama. That's where I'm from; remember? I don't think anybody would come looking for us down there."

"That's for sure."

"We wouldn't have to stay long, maybe only a few days. The newspapers will tell us when the cops catch the murderer. Easy. See?"

"Where're you from in Alabama?"

"Union City." She squirmed. She hadn't mentioned it before. She knew city people were generally disinterested in the particulars of Southern states. In their minds, the country folds at the Mason-Dixon line into two, separate-and-unequal parts.

Raymond's head was splitting from trying to come up with a superior alternative. "Well, all right. Union City, it is. Get some rest. I'll take the first leg." The car clipped along I-95 into the starless night. An icy rain began to fall.

CHAPTER 8.
▲▲▲▲▲▲▲▲▲▲▲

Amber rays of sunshine kissed awake the sleepy blue South Carolina sky, but the contrast of majestic colors was wasted on Raymond whose ire burned red hot. On a normal Thursday morning, he'd be calling the shots in his Manhattan office. Instead, he'd been forced to run for his life by a faceless assassin, and he loathed the intrusion. His resentment had gained momentum through the long night as he sped southbound on their escape route, Lottie at his side.

Daybreak found them in Deedmore, and he pulled off I-95 at the Delight Cafe. Anxious to surrender the wheel to Lottie, he stopped off for a hot breakfast before making the switch. The subdued little establishment backed up to I-20, which would deliver them on the next leg of their journey to Birmingham.

"Yeah." Raymond snapped at the waitress. "While you're at it, bring me some smoked ham, three eggs, a short stack of pancakes, and keep the black coffee coming."

"Honey, ham ain't the only hot thing on my menu," the pert, young waitress said, resting her hip alongside Raymond's shoulder. "Sure I can't get you something else?" Her gingham-checked apron was crisply starched, and black bobby pins secured the matching hat to her peroxide-blonde curls.

"Whenever I want more, *Honey*," Raymond snarled, "I'm the one to do the asking."

"Sure thing, *Honey*." Her cheeks were ablaze. "Your loss." She plopped her pencil into her apron and flounced away.

As the sparks flew, Lottie got a chance to examine Raymond's appeal with the ladies. *I guess it's his muscles and those sexy eyes. He can be charming. But he can turn it on and off, and that kills it for me. I like my men. . . real.* "Now, that's a rare breed—"

"You say something, Lottie?"

"No. Nothing. I was just thinking I didn't know about your private line. Maybe I ought to check and see if we have any messages. Anyway, considering the way you treated that poor waitress, it'll be a l-o-n-g time before we get anything to eat around this place."

"Well . . . why not. I guess I'd better satisfy your curiosity before you pop. He gave her the number, and Lottie scurried to the pay phone near the ladies room.

"Last Chance!" A man bellowed in a rich baritone on the other end.

"Aah . . . yes . . ." Lottie said. "Exactly where are you located, please?"

"Same spot I been located for the last 25 years--514 Raytheon Avenue; Tucson, Arizona; Zip Code 85713. Ma'am, this here is Rex, the owner, speaking. If you'll just let me know what you want, maybe I can help ya.."

"I . . . I'm an associate of Raymond Beck. My name is Lottie . . . Lottie Garrett. He . . . uh . . . Raymond that is, asked me to check this number to see if he's received any messages."

"Raymond?" Rex laughed long and hard. "Well, why didn't you say so, Little Miss; that Ole Cuss. But why're you the one doing the asking? Is the Boy all right, Lottie? Why can't he ask me hisself?"

"He's fine. It's just that--"

"Oh well, anyhow, don't matter much who's doing the asking. I'm just glad he had the good sense to keep in touch." He chuckled.

"And to answer your question: No, ma'am, Raymond hadn't got no messages. But then again, Little Lady, this here's a diner, not a telephone answering service. I been busy. I don't have time to catch the blasted phone every time it rings."

"Well, thanks anyway, Rex. I'm always happy to meet one of Raymond's friends, even if it is over the phone," she said. "I'll have him call you real soon."

"Tell him I said, 'hey'. Okay. Bye-bye."

"Hey!" Lottie said, returning to the table where Raymond was attacking his food. "That's your message from Rex at the Last Chance Diner in Tucson." She stamped her foot excitedly. "Raymond! When will you ever let me in on things? Tucson? Why Tucson?"

"You're not the only one with a hometown, Lottie," he said, taking a hungry bite of his syrupy pancakes. "Tucson is mine. Sit!" He pointed to her waiting food. "Eat!"

"You've never spoken about your childhood," she said, chomping on a strip of her crisp bacon. "Tell me. What was it like growing up in Tucson?"

"Nothing much to tell." He slid a quarter into the jukebox console at their booth and punched in B9. A female vocalist belted out a country ballad in waltz tempo. It filled the cafe with visions of lonesome prairie and clear blue sky. "Hey you!" Raymond hailed the spurned waitress. "Bring me two longnecks and make it snappy."

Beer for breakfast? Another one of his well-kept secrets?

"Tucson was Tucson," Raymond said with a shrug. "Not all that different from anybody else's hometown, I'd imagine; except maybe, I lived in a trailer instead of a house. I lived there with my Mom and Dad, went to school, grew up, and moved away; like everybody else." He studied his empty plate. "My Mom's dead, now," he said. "She once worked for Rex at the Last Chance, helped him get his start."

"Oh, I see, so that's your fascination with diners."

"Yeah, probably. I enjoyed many-a-day hanging around the Last Chance waiting for Mom after school while Rex served me up the day's Blue Plate Special. Rex said Mom was his 'No. 1' waitress, and I was his 'No. 1' pal."

Raymond took a long draw from his first beer and his smile went sour. He twisted nervously on the squeaky vinyl, choking out each word. "I could tell Rex things I couldn't tell my own Daddy. He was a trucker. In the good times, he was kind. He'd let me ride in the cab of his 18-wheeler on long weekend hauls and tell his trucker buddies I was his 'No. 1 Sidekick.'"

Raymond downed the remains of his first longneck. The beer was loosening his tongue, and he was talking as much to himself as he was to Lottie. She didn't dare interrupt. "But when he was drinking . . . my Daddy was a different person--nasty. He even accused Mom of Rex being my daddy," he said, eyes darkening into slits of rage. "I hated him for that. I was born before him and Mom ever met Rex."

He turned up his second brew and ordered another. "My Daddy was like that though. He didn't let a little thing like the truth stand in the way of his foul mouth. He'd say, 'You took after your Mom--worthless trailer trash.'" Raymond's jaw set in a rigid line and his eyes into a trance. "'Together, y'all ain't worth two dead flies. Not worth the bullet it'd take to kill ya.'"

A strange pallor overtook his face, and he rocked like a lost child. "When I was real little, my Mom would protect me with her own body, or hide me in a closet when my Daddy's temper blew. She'd whisper softly through the locked door," he said, mimicking her soothing tone. "'Shush, sweet Baby. Close your eyes and sleep, now. This'll all blow over like an evil dust devil. You'll see. Everything's going to be all right.'"

Raymond stilled himself and sat stone straight. He cleared the tears from his husky throat. "In spite of . . . or maybe because of my Daddy's drunken and shiftless ways, I excelled as an athlete and was a pretty good student, too. Long hours in the library and the football field, beat coming home to my parents' constant fights."

"If Mom could see me now, she'd be so proud," he said. "She said I'd be great in spite of that man. I've proved her right and him wrong. I'm not worthless like he predicted. I'm successful, and my accomplishments have vindicated me and Mom from that man's bald-faced lies." His voice cracked pubescently.

So this is what makes Raymond Beck tick. Since their first encounter, Lottie had marveled at his relentless drive and continuous need to raise the bar. Despite accolades and enviable business results, he hammered himself day and night to exceed even his stretch goals. *Hatred.*

"My Mom died before her 50th birthday, Lottie. Too soon. Too soon. Too much hard work. Too many lonely nights. And too many blows at the hands of my Daddy," he said, hanging his head. "And what of me, you might

ask? Where was I when my Mom needed me most? Too busy hiding, I guess--in my own world. But bottom line, I let Mom down. I didn't keep her safe." He raised a clenched fist, and then dropped it harmlessly to the table again.
Poor Raymond. He can't see it, but he— not his daddy--is hatred's intended victim.
Raymond shifted self-consciously in his chair and downed the last of his third beer. He hadn't intended to expose himself like this.
"So, Arizona." Lottie played along. "Is that where you got the beautiful rug for our office? You said, 'out west.'"
"Yup. That's it. The amazing colors of the desert." He consulted his watch and called for the check. "Okay, it's 7 a.m.," he said, shoving his credit card into the hand of the gingham-clad waitress. "Time to hit the road if we're going to make Union City by nightfall."
Lottie took the wheel, and Raymond flopped into the passenger seat, quickly falling asleep in an alcohol haze. At the I-20 junction she had the strongest urge to turn back, but the graphic images of her ransacked home and the hairy-armed attacker persuaded her to join the westbound traffic to Birmingham. *Please, Lord, let this be over soon so we can get back to our lives.*

CHAPTER 9.
▲▲▲▲▲▲▲▲▲▲▲▲

Lottie tuned into a local oldies station and kept the volume low so as not to disturb Raymond. She glanced over at his sleeping form, which had been riddled with hostility only moments before. *I can remember the time when hatred had me by the throat like that, too.*

▲▲▲▲

It had been one of those clear spring days in Union City, the day of *the incident*. Lottie was attending Folsom High so she could ride home every afternoon with her mother from the Poteet Mansion. Miss Charity had cared for old man Frank Poteet ever since he suffered a stroke six years prior.

Of course Lottie knew the family; everyone did. They were one of the richest families in Red County. Three generations of Poteets lived together in the restored ante-bellum mansion on the north end of town with its massive white columns and splendidly manicured grounds.

When Lottie transferred to Folsom High, she was in the same class with the snotty Poteet grandson, Charles, or Charley to his friends. Charley and his buddies made great sport of heckling her each day. They appeared to derive enormous pleasure from it. She had half-expected they would tire of their childish taunts as soon as the novelty of her being the new kid wore off, so she paid them very little attention. Neither did she want to do anything to jeopardize her mother's job; they needed the money. And anyway, in Lottie's estimation, they were a pack of stupid boys and not worth the bother.

It had puzzled her, however, how Charley had changed so dramatically over the years. When he wasn't looking, she'd search his manly face for traces of the boy she once knew. As kids, the two of them had played together in the Poteet orchid under the sprawling pecan trees until they were sweaty and sometimes bloody. They shared whispered secrets and pledged their allegiance to each other, to equality, and to mutual respect.

But when it came time for them to go to high school in their respective neighborhoods, Charley had betrayed those former days. The games of childhood were tossed aside in favor of the tribal rites of adolescent boys. Charley had bonded with his peers and completely annulled his acquaintance with Lottie.

The Friday afternoon of *the incident*, Lottie would have been in school, except Folsom released early that day for a special teacher's meeting. Knowing her mother would put her to work at some menial task if she showed up early at the Poteets' kitchen door, Lottie decided to hide out in their barn for a few hours and show up just in time for the ride home.

She sprawled out on a haystack near the stall of Charley's new pinto pony that he'd received for his eighteenth birthday. She placed the pony's saddle blanket over the haystack, careful not to get straw on her brand new blouse and give away her deception. Her computer-programming project had been particularly difficult that day and she tackled it with deep concentration.

Suddenly, she realized someone was standing over her, leering. She hopped up to explain her unapproved presence when he pushed her down to the floor with a thud. While she scrambled desperately to recover her footing, he lunged on top of her and pinned her down. Straw and dust flew in every direction as she writhed madly to free herself from beneath his weight. Panic stricken, her cry for help stuck fast in her throat. In her defense, she clawed frantically at his exposed flesh--neck, face, eyes--anything she could grab and gouge. The commotion frightened the pony and he whinnied wildly, kicking against his stall.

The glassy-eyed attacker jeered at Lottie's feeble attempts to free herself. Violently, he skewered her shoulders into the floor and roughly kissed her face, blowing the stench of alcohol into her nostrils. She thrashed her head from side to side to ward off his advances, but he slapped her hard across the ear to win the advantage.

He planted his knee sharply into her midsection and speared her slender frame to the floor. With savage force, he pried her legs apart while she locked them together in rigid defiance. In spite of the piercing pain in her gut and the pounding in her head, Lottie wrestled and squirmed, resisting with all her might. But her strength was no match for his.

▲ ▲ ▲ ▲

Orange flags whipped in the stiff breeze alongside the South Carolina interstate, alerting motorist that bush-hog mowers were in the area. Lottie struggled to reel her mind back to the present. Tears blurred her vision. She could barely make out the friendly man waving to her from the tractor. Her palms broke into a cold sweat, every muscle tensed. Her foot slipped on the accelerator and the Lexus sputtered spasmodically. She clutched the steering wheel tightly, regretting having invited in this specter. *I can't turn back now; only the truth can prepare me for Union City.* She gathered herself and drove on.

▲ ▲ ▲ ▲

As she fought to fend off her attacker in the Poteet barn, the door creaked open. A stream of light filtered through and rested on Lottie's face. When her attacker saw it, he jumped off her and fled from the barn, past the ashen-faced figure planted in the doorway. The onlooker was stunned, immobilized, and he made no attempt to help her. Rather he stared after her attacker long and hard until he was out of sight. When he finally thawed, he stumbled from the barn, slamming the door behind him.

Ashamed and scared, Lottie gathered her things and ran through the woods for home. Her embarrassment grew as she ran, and bitter tears streamed down her face. Faster and faster she sprinted through the woods, tripping and stumbling as she ran. She attempted to outpace her damning conscience with every stride. *It was your fault for being there without permission.* "It was not! It was not my fault!" She yelled into the empty woods. "I did nothing to deserve this. Nothing!" The pine needles that scrubbed her face and the dried brush under her feet were her silent witnesses.

When she emerged from the woods at her house, Lottie stripped off her torn clothes and took a long, hot shower. She pitched her tattered blouse and soiled jeans into a ball under her bed and curled up on top of it, waiting for her mother in the dark.

"Where have you been, Lottie?" Miss Charity said when she arrived home. "I waited and I waited for you."

"I . . . I had lots of homework. I needed to get started. It'll take all weekend."

"But I told you . . . oh, never mind. You don't have the sense you was born with no how. Mr. Frank had a bad day. That last stroke o' his left him low sick, and I'm too tired to have to fool with you, too." She drug into the kitchen and prepared Friday's meatloaf.

Although her mother's meatloaf was one of her favorites, Lottie shied away from dinner. She pretended to be busy with homework behind the closed door of her room. As soon as her mother put the dishes away, she stole back into the kitchen and searched the drawers until she found a knife with a short blade.

Silently, she crept back into her bed and hid the short blade knife under her pillow. She shivered under the heavy blankets. Her insides were cold. Each time she closed her eyes, her heart raced furiously when the darkness engulfed her. *I can't tell Mamma. She'd never believe a Poteet would do such a horrible thing. And even if she believed me, there's nothing she can do. The Poteets are too powerful, and my Daddy's dead.* She poured her heart out in prayer and sobbed into her pillow until she fell off to sleep.

The next morning Lottie tagged along to her mother's church meeting to avoid being left alone. Charity Garrett was the secretary at Mt. Zion. There was no pay for the position, but Lottie admired the loving manner in which her mother discharged her duties.

While the grown-ups worked on the budget, Lottie drifted into the sanctuary. The sunlight streamed through the solitary stained glass window over the meager pulpit, but the familiar warmth was missing. The emptiness made her feel vulnerable, and she hurried back to the church office to rejoin the others.

Lottie dreaded returning to Mt. Zion the following day for Sunday service, even though some of her happiest times had been spent there. It was where she was baptized, sang in the youth choir, and frolicked with her friends. But now, even the familiar seemed strange.

"God really loves us," Reverend Jericho boomed from the pulpit, swaging his rotund belly from side to side. "And He wants us to be happy-"

I don't know about that. Lottie struggled to listen. *Every time I even get halfway happy, something bad happens to me.* Her eyes roamed the little whitewashed church that had seemed so void the day before. She studied the faces of the people who had transformed it into a place of worship. She knew them all. Their lives were a patchwork of poverty, disappointment, and pain.

Sister Farror's husband had walked off and left her ten years before she was nearly blinded by cataracts. Deacon Keenon had lost his only son in Vietnam, and his only daughter to drugs. At nearly 70 years old, he was raising his three grandchildren alone. Sister Brown had lost her job after 18 years because her new boss couldn't bear to look at her; her face had been disfigured in a house fire as a child.

Nonetheless, here they were at Mt. Zion, singing songs of praise. *I guess I'm just like them.* Lottie reflected. *They didn't pick what happened to them, and I didn't pick what happened to me. But they chose love over hate.*

As soon as Pastor Jericho gave the call, Lottie went down front with the other worshippers and knelt at the altar. "Lord," she prayed. "I guess you want me to take the talent you've given me and make my own happiness. So I'll just ask you this one last thing, and then I won't bother you no more. Please help me forgive them Poteets. I don't want to end up mean and evil like they are. I want my face to shine with love, like Sister Brown's."

The following Monday morning at Folsom High, a very shamefaced Charley Poteet sauntered up to her locker. "Hi, Lottie," he said. He was alone, and he looked petrified.

"Get away from me," Lottie snarled. "There's nothing you can say." She removed the short blade knife from her pocket and palmed it for him to see.

Charley shrank back and buried his eyes into the floor. "I just came by to talk, Lottie," he said. "Try to make things right--"

"Hush. Don't say nothing to me."

"Well, what can I do--"

"Do? There's always something y'all rich Poteets can do," Lottie said, alertly seizing the opening. "I don't want nothing for myself, mind you. There's nothing on earth you or your family can ever do to make up for what you've done to me. But it's my mother," she said, formulating her strategy as she spoke. "I want you to promise that when she's finished caring for your granddaddy that you'll pension her off at twice the salary she makes right now, and for the rest of her life, too. Cause if you don't, I just might have a little talk with my friend, Ruth Ann's, brother. You know, the one that's the sheriff."

"Don't you dare tell a soul, Lottie! What you're asking sounds fair," Charley said reticently. "I'll ask my Daddy--Jarrett. I'm sure he'll go along, if you keep your mouth shut."

"My Mother better not find out, neither," Lottie said. "You'd better keep your mouth shut, too. You hear me?"

"You've got my word, Lottie. See you at the prom Saturday night?"

"I ain't going."

CHAPTER 10.
▲▲▲▲▲▲▲▲▲▲▲▲

"Where are we?" Raymond yawned widely, rubbing his red-rimmed eyes; the stench of alcohol lingering on his breath. "I'm hungry."

"Next stop, Georgia state line." Lottie announced like an Amtrak conductor. "See the sign for Augusta?"

"Well, when we get there, pull over and let's grab a bite to eat."

"Sure thing. Gotta gas up anyway. In the meantime, why don't you take another look for the Clayburn file in my briefcase. Maybe you can come up with something I missed."

"Why not," he said, stretching himself drowsily. "I suppose I should take a shot at it." He read the file labels aloud. "Clabbert, Reese?" He scanned the contents. "Oh, I didn't recognize this one, Lottie, because you opened the account. Clark, Ramona. Ramona Clark?" He pushed the remaining files to the floor. "This file's not ours."

"No?"

"No. Not ours," he said, fingering the pages. "It's the beginning of a deposition, and there's an old newspaper clipping in here, too. This is my friend Terry's file," he said breathlessly. "I recognize his handwriting. And the newspaper article features one, John R. Clayburn; none other than the principle of Clayburn and Clayburn Investments."

"What?"

"See, here." He perched the yellowing clipping onto the dashboard. "It's a picture of Clayburn climbing into his limousine." Raymond raised the aging photo to the sunlight and squinted for a closer look. "His chauffeur looks vaguely familiar, too, but—"

"So what's it saying about Clayburn?"

"It's a collection of high profile interviews with Southerners who've made it big in Manhattan--*Taking a Bite of the Big Apple and*

Tasting Sweet Success. It gives a brief bio on the firm and John R." He read aloud. "'John R. Clayburn, the founding and managing partner of one of Wall Street's brightest stars, is a native of Birmingham, Alabama . . . was a member of the 1968 graduating class from prestigious Judson University in Dothan, Alabama, and received his MBA from Harvard University in 1971.'"

"It goes on to talk about Clayburn's political aspirations . . . his family," he said, reading the salient highlights. "His second wife of 15 years, Martha, lost her life in a private plane crash . . . their young son, Bradley, was the lone survivor of passengers and crew. John R. and his younger brother, Thomas P. Clayburn, founded the firm in New York in 1975 and it has had a glorious climb--" Raymond sputtered; his professional jealousy getting the better of him. "I wonder what the deposition from this Ramona Clark woman has to do with Clayburn?"

"Who knows? Let's eat," Lottie said, swinging into the parking lot of a restaurant with a belching smoke stack. Being this close to home gave her a hankering for pit barbecue. "Let's look at the file inside."

Spreading the contents over their table, Lottie scanned the newspaper account while Raymond read Ramona Clark's deposition. "It seems this Clark woman is a college co-ed who accused one of her school chums of date rape," he said, condensing the account. "Her statement must have been interrupted because she didn't complete the details of the attack, nor did she supply the name of her attacker; or at least Terry didn't write it down. Apparently, Ramona Clark was dating this man while attending college at New York University. According to Ms. Clark, although they dated frequently, the couple hadn't been sexually intimate. Then one night without warning, she says, the man raped her."

Raymond stirred his fully loaded potato while Lottie slapped extra pungent barbecue sauce onto her slab of pork ribs. "See," he showed her between bites. "Here's Terry's notes at the bottom of the page. 'Investigate!! Be Sure!!' And look here in the corner, looks like the letters *CB*, or maybe *BC*. With Terry it's hard to tell."

"I see what you mean."

"I used to kid him about his puffy doodles. He was forever interlocking letters on napkins at J-J's when he had a few too many, backwards and forwards, like clouds. He was ambidextrous, you know. The man had a brilliant mind . . . remarkable fellow. Such a loss . . . such a loss."

He signaled the bartender. "Bring me a mug of what you've got on tap. And keep it coming."

"And it looks like a useless loss, too," Lottie said, sipping her sweet iced tea. "Surely this file isn't what the killer was after. This can't be what Clayburn's man came looking for. What's this poor girl got to do with them?"

"Nothing. Based on his notes, Terry advised Ramona Clark to reconsider her story carefully before pressing charges." Raymond snorted on his beer. "I've heard him say that rape is a hard charge to stick, particularly if you've dated your attacker." He clutched his second mug in both hands. *What possessed Long to take on a nothing case like this? It's not his style. He was a top attorney, not an ambulance chaser.*

"You all right, Raymond?"

"Yeah. Just thinking." He slurred after his third mug. Why not stop off in Birmingham and find out more about native son, John R. Clayburn. I'll drive when we get there." He signaled the bartender for another round.

"That's a great idea," Lottie said, secretly hoping he'd be fit to take the wheel by Birmingham.

Raymond threw his credit card on the table, and Lottie returned it to his hand. "Pay with cash. Credit cards can be traced."

"Good catch." He burped. "Should've remembered that at our last stop. Go ahead. I'll pay at the register, after I use the phone."

After downing four mugs, Raymond's gait was remarkably steady. Lottie was reminded of her daddy's conviction. "A man what don't stagger when he's drunk is a man what's on regular speaking terms with his bottle."

"Hi, Rex!" Raymond greeted a little too loudly.

"Raymond?" Rex whispered into the phone. "Is this really you?"

"Who else—"

"Don't talk, just listen," he said. "Man, this joint's been crawling with men in dark glasses and trench coats. They're hunting for you, Boy."

"Wh-what--"

"Yup," Rex said. "At first, you got a passel of phone calls on your private number and nobody'd be on the other end. And then the next thing I know'd, a mean looking pair o' gents is in my face asking me your whereabouts. Man-o-man, it's a good thing I own this joint and my friends guns was bigger than theirs, or else I don't know what might o' gone down in here. Everybody was packing heat."

"Guns? What did you say?"

"I told 'em the truth. I ain't seen ya in over a year. And that seemed to satisfy 'em for the moment, but I hear tell they been asking round elsewhere. Gosh darn, Raymond. What you been up to?"

"Can't talk right now. Lottie and me are fine. We'll be in touch with you real soon. See ya, Good Buddy."

Raymond caught up with Lottie at the pump at the service station next door. "We've got to get outta here right away," he said, looking over his shoulder.

"What's the matter, Raymond?"

"Just toss me your keys. I'll drive."

Welcome to Alabama. The road sign whizzed pass their windshield. *Drive Friendly.* Lottie's heart raced at the sight of the familiar scenery. The steep, forest-covered ridges, and the imposing statute of the perennial Iron Man, welcomed her back across the threshold of northern Alabama. The tree line of brilliant fall colors--blazing hues of reds and yellows--pointed like a finger southward. The afternoon sun kissed her face.

While their stop was unavoidable, Lottie yearned to continue on to Union City. There the craggy peaks of northern hills would give way to majestic tall pine forests, rolling grasslands, and low croplands; and she'd be home. But her homecoming would have to wait. They had more pressing business at the Birmingham Public Library. She tilted her head onto the soft leather headrest and lost herself in the optical illusion of emerald hills touching azure sky.

"Who?" The pinched-faced librarian inquired over her glasses. "My word, Young Woman. Speak up; don't mumble," she said, cupping her ear. "Now, which of our native sons is it?"

"John R. Clayburn, ma'am," Lottie repeated. "He attended high school here in Birmingham, and attended Judson University down in Dothan. He's running for governor of New York in the election next month."

"Why, of course," she drawled. "Everyone knows John R. He'll make a fine governor. I just didn't catch the name at first," she whispered. "But what is your interest? You're Northerners. I can tell." She fanned her lace handkerchief briskly at her high collar. "Are you reporters?"

"Yes, ma'am." Lottie fibbed. "We need to get as much information as we can and get back on our private jet before nightfall."

"This is so exciting." She guided them to a number of periodical selections on John R. and reluctantly left them to their work. The articles, however, provided very little new information. John R.'s childless first marriage had ended tragically when his wife died of cancer after a lingering illness. The poignant details were given of the plane crash that had killed his second wife, who was 10 years his junior. There was a litany of accounts along the theme of "local boy makes good."

"This is getting us nowhere," Raymond said. "What does John R., the all-around good guy, philanthropist, and aspiring politician have to do with us?" He stood up and nearly toppled over the table in the study carousel that he shared with Lottie. "How have our lives gotten sucked up in his wake?"

"Shh-hh." The librarian scowled.

Raymond thudded to his chair and lowered his head to the table in frustration. While he lay there, Lottie seized upon an idea. She checked her watch. The library didn't close until 6 o'clock; she had time to pursue it. The librarian directed her to the stacks in the lower level basement, and she slid back the reluctant metal gate on the creepy elevator.

After checking a number of the stacks in the dimly lit basement, Lottie stumbled over a pile of books that had been laid aside in a dusty corner--Judson University yearbooks from the

1950s and 1960s. Lottie hurriedly cleared a spot near the single raw light bulb and settled down to page through the yearbooks--1960. . . 1965 . . . 1967. And then it happened.

On the pages of class pictures in the 1968 album, Lottie stumbled across a captioned shot of John R. Clayburn. Without the caption, she wouldn't have recognized him. She grimaced at the inevitability of the aging process. The slim, muscular face on the musty page bore no immediate resemblance to the pudgy, slack-faced gentleman in the newspaper clipping. But there he was, John R. Clayburn, senior class, and member of Sigma Gamma Sigma Fraternity.

Lottie flipped through the dry, cracking pages of the album until she came upon the group shot of the SGS Fraternity. With her finger, she skimmed through the names in the caption that held no significance, except one. There he was, John R. at the pinnacle of youth, sitting smugly with his fraternal clique. The twenty or so young men sat poised around their fraternal shield in the stylized motif of the period. The group exuded fine breeding and good fortune.

As she skimmed the names, Lottie's finger stopped on another entry she recognized. A name she hadn't expected to find; a name from her own past. Jarrett Poteet. Jarrett Poteet of the wealthy Union City Poteets, Charley Poteet's daddy, and her mother's benefactor. From the looks of it, both John R. Clayburn and Jarrett Poteet were in the Class of 1968. Among the remaining names was Thomas P. Clayburn, John R.'s younger brother, a neophyte in their fraternal ranks.

Lottie grabbed her pen and paper and listed each name they encountered: Terrence Long; Ramona Clark; John R. Clayburn; Thomas P. Clayburn; Bradley Clayburn; and now, Jarrett Poteet. There was no obvious connection. Studiously she compared the list with the puffy initials that Terry Long doodled in Ramona Clark's file. "*CB* . . . *CB*." She repeated against each name. Then she turned the initials the other way round. "*BC* . . . *BC* . . ."

Suddenly, she lurched up from the stacks of books sprawled about her, stubbing her toe on a nearby box. She grabbed her notes and the 1968 yearbook and ran to the elevator to rejoin Raymond. When she reached the main floor, Lottie flung open the metal gate and bolted from the confined space. She crashed headlong into Raymond, who had been looking for her, too.

"I know who *CB* is," they chimed in unison.

"Shh." Raymond cautioned. He led Lottie back to the study carousel, where he had left their things. "You go first," he whispered.

"Look at this Judson yearbook from 1968." Lottie pushed it toward him, and he eagerly obliged. "Now, this," she said, speaking at a blistering pace. "Look at this list of names I compiled from our research. The initials that Long doodled in Clark's deposition were not *CB*, but *BC*!" she said. "It's the only thing that fits. The initials stand for Bradley Clayburn, John R.'s only son." Her eyes twinkled. "See?"

"Yes. I believe you're right," Raymond said, nodding briskly. "I arrived at the identical conclusion based on what I uncovered. Read these." He showed her a number of snippets that chronicled the doings, or the wrong doings, of one, Bradley Clayburn.

It appeared that Bradley had been accepted at Yale upon graduating high school with honors. After that, he drifted into a downward spiral of pranks, violence, drunken episodes, and expulsions. Bradley had been expelled from Yale midway his freshman year after a hit-and-run accident left another motorist injured. No charges were filed, but Bradley had landed at Judson University the next fall. He had abruptly left Judson for "unexplained reasons," seemingly bound for New York City. It was not clear, but the final account intimated that Bradley might be completing his college career at New York University. And from there, the trail went cold.

"NYU?" Lottie's brow knitted. "That rings a bell." She fished out the Clark deposition from among the growing pile. "Ramona Clark was also attending NYU when the alleged date rape occurred."

"It's got to be more than a coincidence," Raymond said. "We need to check out this guy, Bradley. But we're here, and he's there--"

"And that's the way it has got to stay. Right? At least until we know more about this situation. We need to stay far away from the City--for our safety sake. Right?"

"I guess." Raymond nodded reluctantly.

"Based on what we know so far, this Bradley Clayburn character is a bad-actor, spoiled-brat type," Lottie said. "He dated Ramona Clark, who spurned his advances, so he rapes her, or so she says. So, now, when Ramona reports the rape to your buddy Terry Long, Bradley Clayburn, spoiled brat that he is, kills Long to cover up his latest misdeed." She smirked ruefully. "Sorry, Raymond. It just doesn't add up. If he were going to kill somebody to cover up, why wouldn't Bradley simply kill Ramona and stuff her away somewhere? Why kill Long?"

"You're right. There's a missing piece here. Or else maybe Ramona Clark is already dead," he said, snapping his fingers in recall. "I've got it! I've got it!" he yelled noiselessly. "Yes! Yes! We can't check on Bradley, but we can get what's-his-name to do it."

"What? Who?"

"There's this guy, a cop, that me and Terry used to drink with in the old days down at J-J's. I can't remember his name . . . but I do know that he was once stationed as a rookie beat cop in the East Village," he said. "Actually, this guy was a closer friend to Terry than he was to me. But I used to see him come in and we'd toss down a few with Terry. I haven't seen him in years, but I know he'd be interested in this case, if only I could remember his name." Raymond banged his forehead with his closed fist.

"Lighten up, Raymond—"

"That's it! That's it!" He remembered. "Lt. Thrush . . . Leland Thrush. Yeah. That's it. Lt. Leland Thrush of the 61st Precinct. I remember the night he made lieutenant. He came by J-J's to celebrate with Terry and me. He was drinking heavily, and he kept repeating this silly sing-song, 'Lt. Leland Thrush--Heart and

Soul of the 61st.' He could do it for us. He could check out ole' Bradley Boy and nobody'd be the wiser. He'd probably jump at the chance, too, considering poor Terry and all."

"Wow! That's great!"

"We'll get in touch with Thrush when we get to Union City," he said, happy for some news to put him back on top.

Raymond and Lottie were the last pair to leave the library at closing time. The librarian showed them out and locked the doors behind them. From the landing of the massive staircase, they spotted the glowing neon sign from *The Green Door*. Jaded and hungry, they succumbed to its invitation.

"This'll be our last stop," Raymond said. "After we eat, we'll drive straight through to Union City, even if it means we arrive in the wee hours of the morning."

Upon entering the restaurant, the tired pair was warmed by the wood-burning fireplace. Its giant, fragrant logs crackled invitingly, spewing colorful sparks up the sturdy chimney. They gratefully accepted the booth offered them by the white-jacketed maitre'd.

Lottie pushed her back against the painted bricks and stretched her legs out on the vinyl seat. Her weary body sank low and her heavy eyelids successfully pled their case; she allowed them to close. Raymond slipped away to the pay phone to check-in with Rex.

"Am I glad to hear from you," Rex said. "I was hoping you'd call."

"Why? What's up, now?" Raymond pressed. "Talk up."

"When you cut our last conversation so short like," Rex spoke quietly, "it got me to thinking. Them bad jokers mighta thought to trace your calls, like they do in the cop shows on TV."

"Wha--"

"Well, acting on a hunch, I checked the insides of the phone on the bar and found a small magnetized, disc-looking thing that didn't belong there. I hadn't never seen no bugging device before, Raymond, but I'm fairly sure that's what it was. Anyhow, to be on the safe side, I relocated that little bugger to the mouth piece of the pay phone over there in the corner." He chuckled. "Eavesdropping on these truckers, they're gonna get an earful of wine, women, and song."

Raymond joined in on Rex's sneaky laugh, "For sure."

"Son, you sure y'all all right? This is looking dangerous. Do you need anything? How're you holding up?"

"You know me," Raymond quipped. "Play 'til the horn sounds. We're a little saddle sore, but--"

"Raymond. I hate to tell you at a time like this, but your daddy came around asking about you the other day. He's slipping away, Son. You ought to--"

"Not interested. If there's nothing more--"

"I give him the money you send for him," Rex said. "You've made your point. He knows you're well off. But, Raymond, you've got to come and see him. Talk things over with him and get things straight . . . before it's too late. He's your daddy, for God's sake, and now he's just a sick, tired, old man--"

"Take real good care of yourself, Rex." Raymond side-stepped. "When this is over, I'll come around and we'll have some laughs; just the two of us, like old times. Bye."

After their meal came and went, the ice shifting in Raymond's second glass of bourbon was the solitary sound at the booth they shared. Lottie was satisfied with the arrangement since her thoughts had wandered back to the last time she'd seen her mother. *I don't know why I never called her over these ten years. Maybe Mamma represents the disappointments I left behind. Or maybe I felt guilty because I didn't tell her I was leaving, not even a note. But whatever my reasons, it's just about to come to a head.*

Raymond ordered his third double. Rex's appeal was ringing fresh in his ears, and he remembered his mother, too. *Why's she dead, and that man's still alive? Some cruel twist of fate, perhaps? Some other-worldly mix-up? Mom deserved life more than him.* Beautiful, glistening raven hair falling below her waist, and a kind, gentle manner that hog-tied everyone's heart with a velvet rope. His pulse thumped violently and his stomach twisted in knots. *I miss you, Mom. I'll always hate that man for taking you away from me. He's no Daddy of mine.*

"Time to go." Raymond downed the last dregs of his drink and banged his glass on the table. He slapped some cash on the counter and fingered the remaining bills in his thinning money clip. Grudgingly, he passed a tip to the waitress.

As he drove them southward on I-65, Raymond's morose mood matched the ominous night sky, thick with fog. The alcohol didn't help him, and neither could Lottie. She feigned sleep and maintained a steady vigil; keeping an eye out for Alabama State Troopers, who were known to haul out-of-towners to jail for drinking and driving, and she kept even a closer eye on Raymond.

Over the 100 miles from Birmingham to Montgomery, she peeked at his intensely pinched expression that carved deep furrows into his brow. Silent tears reflected off his cheek as the headlights from oncoming vehicles pulsed through the windshield. Lottie pretended not to hear his grinding teeth and fitful murmurs, but his state of mind concerned her more and more.

As the lights on Montgomery's capitol dome grew brighter, it was nearly midnight. The narrow, two-lane road between Montgomery and Union City would be teeming with fully loaded pulp wood trucks and 18-wheelers making their nightly runs to Florida. No place for a tired driver, and Raymond needed rest.

"Who cares if he dies, anyhow?" Raymond yelled, and Lottie shot straight up.

"Raymond," she said. "You're tired. Stop for gas. I'll drive the rest of the way."

Under the cover of darkness, he tried to explain away his outburst when Lottie relieved him at the wheel. "It's just this trouble--it's stirring up some pretty tough emotion," he said.

"I don't like it. It's shaking up everything--our business, our schedules, our lives. We've got to get to the bottom of this thing--and fast--and put our lives back on track."

"I agree, Raymond, but . . . life is what it is. We can't always keep things in neat little packages, or keep our emotions under wraps. Sometimes, a 'purposeful shaking up' is what we need."

"You're making no sense, Lottie."

She chuckled faintly. "It seems the closer I get to home, the more my Daddy's words tumble in on me. Anyway, my Daddy used to say, 'a purposeful shaking up' clears the air, puts things into perspective, and makes us come to grips with things as they are, rather than how we want them to be. He'd say, that's the time to 'hold your holt, Baby, and keep the faith,'" she said. "I don't like this mess any more than you do, Raymond, but we've got to deal with it. What choice do we have?"

"I suppose you're right. We've got to process through this somehow. How much farther to Union City?"

"Close." Her voice smiled.

Raymond spotted the road marker first and read it smugly. "Union City, 26 miles."

CHAPTER 11.
▲▲▲▲▲▲▲▲▲▲▲▲

Turning off Highway 82 onto County Road 49, Lottie drove Raymond to a little motel on the outskirts of town. The "V" flickered spasmodically on the neon "Vacancy" sign. He looked at her, eyes wide, and back again at the run-down bungalows. "Whoa." He laughed uneasily. "You're really leaving me here?"

"It's clean," she drawled. "Y'all is down South now, suh." She checked her watch--1:47 a.m. Friday morning. She didn't want to have to explain Raymond to her mother.

Lottie parked the car next to a pick-up truck, and Raymond reluctantly climbed out. He stretched his achy joints and retrieved the Beckmobile from the back seat. The cold, crisp air was loaded with the pungent smell of wood-burning fireplaces. Lottie waited until he got his room key from the tiny office.

Back on Highway 82, she headed east for the twenty-minute drive to her mother's house. The double yellow lines and snake-like arrows mounted on warning markers bade drivers to heed the winding curves along the way, or face the disastrous duo of soft shoulders and steep drop-offs. The roller-coaster roads and narrow bridges allowed no margin for error.

When she reached Saw Mill Road, Lottie took the turn to her mother's house. When she was a child, this had been a red clay road that had to be wet down periodically to settle the dust. It had since been paved with pitch and pee gravel, but it was pitted with potholes by the heavy truck traffic from the sawmill plant where it dead-ended. The trucks usually moved through late at night bringing loads of spindly pine saplings to it and finished wood products from it.

When she reached her mother's front gate, a semi-trailer truck from the mill slowed down to take a look. Blinded by its headlights, she vigorously shooed away the silhouette of a man who was peering down at her from his elevated cab. "Still some nosy folks down here." She grumbled.

Lottie turned into the uneven gateposts that marked her mother's front yard. Her headlights swung onto the lush fall garden, heaping with broad-leafed collard greens, turnips, and dark-hued beets. A sweet potato mound covered in protective pine straw was set over into the corner where a chicken coop once stood. Apparently her mother had gotten rid of the chickens that once roamed the yard freely, but everything else matched Lottie's recollections.

She parked her car and collected her personal items, locking up securely. Although she didn't expect thieves, she took every precaution to secure the precious information they'd gathered in Birmingham.

The sky was filled with stars that twinkled brightly over the housetop and lighted her way. It was a celestial spectacle that would have been obscured by bright lights back in the big city. The fresh scent of pine mingled with the tell-tell stench of wet manure from Mr. Joe-Joe's cow pasture next door. Gingerly, Lottie mounted the steps to the wrap-around porch. The second step creaked in its old familiar way, reminding her of the hot summer nights she'd spent there as a girl.

▲▲▲▲

The second step had been her favorite ringside seat when the family gathered on the porch to drink ice-cold lemonade and play a game called, "I See Something You Don't See." On those hot summer nights, each of them in turn would call out clues for an object that they hoped no one else had spotted. This would go on until either someone guessed the object from the clues and won the game, or the object had to be revealed to everyone by the clue-giver. In which case, the clue-giver won.

They would laugh and play the game for hours. Those times together as a family had been some of her best. Except for her sister, Rose, who had been known to cheat; she would change the identity of her object when someone guessed it correctly.

▲▲▲▲

The front screen door whined when Lottie opened it. Her heart raced into her mouth and her knees went weak, like the marrow had absented her bones. She knocked softly on her mother's front door. No answer. She rapped a little louder the second time and heard some rustling inside. She drew in her breath when the front door parted. The blood gushed through her neck and pounded violently against her skull. She felt dizzy; her vision blurred.

"Who's there?" Miss Charity called out.

"It's me, Mamma," she said, managing to unstick her tongue, which had cleaved to the roof of her mouth. "Me . . . Lottie."

"Lottie? " Her mother gasped. She flung open the front door and blinked in disbelief. "Chile, is that you? Lordy, mercy!"

"Mamma!" Lottie grabbed her slight frame and hugged it tightly. The time and distance between them melted in an instant. They clung to each other like victims of a shipwreck. Lottie's tears flowed silently down her mother's back. Had she not been caught up in the moment, she would've felt her mother's tears watering her shoulder, too.

"Lottie?" Her mother pushed her away, and frowned accusingly. "What you doing here, Gal? You in some kind o' trouble? Miss Charity Garrett was not known for her subtlety, and her intuition was renown. Very little escaped her notice.

"Ma-ma," Lottie said in an agonizing whine, the dimly lit porch concealing her flushed face. "I'll give you the whole story in the morning. I promise. But right now, I'm very tired." She faked a deep yawn. "And if it's all right with you, I need some sleep."

"Well, of course you do," her mother said, gently patting the back of her hand. She stepped aside and allowed her to enter. "What am I thinking of? You must o' been driving for a long time, all the way from New York City. And all by yourself, too." She observed. "The back bedroom is made up as usual. But if I was you, just to be on the safe side, I'd shake them covers out a bit to be sure no spiders or nothing done camped out in there. You wouldn't want none o' these backward-acting black widows climbing into bed with you on your first night back in the country, now would you?" She snickered, pleased for an opening to poke a little fun at her daughter. "You hungry, Chile?" She called from the kitchen as Lottie closed the bedroom door.

"No, Mamma. Not hungry, just sleepy. See you in the morning." Obediently, she turned back the bed and shook the covers.

Lottie awoke to the savory smell of smoked bacon frying and chicory coffee brewing, welcomed smells that reminded her she was home. She stretched out in her bed like a supple cat soaking up sunlight in a big bay window. Her bedroom was toasty warm and cozy. Her mother had seen to it. As was her custom, Miss Charity rose early before anyone else in the house, and lit the space heaters, particularly in the "girl's" room. Lottie drew a robe around her that she found in the closet, which was filled with empty wire hangers. She couldn't remember if the robe had belonged to her, or Rose.

▲▲▲▲

In the old days, she and Rose had shared the bedroom; one of two in the house. They had shared their sibling fights there, too. Rose had squabbled with her incessantly, over shared quarters, personal clothing, and parental affections. She lorded over her, imposing her will as the older sister, and Lottie had fiercely resisted the imposition. Their episodes had become terribly fractious at times. The bedroom walls bore the scars to prove it.

After she left home, Lottie didn't keep in touch with Rose. Since they didn't get along, she didn't see the point. But Ruth Ann, Lottie's friend in The Bronx, kept her up-to-date on the latest hometown gossip. She filled her in when Rose married a man in the military, moved to California, and had her first child. Although happy with the news, Lottie had made no attempt to contact her. They were bonded by blood, and Lottie loved her, but it had been proved to her satisfaction that the best relationship with Rose was one maintained at a distance.

▲▲▲▲

Lottie slid her feet into the slippers she found under the bed to ward off the chill of the linoleum floors. She scooted briskly down the narrow hallway toward the kitchen. She felt like a kid again, waiting to face the music with Miss Charity.

"Good morning, Mamma." She took the offensive. "Can I do something to help?" she said, safely expecting to be turned down. Miss Charity could prepare a meal and clean up quicker than a two-man assault team, and her kitchen was categorically off limits to even well intentioned intruders.

"No. I thank you, Miss; and a very good afternoon to you, too. It's well past 9 o'clock. Did you get your rest out?"

"Thanks. I slept like a log, and I feel wonderfully rested. It's this great country air."

"Well, sit down and join me. Let's eat a little something and *talk*."

Miss Charity's inflection on the word sent chills through Lottie. She retreated to the kitchen sink, putting her back to her mother. Slowly, she washed her hands under the soothing hot water and stalled for time to invent an alibi for her unplanned homecoming. She wanted to keep it light, anything that would throw her mother off the scent of the truth.

The glistening sunlight streamed through the bare window over the sink and drew Lottie's attention into the yard. Two dogs were frolicking near the broken-down utility shed, or *corncrib*, as the locals called them. *Only in rural Alabama would dogs be allowed to run loose, and that sorry excuse for a corncrib be left standing.* They let things around here crumble under their own weight. From her safe distance at the sink, Lottie remarked, "Still letting those mangy dogs run loose, I see?"

"They my dogs," Miss Charity said. "Anyway, it's been over ten years since you was here. Those ain't the same dogs you recall. Both the old ones got run over by them pulpwood trucks what roar through here every night. These are some of their pups."

"Then why don't you tear down that old corncrib? It really looks a mess, Mamma."

"You talk mighty pretty, Miss Lottie, with your New York accent and all. Your lips is moving, but you ain't saying nothing. If you've finished dissecting my business, maybe you could sit down and shed some light on your own. Why're you here, Lottie?"

As instructed, Lottie slid over from the sink and took her seat at the table across from her mother. She flopped her hands limply into her lap and buried her eyes into her breakfast plate, trying to buy some time. Lies wouldn't go far with Miss Charity. The truth was her single option. She drew up her courage and let it fly.

Lottie brought her mother up-to-date on her college degree, and her work at Beck. She filled her in on the recent murder of Raymond's friend, Terry Long; his misplaced file; and, ultimately, the break-in at their offices. In deference to her mother's peace of mind, she held back both the attack on her life, and their trip to the Birmingham library. She hesitated to divulge their findings until she and Raymond could put all the pieces together.

Since John R. Clayburn and Jarrett Poteet, her mother's former employer, knew each other, she withheld Ramona Clark's charges of date rape against Clayburn's son, Bradley, too. Lottie didn't want to make her mother anymore complicit in the matter than she already was due to her association with her daughter, the fugitive.

"Mamma, I didn't come down here alone," she said, squirming until the cane bottom on her high-backed chair squeaked. "Raymond and I came, together."

"I figured as much," Miss Charity said, and her countenance didn't so much as ripple.

"We were alone together--all the way from New York City."

"Good. I'm glad he's here. Seems like the only wise thing y'all could do under the circumstances. So, where is he? Where is this Mr. Beck? Outta harms way, I hope."

"Uhh . . . yes. I left him at Motel 49." Her eyelids fluttered in disbelief. Stunned that after years of neglecting their relationship, she could discuss her dilemma with her mother--one adult to another—no reprisals, no fireworks, no condemnation.

Lottie had underestimated her once again. Although her mother had never been so much as 200 miles from Union City, her grasp of the complexities of life was a marvel. Had Lottie the nerve to press her for an explanation, Miss Charity probably would have told her, "My Bible tells me ain't nothing new under the sun. Folks been doing bad things to each other since the world began. And don't none o' us know what we'll do 'til we're put to the test."

But Lottie wasn't granted the opportunity to explore her mother's wisdom. Miss Charity was satisfied with the facts in the matter, and she closed off the discussion. "Well," she said, rising stiffly. "I've got quite a few little chores to do, and I best get to 'em." She nodded vacantly. "If you want to, you can bring that Mr. Beck fella by for supper this evening."

"Well—"

"No need to answer me right now. I'm gonna fix enough food anyhow. The frost fell on them collard greens last week and they're fit to eat." Before she could say more, Miss Charity moved to the sink, humming. It was the signal she'd been dismissed. Lottie gently kissed her on the neck.

Back in her room, Lottie examined the pile of small boxes she'd noticed earlier. They were stacked in the overstuffed armchair by the window. As it turned out, each of them contained a gift addressed to her in her mother's crude handwriting. There was a gift there for each birthday and Christmas she'd been away.

Carefully, Lottie placed the handkerchiefs, gloves, and assorted trinkets side-by-side across her bed. The chain of tender tributes broke her heart. The love they represented out-measured every laudable thing she'd accomplished in the city. *Oh, Mamma! You do love me! You always loved me!* She knelt by her bed and wept bitterly over the irretrievable years she'd missed with her mother.

▲▲▲▲

Back at Motel 49, Raymond paced the floor of his small, musty room like a caged lion, wondering when Lottie would call. He hadn't slept well on the lumpy mattress, and he hated the seclusion. His nerves were too raw to bear it. He needed some air. He got dressed and took a brisk walk across the parking lot littered with 18-wheelers to the stingy main lobby. He used the pay phone to call Rex.

"Last Chance."

"Rex. It's me. Raymond."

"Oh, hi Ra--. It's about time you checked in," he whispered anxiously. "Some real tough guys was by here again, interested in your whereabouts. They must've camped out 'round here when they found out you had kin in the area. As best I can tell, they're hold up at a motel nearby, cause they come checking every so often."

"Rex, you can slow down. I'm on a pay phone and this call can't be traced. We're doing okay where we are. I just called to see if you're all right."

"Yeah. Yeah, Raymond. I'm okay, but I'm telling you, you'd better watch your back, Son. These are some real tough customers."

"Okay, Rex. And thanks--"

"Wait. Before you go. Have you called your dad--?"

Raymond used his calling card again; this time to dial his office in New York. He was greeted by his own voice on the recording. He punched in his remote code and retrieved his messages. There were a number of client calls, but he'd get back to those later. He fast-forwarded until he came to a message from his secretary, Mary.

"Hi Raymond." Mary's voice sparkled in her familiar prissy manner. "I remain grateful for the unexpected vacation. My very deserving gubernatorial candidate is gaining ground as the race heats up, and this sabbatical allows me to stand shoulder-to-shoulder with my fellow supporters to push him over the top. The more I follow this campaign, the more I'm convinced that the people of this state do not deserve a man like, John R. Clayburn. Brrr. He's as cold as ice. Since I don't know when you want me to return to work, I expect you to call me at least one day in advance. Time is ticking. Hope we can count on your vote in a couple of weeks."

CHAPTER 12.
▲▲▲▲▲▲▲▲▲▲▲

After a good cry in her bedroom, Lottie pulled herself together to meet Raymond at Motel 49. She expected him to be hungry and more than a little antsy. On her way to the car, she saw a figure hiking across the field, dressed in a man's tattered coat and hat, and boots loaded down with thick red clay.

"Whew! Hey there." Miss Charity waved, in answer to Lottie's quizzical look. "Had to make sure that mare of mine didn't catch herself in no mud bog during that last heavy downpour. You'd think horses had more sense, but sometimes they're awfully dumb, and have to be saved from themselves." She snickered behind a gloved hand. "Sort o' like some people I know."

"What's that you say, Mamma? Your mare all right?"

"Oh, nothing, Daughter. Nothing." Miss Charity muzzled a grin. "The mare, she fine. And that's a mighty fine car you're driving there, too, Little Miss. Mighty fine."

"By the way, Mamma," Lottie said, reminded of the cache of information she had stashed there, "whatever happened to mean ole Charles Poteet?"

"Little Charley? Well, believe it or not, he finished off to be a fine young man. Graduated from Judson with honors and went to law school back east somewhere, and now he's got clients coming out the woodworks they tell me."

"Finished off well? He just should have. He had every advantage money could buy. So what's he up to now?"

"Still living on the family estate, o' course, but he got a law office in town, too. Why--"

"Gotta go now, Mamma. See you at dinner."

Pausing at the front gate, Lottie took stock of her homeplace in the daylight. One by one, her unaltered childhood memories fell like straw men. The tin roof, which had once sparkled in the sunlight, was dull and in need of repair. Sap from the branches of the pecan trees, which hung dangerously close, had tarnished it. The trees once yielded a bountiful fall harvest of the meaty nut, but now they looked scanty and in desperate need of attention. The pine planks covering the base of the elevated front porch resembled the snaggled-tooth smile of a seven year old. And the wooden fence bounding the property, which had once stood erect and proud, was shamefully bowed by the invasion of termites, barely agile enough to serve its purpose.

Lottie's heart sank as she squinted into the sunlight. *Whew! Time is a monster. Mamma's been without a man for a long time, and it shows. Maybe . . . it's my turn to give the Garrett Place back its shine.* The pair of rangy yard dogs charged her, wagging their tails and sniffing at her ankles. She closed the car door on their cold noses, but they tagged playfully alongside the car for a ways as she pulled onto the blacktop to meet Raymond.

When she arrived at Motel 49, a baggy-eyed Raymond was standing outside his room, leaning against a chinaberry tree carved in romantic graffiti. He was smoking a cigarette he'd bummed off a trucker whose red-white-and-blue cab had a shotgun mounted in the window.

Lottie was surprised. She didn't know Raymond smoked.

"Hey there, Big City Slicker!" She called out through her open window. "Trying to pick up a Southern Belle?"

"Where've you been, Lottie? Were you planning on leaving me in this God-forsaken place forever?"

"Hop in. I'll buy you some lunch."

"It'd do you good to remember we're not down here on vacation. We're here to get our arms around our situation. That's it. We've got to contact Lt. Thrush, or have you forgotten?"

"Then get in, Raymond. We're wasting time." She pretended not to notice the trucker eyeing them with the third-degree.

Raymond turned to see it, and growled under his breath. "Trailer trash."

As they approached downtown Union City, the two-lane road ushered in a divided four-lane boulevard, bounded on both sides by a sampling of ante-bellum homes. Huge potted ferns, holdovers from the summer, swung charmingly in the breeze on some of the sprawling porches, while wind socks of Confederate flags flapped happily on others.

"You should come through here in the springtime," Lottie said, pointing proudly to the dormant plantings in the median. "When the magnolias and azaleas are in bloom, the colors and smells on this one little street can rival any in the world."

"It's some wonderful old architecture, all right." He pointed to the Shortner Mansion. "The Civil War movies don't do these houses justice."

"My mother did some day-work at the Shortner, and says it's beautiful inside, with winding staircases fit for a fairy tale wedding."

"I bet it was great living in these wonderful old homes during their heyday."

"Yeah. I bet." Lottie smirked. Undoubtedly, her image of life in those old houses differed from his.

At the first traffic light, one of three in downtown, she waited for her turn to circle the square. All traffic was routed around it in honor of the granite monument of an unknown Confederate soldier bearing arms. She pulled into one of the parking spaces in front of the only sit-down restaurant in town, and they got out.

"Where is everybody?" Raymond said. "Is this a ghost town or what?"

"Noon hour's nearly over. And down here, working people *really* work."

"Whatever." He shrugged, rubbing his hand across his stubby face. "Help me remember to buy a razor."

Like Raymond, this was Lottie's first time to set foot in the Old South Restaurant. As they entered, she was distracted by a weathered sign tacked to the doorpost. The whitewash had failed to cover the words scrawled beneath-- *White Only*. The chilly reminder of Jim Crowism sent Lottie hurrying to catch up with Raymond at their table.

"How's your Mom?" he asked politely.

"As perceptive and ornery as ever." She smiled. "Thanks for asking."

"Did you tell her about me--?"

The waitress plunked down two glasses of water onto the checkered oilcloth. "What y'all want," she said, glaring between them.

"For starters, *y'all* can bring us some menus," Raymond said, sending her cowering to retrieve them. "Lottie, what's with these people down here? Whatever happened to that southern hospitality you're supposed to be famous for?"

The waitress returned and Raymond ordered in rapid fire, without so much as looking at the menu he had demanded. "And give me whatever beer you have on tap, too," he said unyieldingly. "I want my beer in a mug, not a glass. And you give the Lady, here, whatever it is she wants."

The waitress wrote vigorously on her pad, eyes pleading to Lottie for relief. "Lunch special." She obliged.

"What're we going to tell Thrush?" Raymond said, as the waitress skulked away.

"He's your buddy, Raymond. What'll move him to action?

"I can tell him about Long's murder, the attack on your life, and the missing file. But we've got to be careful. We can't go bantering around the names of highly influential people without hard and fast evidence."

"But how can we convince Thrush without it?"

"Well . . . I could throw in the fact that some real dangerous types have been hunting for me in Tucson—"

"Tucson? You didn't tell me--"

"I'm telling you now."

"How do you--? Are we safe?"

"Rex told me, but I didn't want to worry you. There's nothing we can do about it anyway, and they didn't find out anything from Rex. We should be safe for now."

" Raymond, you should've told me."

"For now, let's just stick to the Thrush angle. Okay?"

"Um-hum," she said, rubbing her cold hands together. "I hope your lieutenant realizes when two very sane people take off in the middle of the night in fear of their lives, the threat is real, not hype."

"Yeah. But just the same, I think I'll spare him the details about John R. and the possible southern connection."

Raymond downed his burger in four big bites, each one followed closely by a giant gulp of beer from his mug. Lottie was amused when a different waitress delivered their check. Southern prejudice had met head-on with northern audacity, and the north had won, again.

"Well, would you look at that?" Lottie motioned to the turn-of-the-century telephone booth at the side exit.

"No time like the present," Raymond said, sliding back the accordion door.

"Yikes." She shuddered at the sound, like a thumbnail scratching on a chalkboard.

He dialed a long string of numbers while Lottie paced the wall. "Lt. Leland Thrush. Tell him it's Raymond Beck from J-J's. He'll know." He dug his knee into the seat and fidgeted with the door and waited.

"Hello, Thrush." He signaled Lottie. "Remember me? I know. It has been a long time. I hope you're sitting down, Good Buddy. Have I got a story to tell." Without pause, Raymond launched into the details that had inaugurated their fugitive status. Lottie could pick up only bits and pieces of the one-sided conversation, but his body language told the story. His voice traveled the scale, from pleading to yelling.

"Man!" He finally exploded. "This is not a hoax! Lottie's got the bruises around her throat to prove it. Look at my office if you don't believe me. We're not crazy here." Finally, the veins in Raymond's neck settled down. "Thanks. Thanks ole Buddy. I knew Terry could count on you. We're in trouble, real trouble, and we desperately need your help." He recited Lottie's local telephone number. "Please. Let us hear from you real soon."

"Well?"

Raymond wiped his brow, embarrassed for her to see him sweat. "The deed is done."

"You said you weren't going to mention John R."

"Did I have a choice? You heard. He wasn't buying. I had to give him something."

"I guess. Anyway, come with me." She pointed in the direction of the town square. "See that five-and-dime over there. It's been in business since I was a little girl. It's got the best hand-dipped ice cream you've ever tasted."

"Ooo-wee!" He mocked her small-town excitement. "I'm sure I can hardly wait."

"Come on, Little Boy," she said, aware his throne was up-ended, and he wasn't fairing very well without it. "You can relax, now. You're in my town."

They crossed over the square past the white gazebo. A wooden glider swung idly in the breeze, and the massive oaks marked the path with their shedding leaves. The bricks in the walkway bore the names of the founding fathers, dating back over a century.

"This was the site of Red County's slave auction," Lottie remarked somberly.

"Slave auction?" The year, 1858, jutted from under Raymond's shoe, but judging by Lottie's mood he decided to hold his questions for later. "Ouch!" He yelped, as he banged his head against a low-hanging storefront shingle.

"What? Well. Well. So this is it." Lottie read. "Poteet and Brunson, Attorneys-at-Law."

"Jarrett Poteet? John R.'s classmate?"

"No. Charles Poteet. His son. My classmate."

"You didn't tell me you knew the Poteets."

"Like you said, 'I'm telling you now.'"

With Lottie in tow, Raymond bounded as casually as his excitement would allow into the mahogany-rich offices of Poteet and Brunson. He approached the receptionist with one of his patented snake-oil smiles. "We're here to see Attorney Poteet."

"Do you have an appointment, sir?" The cherub-cheeked receptionist frowned.

Raymond flashed his business card like a badge of honor. "We're here from New York City, only for a few days. It's imperative that we speak to Mr. Poteet on an urgent matter."

The receptionist didn't appear particularly impressed with Raymond's come-on, but she politely excused herself, business card in hand. She entered an inner chamber and gently closed the solid doors behind her.

The waiting area smelled of rich woods and old money. Elaborately etched glass doors enclosed the floor-to-ceiling bookcases, weighted down by impressive law tomes. An array of gilded plaques validated the professional and charitable accomplishments of the principles. An exquisite pair of bronze eagles, perched on matching marble pedestals, made quite an elegant statement. But Lottie wasn't impressed. She knew Charley Poteet.

"How do you do, suh?" Mr. Poteet's private secretary emerged from the inner chamber with the receptionist trailing at her heels. "Mr. Beck, is it?" The mature woman glanced at his business card. "Mr. Poteet is tied up in conference at the moment, but he will make every effort to see you directly," she drawled. Raymond joined Lottie in the waiting area, and sat down amid the distinctive swish of leather.

In due course a cadre of gentlemen, clad in rep ties and investment banker shoes, trailed out of the inner chamber. An amiable young man in his early thirties bid them farewell. His imperious bearing and relaxed manner identified him as the man at the helm.

"Mr. Poteet?" Raymond waded upstream through the departing guests and shot out his hand. "Raymond Beck, here," he said, claiming first strike in the customary joust for male dominance.

"Yes. I am Charles Poteet," he said, swinging the momentum clearly in his favor. "I only have a few minutes before my next appointment. But please, let's move into my office." When Lottie rose to join them, Charley flinched. "Lot-tie? Lottie Garrett? Is that you? Wh-hat on earth are you doing in Union City?"

"Mr. Raymond Beck, of Beck & Associate, New York City," Lottie enunciated eloquently, "I would like you to meet Mr. Charles Poteet, of the Union City Poteets, Attorney-at-Law."

"Let's move this into my office," Charley said quietly.

"Well, Charley. How's tricks?" Lottie took the seat he offered her.

"What? Why're you here, Lottie?"

"Simple, Charley. "We need your help."

"I don't understand." He shot a bewildered glance in Raymond's direction.

"My firm . . . " Raymond came to her rescue. "My firm is in stiff competition with another Wall Street firm on a daily basis."

"Clayburn & Clayburn." She followed. "You should know--"

"And since we planned to visit Lottie's hometown, anyway, I thought I could do a little amateur sleuthing while I'm here to find out as much as I can about my competition." Raymond winked. "To give myself a leg up."

"And . . ." Charley motioned impatiently. "I fail to see how it involves me."

"The principle of Clayburn & Clayburn is John R. Clayburn," Raymond said. "He's campaigning for the Governor's Mansion in our state?"

"You should know." Lottie chimed in. "Isn't he your daddy's friend?"

Charley plucked at his intercom. "Hold all my calls." He barked. "Mr. Beck, are you some sort of investigator? Are you trying to say there's some connection between my father and the Clayburn campaign?"

"No, of course not." Lottie softened. "Nothing like that. It's just that Raymond and I . . . made a little wager. He bet me he can piece together John R.'s entire background in the short time we're here. I bet him, he can't." She flushed at her lie. "It's as simple as that."

Charley was inattentive through much of Lottie's explanation. Her words drifted in and out. As he watched her, his mind returned to *the incident* in the barn so many years before, and he remembered her knife. *What's she really after? Back to exact her pound of flesh? I guess I have to help her. I owe her that much. She's grown into a lovely young woman. But there was always something quite special about Lottie Garrett.*

"Charley?" Lottie prompted. "Take a look at these."

The duo from New York littered his desk with copies of old pictures. "Sure, I recognize the photos," Charley said. "They're from the Judson yearbook. My Daddy is quite the passionate alum, even if it has been nearly 30 years. There he is. And there's John R. Clayburn."

"So you knew they were classmates?" Raymond said.

"Of course. It's no secret. I've heard of their sophomoric exploits for most of my life, 'til I'm sick of the stories."

"Then you know John R?"

"Not personally. Only what I read in the papers. My Daddy thinks the world of him, sort of like a friendly foe. Interestingly enough, though, he doesn't think very much of his chances in next month's election. Aside from that, y'all probably know more about the man than I do. Did know his son, though."

"Huh?"

"His son?"

"Bradley Clayburn. I met him when his daddy sent him down here to attend Judson after he'd been kicked out of Yale, or Princeton, or one of those Ivy League schools back east. I first met

him when he came out to the Mansion to pay his respects to my Daddy."
"What's he like?"
"Nice enough kid. Came down here as a freshman, driving a shiny new Porsche . . . spoiled little brat . . . but very handsome and likeable. You know, the kind o' kid you love to hate. But he didn't stay around very long. Ran into some trouble with the administration. I guess too much drinking, or womanizing, or something. In the end, he was quietly booted out of Judson, and I never saw him again. Don't know anymore than that."

"We want to find out as much about old man Clayburn and his son as we can." Raymond said. "I've got to win this bet, or I'll never hear the end of it."

"Charley." Lottie edged in cautiously. "Maybe we could speak to your daddy about this. He's known him the longest."

"Out of the question." He glared at her as though he had uncovered her motive.

"Charles," she said reassuringly." We won't upset your daddy. And if it'll make you feel better, I won't even be there. I promise."

"Promise." Raymond raised his right hand.

"That might be all right," Charley said. "Tell you what. I'll set up the meet." He handed Raymond his business card as he showed them to the door. "Call me tomorrow."

By the time they reached the street, Raymond's curiosity was running wild. "This is a strange town, and what's with you and this Poteet fellow? I sense some long-standing hostility."

"Hostility?" Lottie threw her head back in a gigantic laugh. "Raymond, you're coming home with me. Mamma wants you over for dinner."

"Well, okay. Fine. When we stop off for my razor, we can get her some wine for dinner. Which would she prefer? Red or white?"

Lottie was dumbfounded by the suggestion. Charity Garrett had probably never drank anything stronger than homemade grape juice in her entire life. *Besides, what vintage would be suitable with collard greens?*

CHAPTER 13.
▲▲▲▲▲▲▲▲▲▲▲

Their last stop on the edge of town was at the state-regulated Alcohol Beverage Control store, affectionately termed, *ABC*, by its frequenters. Raymond stashed the precious contents of his brown paper bag safely underneath the passenger seat and scrunched down into its contours to rest his heavy eyelids. He looked beat, and Lottie took the long way home. She wanted to give him ample opportunity to gather his wits before his first meeting with Charity Garrett.

Winding along her favorite stretch of country road, Lottie drank in the color spectacle-- vibrant hues of red and orange. The setting sun flickered through the dense green forest, like ticker tape in a parade given in honor of her homecoming. Lottie choked back happy tears.

Suddenly, without warning, a skittish deer hurdled across the front of her car. She slammed on the brakes just in time to prevent it from crashing through the windshield. Dusk was the most dangerous time in these backwoods. Deer blinded by headlights killed more motorists than the sum total of eight-point bucks hauled out by hungry-eyed hunters.

Raymond bolted upright during the disturbance, and he remained on wide-eyed alert for the balance of the trip. His vigilant sentry could not have prepared him, however, for the leanness on Saw Mill Road. *Who would have thought Lottie came out of a world of half-breed cattle and red clay ruts? No wonder she never mentioned this place.*

When they pulled in through the gate, Miss Charity was sitting on the front porch with a wool shawl tightly drawn about her shoulders. She was rocking in a primitive-looking contraption, fashioned by hand from sturdy twigs and thin leather strips. She hummed a dirge of a hymn in tempo with the thump on the porch.

"Hi, Mamma," Lottie waved from the car, realizing she'd probably kept her waiting past her customary dinner hour.

Raymond awkwardly combed his fingers through his hair and self-consciously ran his hand over his stubby face. He rearranged the collar of his crumpled shirt and shook the creases back into his pant legs. The dogs skipped happily around his ankles, sniffing out the newcomer, but Lottie shooed them underneath the porch.

"Glad y'all could finally make it," Miss Charity said when they mounted the steps. She was dressed in her best gray flannel chemise. She raised herself by the banister and led the way. "Y'all's dinner is getting cold."

Once inside, the house was filled with the welcoming aroma of collard greens and bell peppers simmered in ham hocks. "Sit here, Raymond." Lottie fidgeted nervously. "I'll go help Mamma." She eased into the kitchen to gauge her mood. "Umm. . . Mamma. Something sure smells good. Can I help?"

"Let the man wash up, Lottie. Did you leave him out there all by hisself, without the benefit of heat nor light? Use some common sense, Gal."

In the living room, Raymond had begun to feel like a perspective beau on his first date, an idea he categorically rejected. He followed the voices into the kitchen. "Hi," he said, poking his head around the corner. "I'm Raymond Beck, Beck and Associate, New York City."

Miss Charity scrubbed her right hand on her apron and shared his handshake. "Yes, suh," she said, nodding with a mischievous glint. "Mighty fine. But I know who you are. I'm the one what invited you." She motioned him to the head of the table. "Have a seat."

"Here?"

"Why, sho, Mr. Beck and Associate. You deserves the best seat in the house, I'm sure. I've just about got everything on the table."

The dinner was superbly prepared and the atmosphere was warm and easy. It was no match for the fine restaurants to which Raymond had grown accustomed, but he didn't seem to mind the wholesome simplicity. He served himself from every dish on the table--peas and okra, hot water cornbread, squash casserole, smothered chicken with gravy over rice; and of course, the collard greens.

"Pass me that dish near you, Lottie," he said politely. "It's the only one I haven't sampled yet." He whiffed. "Smells great. What is it?"

"Uhh . . . a southern delicacy," Lottie said. "Smoked neckbones." *He's out of his league now.* She chuckled to herself. *Particularly since on more than one occasion, I've heard him sternly reject the more uncomely parts of the pig.*

"Umm . . ." He moaned with delight. "Just as I expected. Succulent." He polished off his meal with a hearty helping of Miss Charity's state-fair-winning, hot peach cobbler, topped with hand-cranked ice cream from the summer stock in her deep freeze. "Well, I've enjoyed my stay here so far," he said, over the clatter of knives and forks. "But by far, Mrs. Garrett, this lovely meal has been the highlight of my trip."

"Thank you, suh."

"I saw that healthy garden of yours as we drove up," he said, angling into her good graces. "You do all the work yourself?"

"Yes, suh, I do."

"My Mother had a garden like that once. Loved it. Any bad weather so far? Insects?"

"No, suh. Ain't had neither."

"Mrs. Garrett!" He threw up his hands in frustration. "I'm drowning here. Won't you talk to me?"

"Miss Charity," she drawled in a sweet motherly tone.

"Huh?"

"Just call me Miss Charity," she said. "Everybody else does."

"Whatever you say . . . Miss Charity. I—"

"Come on over here, Mr. Beck." Her bones creaked as she rose to usher her empty plate to the sink. "Help me with the dishes, if you will, and then me and you, we can sit out there on my front porch and have ourselves a fine talk." Her face softened. "It's a nice night. I don't think it'll be too chilly for ya, not if you wraps up real good."

"Yes, ma'am." He rose obediently and moved toward the sink.

Help me with the dishes? Lottie mouthed behind her hand. *What's she up to now?* She had watched her mother sizing him up, and stayed far away from their awkward exchange. She knew better than to get in Miss Charity's way. *She's got him in her sights now, and I don't want to be around when the straight shooting starts.*

Lottie retreated to her room, taking the *Montgomery Chronicle* off the sideboard on her way out. She hoped the local daily would have some news on the Long murder, anything that would jettison them out of Union City and back into their proper orbit.

Raymond chatted fluidly as he opened the squeaky front screen and claimed the chair beside her rocker. "Like I said, Miss Charity, I haven't had a meal like that since . . . since the last time my Mother cooked for me. And that's been some years ago. You put a lot of love into your recipes, just like she did." He rubbed his hands together appreciatively. "Yes, sir. That was some fine meal."

"And by the way, Miss Charity," he gabbed on non-stop. "You can be very proud of your daughter. Lottie is a true credit to her profession. What she can do with a computer, most folks will never comprehend. It's like she becomes one with those blasted machines." He chuckled like a used car salesman. "Lottie is one of an elite few, I tell you. She has a limitless future in New York. But, what am I saying?" He banged his forehead demonstratively. "She's your daughter, right? The nut doesn't fall too far from the tree . . ." He bobbled to a halt like an expiring spinning top. " . . . Or something like that, right?"

"You have a very busy heart, Mr. Beck," Miss Charity said when she'd heard enough. "And you sho' can run off at the mouth. But as for me, I'm a woman living on her faith." She raised her eyes adoringly toward heaven. "Blessed to have my two daughters. They're my only earthly possessions of any value, whatsoever."

She rocked her chair at a steady pace. "Now, don't let this trouble y'all's having overtake you, you hear? If you needs yourself some help, git some. And put this thing behind you so you can move on."

"Yes, ma'am," he said, motionless. *Did Lottie tell her? Or is this shrewd old woman setting a trap for me to incriminate myself?*

"I know Lottie don't think much o' him," she said. "But Charley Poteet done turned out to be a real credit to this community, and he helps folks in need in this whole county. He might be able to help y'all, too." She rocked faster. "As for Charley's daddy, Jarrett Poteet, he's a man to be feared, but he ain't no man to be trusted. His daddy, old man Frank, God rest his soul, didn't put no time into raising po' Jarrett when he was coming along."

She rocked pensively. "Them Poteets own nearly half o' Red County, mostly cause o' Mr. Frank's shady land-grabbing deals. Folks round these parts know all about his trickery back then. If you had 40 acres and a mule and Mr. Frank wanted it, he wouldn't stop at nothing 'til he stole it off o' ya, or bought it dirt cheap for taxes. Folks say Jarrett pretty much raised hisself. No Mamma, you know. You hearing me, Raymond?"

"Yes, ma'am."

"Mark my words." She rocked back emphatically. "Every crop you sows, good or bad, bears after its own kind. That's sho-nuff the way it is, and there ain't no getting round it neither. It was all I could do to help po' Charley when he was coming along . . . him with no Mamma to speak of neither."

At that moment, Lottie appeared at the front door and flicked on the weak porch light. The pair on the porch suspended their conversation. It would have to keep for another time. Lottie wiped her hands conspicuously on the kitchen towel. She'd put away the dishes and she wanted them to know it. "I see something you don't see!" she said playfully, lounging across the last remaining chair.

"Whatever could it be?" Miss Charity followed her lead.

Raymond quickly caught onto the rules, and enjoyed playing the game with the women. The good food and warm hospitality had relaxed him. But it was getting late. "I need to get on back, now." He coaxed and Miss Charity did not disagree.

"Oh, by the way, Lottie," she inserted cleverly as they approached the car. "I forgot to mention, a Lt. Thrush from the N-Y-P-D called y'all today. He say, call as soon as possible. He say, with his busy po-lice caseload he'll be working all weekend, so you can reach him at his office. Anytime. I've got the number in here when you're ready for it."

"Oh. Thanks, Mother." Lottie squeezed through locked jaws; her cheeks ablaze. "He's Raymond's friend. We've got the number." *Can't get nothing pass Mamma. And look at Raymond-- the chameleon--waving at Mamma like he's none the wiser.* She spun out of the gate for Motel 49.

Back in his cramped motel room, Raymond kicked off his shoes and poured himself two fingers of bourbon from his brown paper bag. He savored the familiar warmth as it traced his throat. He was glad to finally be alone with the company of his private thoughts and his precious bottle.

He flopped across the bed and flipped the channels on his pint-sized TV until he found a news station. There was nothing at all on the national scene about Long's murder. Disgusted, he tossed his plastic cup aside and took a deep draw straight from the bottle. He was snoring loudly before the sportscast wrapped up.

CHAPTER 14.
▲▲▲▲▲▲▲▲▲▲▲▲

"Hullo . . . hullo," Lottie mumbled sleepily. She was awakened early Saturday morning by sunlight streaming through her bedroom window and the ringing telephone in the hall.

"Lottie Garrett?" A man barked on the line. "Lt. Leland Thrush, here. NYPD."

"Hi, uh, yes." She hopped from one barefoot to the other on the chilly linoleum floor. "I'm Lottie Garrett, Raymond Beck's associate. We've been waiting for your call."

"Is Raymond with you? I need to speak with him directly."

"Sorry. No. He's not here right now. But you can tell me anything you'd tell him. I assure you, we're in this thing together up to our necks."

"Well, as bad as I hate to admit it," Thrush said briskly, "it seems that our mutual friend, Terry Long, did indeed die under some rather suspicious circumstances. He died of a heart attack, true enough, but markings on his body indicate he'd been exposed to some sort of trauma before his death that left burn marks on his arms and legs. To put it bluntly, Long was tortured to death."

"Tortured? But why—"

"I also did a little checking around Raymond's office like he asked, and I didn't like what I found there either. You tell Raymond after we got what we needed, I sent a clean-up crew to that disaster area. Tell him he owes me. Big time."

"Okay. But what about--"

"Also tell him I can't find anything to connect Long's death with that mess in his office. As far as I can tell, one thing had nothing to do with the other. If he wants my help, he's got to give me more to go on. I'm still working the murder angle and maybe I can turn up something there. But Raymond needs to get back with me on what exactly was in Terry's missing file. That might be the key. Any lead would help. I need something solid to go on."

"But didn't he tell you--"

"Oh, and by the way." Thrush moved at a fast clip. "John R. Clayburn was in the news this morning. He's climbing rapidly in the polls. So tell Raymond to be careful how he flings his name around. The election's in a few weeks, and by all accounts he's going to be our next governor. And I'm not telling a single, solitary soul about Raymond's crazy suspicions until I have enough hard evidence for an official investigation. That's evidence mind you, not guesswork. I'm not putting my pension on the line for Raymond, or anybody else. Is that clear?"

"It's clear, but--"

"Hold on--" He spoke in muffled tones away from the receiver. "Got to go now." Thrush returned to the line. "I'm a busy man. I've got some real murder cases to solve. If he wants my help, you tell Raymond he needs to call me--himself--right away. Got it."

The dial tone was screaming in Lottie's ear when she hung up the phone. She searched the house for her mother, but was not surprised she wasn't there. Miss Charity was in the habit of rising early for her daily devotions. By now she'd probably be running errands, or performing *helps* for one of the neighbors. She had a full life and financial well-being. Lottie had seen to that.

It made her feel far less guilty for neglecting her mother over the years.

Hearing voices on the front porch, Lottie slid over to the window to investigate. She couldn't barge outside in her pajamas so she stood behind the drapes and eavesdropped. A teenaged girl, she didn't recognize, was crying bitterly on Miss Charity's shoulder.

"He's gone and it's all my fault." The young girl wailed mournfully. "It's God's way of punishing me for my sin--having my baby out of wedlock." She whimpered pathetically. "My Mamma taught me better, Miss Charity. I just didn't listen. And now, my baby, my precious little one-year-old boy is dead and gone, forever."

The young girl's heart was wrenched with sadness, the likes of which Lottie had never seen before. Her fragile body heaved with violent tears as she clung desperately to Miss Charity for consolation. She appeared to possess neither the physical maturity nor the emotional stability to be a mother, not to mention coping with the death of her baby. The bewilderment, reflected in her grief-stricken eyes, broke Lottie's heart. It reminded her of the reason she'd escaped Union City when she did.

▲▲▲▲

Before leaving home, Lottie had been sick to death of seeing unmarried girls swaging babies on their narrow hips, and living on welfare crumbs with their mammas who already had too many mouths to feed. Poorly educated young girls, who couldn't expect husbands and families of their own, because their men folk had mortgaged away their futures with drugs and alcohol, and a bogus perspective on life.

She witnessed young men her age huddled on street corners, unaware of their God-given right to have dominion over the earth. They assigned more worth to cars and clothes than to their own families. They neither understood their value as men, nor their responsibility in raising their children; and thus fulfilling their duty in the circle of life.

Lottie had watched her little town become overrun with drugs. She knew of the devastating effects they caused in big cities, but those were strangers, not the people she loved. Not people like Ruth Ann's baby brother, Ned, who died of a drug overdose the month before Lottie took off for New York City.

No one had found Ned's body for over a week because he'd hid out in a wrecked car in the junkyard to celebrate his sixteenth birthday with his brand new crack pipe. The funeral ripped his mother to shreds and set the whole town reeling. By leaving Union City when she did, Lottie traded one means of escape for another.

▲▲▲▲

Back on the front porch, Lottie looked on while her mother listened patiently to the pitiful young girl. Lovingly, Miss Charity rocked her in her arms. After a long while when the girl's tears subsided, she prayed.

"Dear Lord." Miss Charity entreated confidently. "We trust you 'cause there ain't nothing you can't do. Po Pam's heart is broke cause you took her baby home to be with you. But we know it wasn't no payback, cause you already died and paid for every one of our sins. Help Pam not to wallow around in hers no mo. And please, Sir, let her come out stronger and wiser on the other side o' her grief. We thank you in Jesus' name. Amen."

"Thank you, Miss Charity." Pam sniffled, lifting her head from her bosom. "I know you're right." The younger woman tenderly kissed the older one on her cheek. "I know it's gonna be all right. He knows best. But sometimes, it just hurts so bad." She shuddered. "At any rate, I'll be back at church on Sunday morning."

"That's what I'm talking about," Miss Charity said, smiling tenderly. "Back where you belongs, with folks that love ya." She locked arms with Pam and they ambled off the porch and up the road out of sight.

Lottie returned to her bathroom to prepare to take Raymond to breakfast. Her daddy had added it on when her older sister, Rose, became a teenager. He wanted to give her more privacy. He could do wonders with an idea scribbled on a scrap of paper, some two-by-fours, and a level.

▲▲▲▲

"Tee-hee-hee. And don't you dare forget that level." Her daddy would snicker. It was his way of poking fun at the northern notion that southern folk were backward and incapable of quality construction. "We can't have nothing looking crooked on my watch." He'd jab playfully. "What would city folk think? We've got our image to uphold."

Building the bathroom had been only one of a number of projects her daddy undertook around the house. Even after long, difficult hours at the mill, he'd always find time to keep up his premises. "There's no place I'd rather be than taking care of what's mine," he'd say.

He built birdhouses, painted them bright colors, and set them in the yard on high poles. He made a greenhouse out of scrap lumber and heavy plastic for Miss Charity to store her plants in winter. He would be the first in the neighborhood to till his garden in springtime and plant all sorts of wonderful things. (Although he'd sometimes lose interest in midstream, and Miss Charity was left to bring in the harvest, alone.) He planted pecan trees and fruit trees in the back orchard, and named each one of them after a family member.

One day Little-Bad-Johnny-Hurd, the neighborhood bully, taunted Lottie mercilessly about her daddy's idiosyncrasies. The other kids circled them to egg on the fight. The little boy had gotten stuck with the handle because he stole frequently to have enough to eat, and lied compulsively for no reason at all.

"Why Mr. G talk to all them trees he plants?" Little-Bad-Johnny skipped around Lottie, wagging his finger spitefully. The growing flock of kids hummed with excitement. "My Daddy say your Daddy, he a Crazy Old Coot. He'll be dead and gone fo' any o' them trees is grown."

Lottie poked out her tongue at the mean little boy, while the other kids jeered. "No, he doesn't," she defended passionately. "My Daddy doesn't talk to all them trees. He only talks to the ones he likes. And besides, Little-Bad-Johnny-Hurd." She propped her hands on her slender hips and bobbed her head like a fishing cork. "You don't even *know* your Daddy." With that, the rabble disbursed with a loud roar, spreading the news of Lottie's victory. Her reputation for holding her own was sealed.

But one day when her curiosity had gotten the better of her, Lottie confronted her daddy to set the record straight. "Why do you plant those trees, Daddy, that you may never see grow up? And why do you talk to 'em at all?"

"Why do I call the trees by name?" Her daddy paused a while to consider. "I guess to keep my loved ones in my thoughts, Lottie. That way, they're never really gone. I probably won't live to see these trees mature. But long ago somebody stood in my shoes, and they chose to plant the trees we enjoy today. Now, it's my turn. Besides, the orchards will be a cash crop for your Mamma's little whims."

▲▲▲▲

"Ouch!" Lottie stubbed her toe against the raw edge of the linoleum that had been improperly sealed. *This bathroom is just like my Daddy.* She smiled fondly. *A little rough around the edges, but well suited for its purposes. And as long as we have his projects and funny little stories, he'll never really be gone.*

Lottie took a moment to inspect the silver picture frame setting on her dresser. It was one of the countless childhood snapshots of her and Rose scattered about the house. This particular photo was of the pair of them in their early teens on a fishing trip. Lottie had accidentally fallen from their small paddleboat into the water and had to be rescued by her daddy.

She looked like a drowned rat standing beside Rose who was wearing a radiant smile and holding high the catch of the day. Setting the picture aside, Lottie remembered the pain she wanted to forget.

▲▲▲▲

Everyone who had seen the picture back then had thought it was funny and cute, but not Lottie. That day had been her last fishing trip. She'd never really liked fishing, anyway, but Rose had insisted she come along. She'd used it as yet another opportunity to make Lottie appear foolish in front of their daddy, and her plan had worked.

Rose had learned to fish because it gave her an excuse to be close to their daddy. She adored him and the feeling was mutual--and exclusive. Although Lottie never doubted his love--no, not for a moment--it had been evident to her that Rose had his heart.

"You'd better give it to me, Lottie, or I'll tell Daddy," Rose said, when they tugged over the last apple in their bedroom. "You know Daddy'll make you give it to me if I ask him to."

"I will not," Lottie screeched bitterly. "You got the last one last time. It's my turn."

"Lottie, stop fighting with your big sister." Her Daddy yelled through their closed door. "And give Rose whatever it is she wants. I don't want to hear another peep out o' you."

Lottie had been envious of the bond between Rose and her daddy. She longed for an equally intimate relationship with her mother to somehow balance the scales. Although Miss Charity was deeply devoted to their family, Lottie never experienced the same level of closeness with her as was commonplace between her daddy and Rose. Deep down, Lottie had felt it was her mother's duty to come to her aide and be her defender. But that had not been the case, and she felt cheated and powerless.

"Mam-ma." Lottie sulked pitifully. "It was my turn to have the last apple, and Daddy gave it to Rose."

"Mind your Daddy, Young-Un."

It was back in those awkward, misfit days that Lottie first heard her Sunday School teacher at Mt. Zion, Sister Foster, tell of Jesus' love.

Lottie had watched the *churchiness* of the old folk every Sunday, with their testimonies and shouting; but that had nothing to do with her. She came only because her mother would drag her along.

However, Sister Foster told her class something new that grabbed Lottie's attention. "Jesus wants a personal relationship with you," she said, as though it were the most precious news in the world. "He loves you, and He'll stick by you closer than a brother. He's on your side. And if you ask Him, He'll come into your life and be your very best friend."

Lottie timidly raised her hand. "Closer than a sister, too?"

"Yes, Lottie." Sister Foster assured her. "Closer than a sister, too."

Lottie believed. From that point on, she prayed and talked to Jesus about everything--anything. In prayer she found refuge from her feelings of rejection, and she gorged herself on the sweet promises of scripture. When Rose was mean and cocky about their daddy's love, Lottie ran to Jesus. When her mother's unflappable countenance was a painful mystery, Lottie ran to Jesus.

At long last she had found the friend she craved, a friend whose heart she held. He didn't betray her confidences, or think her problems petty, or her desires far-fetched. Her search for significance was over. No longer needy for Rose's approval or her daddy's attention, Lottie reclaimed control over her life. And from that time forward, Rose found herself at a decided disadvantage.

I'm gonna tell Daddy," Rose said, blustering angrily. "And you'll be sorry." She whizzed a high-heeled shoe past Lottie's face, smashing it into the bedroom wall. "Daddy will *make* Chaney take me to the senior prom, and you can't stop me."

"You go right ahead and tell Daddy." Lottie tossed back the shoe. "If that boy is stupid enough to take someone as mean and spiteful as you to the prom, you deserve each other."

Afterwards, she dealt with the boy who was in Rose's senior class. "You can take Rose to the prom if you want to, Chaney James Masters," she said. "It's perfectly fine with me."

"No, Lottie," Chaney said. "You're the one for me. I'll wait until I can take you to your senior prom. And I don't care what Rose wants, or what your Daddy says. And I'll tell him so, too."

CHAPTER 15.
▲▲▲▲▲▲▲▲▲▲▲

While on her way to Motel 49 to pick up Raymond for breakfast, Lottie made a detour through town to the Piggly Wiggly. She wanted to recruit some locals, who hung out in front of the grocery store on Saturday mornings, to help her with chores at her mother's house. Two of the men recognized her right away.

"If it ain't Miss Charity's Gal." They grinned broadly.

"My name is Lottie." She corrected spiritedly. "And I ain't nobody's Gal."

"Aw, now. Don't go and get yourself all riled up. We know who you are. We was just funning with ya. You ain't forgot us, neither, is ya? Duke and Hamp?"

"Oh yeah, I know," she said smartly. Of course, she remembered the tag team. They were older than her, but not that much older; although they looked ten years older than they should. They were a unique brand of drunk--never staggered, fully capable of a decent day's work, but never more than a quart low of the cheap *'Bird* wine they drank.

"Well, now." Hamp cajoled playfully. "What you doing back down here in L.A.?"

"Yeah, Lower Alabama?" Duke snickered.

"Here to see my Mamma. What else?"

"Here tell you brought you a blue-eyed Mister with you." Duke ribbed. "Tucked away real quiet like over there at Motel 49."

"What? Lottie?" Hamp joined in on the sport. "A white man? You? I didn't know you swung like that."

"Yeah," Duke said, gyrating his hips to further the point. "We didn't know you liked cream in yo' coffee. I'm sho' glad your Daddy ain't here to see his brown-sugar go bad."

"Yeah. What you gotta say for yourself, Young Lady."

"He my boss." Lottie slipped back into the vernacular. "We're on the road on business, and we decided to swing by here, is all."

"Then, who fine car is that?" Hamp said. "Yours or his'n?"

"Mine."

"Well then, you must be doing mighty fine for yourself up North." Duke winked.

"Yeah, we thought you'd be eating chicken feathers and turnip roots by now." Hamp doubled over with laughter, bracing himself on one knee.

"What you telling us, then? That white boy you got stashed over at Motel 49, he your Boss Man, not your Hoss Man." Both men snickered lewdly.

"That's it." She twinkled. "If it's any of your business . . . he is my Boss Man."

"Well," Hamp said, taking a long snort from the brown paper bag nuzzled close to his heart. "Guess we could spend a day doing more than skinning and grinning. What say you, Duke?"

"Yeah." He straightened his back out of respect. "I guess we can't deny Miss Charity. We'll meet ya over there at noon."

▲▲▲▲

It was nearly 11 o'clock. Lottie stopped off and picked up a fast food breakfast for Raymond. When she arrived at his room, he was fully dressed. In fact, he was better groomed than she'd seen him in some time; even though the room smelled like stale booze.

"Good morning to you," she said, leaning against the wall, arms folded "You're in fine spirits. What's up?"

"You made me wait." He smirked. "Now, it's your turn." He ate dramatically slow.

"Raymond. Please!"

He wiped his mouth and flung his napkin aside. "Now let's see. What can I tell you? Oh, yes. I received a call from Charley Poteet early this morning. He called me, unlike some people in this room who shall remain nameless, and informed me that his daddy will be in town today. Home from the state capitol," he blared. "Lottie, why didn't you tell me the man's a state senator?"

"You didn't ask. Anyway, I thought you knew Jarrett Poteet was in politics. Around here, that's how old money keeps their money."

"Anyway, to make a long story short, Senator Poteet is home from Montgomery today, and his chauffeur will be dispatched to whisk me up to the big house sometime this afternoon for an audience with His Highness."

"Charley arranged all this for you?"

"Don't you worry about Charley. He's like putty in the master's hand. Now, shoo. Go spend some quality time with your mom, or something. I've got this handled."

"I've got news, too." She dangled juicily.

"What? What?"

"To make a long story short . . . Lt. Thrush called this morning, and he wants you to call him right away." She filled him in on their conversation. "And Raymond, Terry Long was tortured to death."

"Tortured?"

"But Thrush's not buying John R.'s involvement in this mess--"

"But doesn't he know the same people who tortured Long are looking for us, too?" He grabbed Lottie's shoulders and glared wildly. "Can't Thrush get that through his thick skull?"

"Let go of me, Raymond." Lottie pulled away and moved to the door. "You're losing it. Thrush didn't say he wouldn't help us. He just said he needed more to go on. That's why you need to talk to him."

"Well I don't have time to deal with Thrush right now, not if all he can think about is his blasted pension. Looks like we've got to get to the bottom of this thing ourselves, if we want to stay alive. Thrush is a --"

"Just call him, Raymond. He's waiting for your call."

"Okay. Okay. One thing at a time. I'll get back to Thrush, but first I want to be sharp for my meeting with the Good Senator."

"Have it your way." She threw up her hands on her way out. "You always do."

The sleek steel-gray limousine looked out of place at Motel 49. A few of the pay-by-the-week tenants came out for a closer look. They were duly impressed when the chauffeur, dressed in a stylish gray uniform, whisked open the passenger door for Raymond to enter. They set off for the Poteet Mansion.

A towering wrought iron archway, branded with a gothic P, marked the entrance to the estate. It was joined to a sprawling white iron fence that skirted the perimeter of the expansive acreage. Thoroughbred horses galloped friskily in the side pasture, and beautiful peacocks roamed freely in the distance. The gardener, who was sculpting the shrubs at the apex of the magnificent circular drive, stopped his work to meet the limo. He bowed from the waist and opened the door for Raymond's exit.

Raymond bounded the enormous granite steps, two by two, up to the over-sized double doors. He was expected. The butler responded promptly to his ring and ushered him into the drawing room to wait for the senator.

While he waited, he leaned against the grand piano and looked out onto the covered verandah. The sunshine shimmered off the crystal blue pool and rainbows of light danced on the sparkling glass enclosure. Visions of lazy pool parties featuring long-legged blondes in string bikinis played through Raymond's mind, and he didn't notice when Jarrett Poteet entered the room.

"Good afternoon, Son," the senator said, placing a weighty hand on Raymond's shoulder and toting a half-empty cocktail glass in the other. "I'm Senator Jarrett Poteet, at your service," he said smugly. And judging by his slur, this was not his first drink of the day. The senator had a full head of unruly white hair and was wearing an expensive, yet poorly tailored suit, with bulging pockets that made him appear slightly stooped. It was apparent, however, that he had been quite a striking figure in his youth.

"May I offer you a cocktail," he asked when the butler entered on cue with a serving tray. "Southern Comfort, perhaps, or if its too early for you, Son, a lemonade with a sprig of mint." The senator traded his empty glass for one filled with Southern Comfort.

"The lemonade would be fine," Raymond said, wanting to keep his head in the game. "Sir,

I'm Raymond Beck." He extended his hand. "I very much appreciate your giving me a moment of your time. It's quite an honor to meet someone of your stature."

Senator Poteet huffed as he lowered his bloated body into an overstuffed armchair. "My son tells me you know one of my oldest and dearest friends."

"I don't exactly know Mr. Clayburn, but I'm here to learn as much about him as I can," Raymond said queasily. Charley had obviously robbed him of the element of surprise. "John R. is becoming a very prominent figure in my state."

"What is it you want to know? You a reporter or something?"

"It's funny you should ask." He seized the opening. "A friend of mine in Manhattan is a freelance writer. And when I told him I'd be coming down here for a visit, he asked me to get some first-hand information on John R.'s early years; you know, human interest stuff. Certainly you're aware he's going to be the next governor of New York State."

"I've heard the rumor." The senator smiled ruefully. "Don't know a whole lot about his early childhood, though. John R. and me didn't cross swords 'til he came down here from north Alabama to go to college. Fell in love with the same girl, we did. We were both pretty hard drivers, even back then. We discovered competition and rivalry fueled our accomplishments . . . in school . . . in business." He winked a baggy eye, "And with the ladies."

"Sir?" Raymond prompted.

"Oh, it's nothing, Son, just musing." He slurred. "I won by the way. I got the girl . . . married her, too. John R.'s never let me forget that one. But through it all, we have remained the dearest of friends. I was thoroughly disappointed when his son decided not to complete his studies down here. I had great plans for that boy. The real charismatic type, you know. Not like my boy, Charley . . . not at all. Charley takes life too seriously, too uptight. Just like his Mamma."

The senator cleared his husky throat and swigged down the remains of his cocktail. "But I do remember the time ole John R. and me took the same economics class from two different professors," he said. "We made a bet that we each would get a hold of the midterm exam before test day. Mind you, we wouldn't use it to better our grade. Naw. But we were itching to switch the tests to baffle the professors and get them all riled up . . . just a boyish prank. Nothing more.

"For the life of me, I couldn't figure out a way to sneak that blasted test from my professor. I don't know how John R. did it, but he got his." He leaned in closer to Raymond. "Some say he slipped the professor a mickey, but I never knew for sure. I wouldn't put it past him, though. Since we weren't able to make the switch, John R. scrambled his prof's questions and put them back into the locked cabinet." He snickered wickedly. "I bet that old buzzard is scratching his head 'til this very day. Aw shucks, I had to pay-up the silver dollar that time."

"Silver dollar, sir?" Raymond probed, with the countenance of a junior senate page.

"Why . . . yes," the senator said and rang for the butler to refill his glass. "Our bets are always for one silver dollar. While we were at Judson, me and John R. bought eleven freshly minted silver dollars and stashed them away in a safety deposit box." He downed his fourth glass. "Not worth much back then; maybe, a little bit more today. But, it wasn't the money. Naw. It was the sport."

He glared wildly. "You ever play musical chairs, Mr. Beck? We figured the first man to win six of the coins would be crowned *King of the World* in our little bet. Eleven silver dollars . . . six to win . . . odd man out. Get it?" Poteet spouted enthusiastically. "Aw shucks, Son, you've heard, 'the one with the most toys at the end, wins'. Well, with us, it's the most coins." He chuckled in response to Raymond's bewildered look. "Just a game between worthy adversaries, Son. Nothing more."

The senator waved his puffy hand toward the wall, pointing to five, mint-condition 1965 silver dollars elegantly framed on a bed of deep blue velvet. The sixth, and final, position in the set was empty. "John R's got five just like that," he explained. "We're 'bout even, and the music's still playing." He snickered wryly. "Me and that ole Boy, we're headed for a showdown."

The more he drank, the more the senator spouted off about his college escapades with John R.--the coeds they'd duped, the guys they'd swindled--each account more bizarre and reckless than the one before.

He told the story of a debutante who had left campus and returned home because she thought she was seriously ill. Only to find when she got home to her father, that she was pregnant. The unwitting coed swore that she neither knew the assignation had occurred, nor the identity of the father of her child.

Of course, no one believed her, not even her father. She was brutally shunned. The young woman killed herself and her unborn baby out of remorse for the disgrace she had brought on her family. Her father's grief was irreconcilable. The girl was his only child.

"I don't know all the details," Senator Poteet slurred with ghoulish delight. "And I can't be the one to place blame, but I've as much as heard it said that the baby's father might o' been ole John R. himself. Sush-sh-sh," he said, pressing his flabby index finger against his pursed lips. "It was probably just slanderous talk by jealous men. You know how that goes. You get implicated once, with no hard evidence mind you, for using a mickey, and those weaklings try to pin everything on you from then on. It's a fact of life, Son. Check your history. The warriors of the species always have sniveling detractors. But the only people that know for sure what went on with that girl that night are the people that were there." His cheeks flushed brightly and he flashed a toothy grin, hinting at his complicity in the matter.

"Survival of the fittest." Raymond played along, although he was disgusted by the sick pranks. "Law of nature, right?"

"Right as rain, my Boy. Right as rain," Senator Poteet said, pushing his puffy body off the chair to see him to the door. His inebriated steps sounded an irregular cadence on the foyer's marble floor. "It's always good to meet a man I can see eye-to-eye with, Son." He reared his head back in a piercing wolf's howl, "Hoo-hoo." He nearly threw himself off balance, and Raymond braced him discreetly.

"Thinking about the good old days really gives me a charge. I'm glad I met you Beck." The senator cranked his hand vigorously at the front door. "I'm gonna give ole John R. a call real soon, and I'll tell him so. We've got some unfinished business, him and me."

Once outside, Raymond's face drained in panic. He forced his bedraggled frame into the limo for the return trip to the motel. *Why did I tell that old fool my real name?* He rubbed his head fretfully. *Senator Poteet wouldn't care who I was so long as he could re-live his wretched stories.* Raymond replayed their conversation in the back seat of the limo, and his knees went watery. *If he tells Clayburn. . .we're done for. My stupid blunder could cost us our lives.*

CHAPTER 16.
▲▲▲▲▲▲▲▲▲▲▲

Back at Motel 49, Raymond fled into his room. He poured a shot of bourbon into a plastic cup and guzzled the stinging liquid. His fingers fumbled stiffly through the dial, and he spoke too loudly when the desk sergeant answered the phone. "Lt. Thrush there?"
"No. Out. Leave a message?"
"Tell him, it's Raymond Beck. And tell him. . .it's a matter of life and death. I'm waiting on his call." He tossed the cup aside and chugged the bourbon straight from the bottle.

▲▲▲▲

Meanwhile, Lottie was knee deep in moldy lumber from the remains of the old corncrib. The men from the Piggly Wiggly showed up, surprisingly on time, probably more curious about the reunion between Lottie and her mother than any real commitment to the task.

Even Miss Charity was cooperative. "Makes no never mind." She hunched her shoulders before taking off for the lower pasture. "Tear it down if you want to, Lottie. Since you ain't got no husband, Lord only knows why, this'll all be yours sooner than later, anyhow."

As Hamp pitched shingles on the growing pile of trash, he winked playfully at Duke. "Miss Charity sho' did give us a scare the other night, didn't she, Man?" He apparently wanted Lottie to overhear, but she sensed the sport and pretended indifference.

"Sho-nuff!" Duke played along. "Lottie, did your Mamma tell you 'bout them men--and her shotgun?"

Lottie sucked in her panic. "Nope," she said coolly. "Not a word, so you tell me. What's she been up to now?"

"You mean she didn't tell you?" Hamp sensed a crack in her armor.

"Don't do that, Man." Duke rubbed his hands together greedily. "Don't keep the woman in suspense no longer. Tell her! Tell her!"

"Yeah. I suppose she's got a right to know." Hamp postured. "Well, it was the night before you got back to town. Thursday, I believe it was. Everybody was woke up by some noise coming from Miss Charity's front yard. Sounded like gunshot blasts." He pinched his forehead.

"Anyway." Duke went on. "It seems that some strangers had been parked in the shadows of yo' Mamma's front yard for a long time. Miss Charity had seen 'em when they pulled in, but they didn't see her. When it got close to midnight, them fellas snuck out the car onto her front porch," he said. "And out the side door, Miss Charity fired two warning shots over the car which sent them strangers running for they lives, and it alerted the men down at the mill that something was mighty wrong."

"And by the time the sawmill men arrived, the three strangers were back in the car with the out-of-state tags, and they was trying to back out o' the yard onto the road. The men hemmed 'em in and proceeded to rock the car and try to pull them low-life fellas out of it."

"Yeah, and they might o' killed 'em, too, and turned they sorry butts into sawdust, if it hadn't been for Miss Charity coming out on the front porch when she did. She didn't say nothing--"

"But you could tell she wasn't liking all that hitting and name calling. So the boys from the mill backed off and let them strangers out the yard."

"Yeah, and they hauled they sorry tails up outta here, too." Duke grinned sneakily, spitting his tobacco juice at a safe distance. "And if you ask me, they still running."

"Ah, yeah." Hamp slapped his knee and jiggled with laughter. "They still running 'til yet."

Lottie was shook; the missing pieces hurled into place. *So that's how Mamma knew I was in trouble when I got here that morning."*

Lottie wanted to pump Hamp and Duke for more details, but before she could get answers the phone rang. She willed her legs to run into the house, and she snatched up the receiver before the final ring.

"What's up?" Thrush said bewilderedly. "Raymond called. Said it was 'life and death'? Where is he? What's wrong?"

"He's not here," Lottie said, itching to return to the men in the yard. "He's at a motel nearby." She rattled off the telephone number. "Call him. I'll meet him there."

Hamp and Duke had finished the job when Lottie ran back to the yard. They were loading the last of the trash bags onto their truck. She handed them a pan of her mother's peach cobbler that she had grabbed from the kitchen, and she gave them the gas money she'd promised. Her handpicked crew gladly folded the bills into their grubby jeans and pled to stay longer and help with other chores.

"I've got to go now," she said. "But I certainly do thank you for a job well done. I don't know how much longer I'll be here, but please . . . no matter . . . promise me you'll keep an eye on Mamma."

"Why is that?" Hamp said, attempting to tease away the crease in her forehead. "You know Miss Charity ain't scared o' nothing, xcept hot grits."

"Swear it!" Lottie said. "Swear it!"

"We swear. We swear." Duke and Hamp raised their right hands. "We ain't gonna let nothing happen to Miss Charity. You can bank on that." Lottie hugged each of them and sent them on their way.

"Raymond!" Lottie stormed into his room at Motel 49. "What's this Thrush tells me about 'life and death?'"

Raymond was frantically packing his bags and beads of sweat were swimming on his forehead. Between folds, he filled her in on his meeting with Senator Poteet. "I shudder to think what those two old Farts have done to people over the years to claim those stupid coins," he said breathlessly, citing example after example of their conscienceless pranks. "Who's to say what they'd be capable of if the stakes were high enough? And if you ask me, becoming the next governor of the state of New York is pretty high stakes. It could put John R. over the top in their stupid bet."

"Raymond, slow down. You're going to blow a gasket."

He stopped packing and glared at her. "And that nitwit senator, Jarrett Poteet, is planning to call John R. real soon. Lottie, do you have any idea what that means? His hands trembled angrily. "I'll tell you what it means. It means whoever's been hunting us across two states will know exactly where we are. That's what it means." Raymond strong-armed the zipper on his bag and it ripped. He sunk to the bed with his head in his hands.

"Did Lt. Thrush call you?" Lottie said softly.

"Y-e-s!" he blared. "And I told him everything I know about this blasted case. Everything!" He rifled a look at Lottie, daring her to challenge his decision. "Everything about Ramona Clark's file and Clayburn's bad-boy son, Bradley."

"What did Thrush say?"

"Just what you'd expect. Another dead end," he said snidely. "Thrush wasn't able to give me any details on Ramona Clark, or her date rape charge. But he said he'd look into it, if you can believe what he says." He wrung his hands and paced the tiny room. "This thing is getting away from us, Lottie. It's getting out of hand. It's hopeless." He grabbed the rusty burglar bars in the narrow window and shook them like a caged beast.

"Stop! Stop already!" Lottie dropped onto the bed. "We can't whip this thing if we give up. We've got to take it one step at a time. I know it looks bad," she said consolingly. "But there's always hope."

"Hope? Hah!" He dropped to the bed.

She placed her slender arm across his broad shoulders for comfort. "I don't know how to tell you this," she said evenly. "But it's not two states we're being hunted in. It's three."

"Three!" Raymond hopped up.

"They've traced us here, too," she said grudgingly. "I told you any half-rate hacker could follow your credit card trail." She gave him the full report on the attack against her mother she'd learned from Hamp and Duke.

"They came after Miss Charity?"

"Yeah. And I had to hear about it from strangers."

"She probably didn't want you to worry," he mumbled foggily.

"She's quick to say, 'The Lord will take care of me.' But when it comes to her *girls*, she's as protective as a she bear with cubs. Her treating me like a child, no matter how well intentioned, makes me feel . . . impotent. One of the very feelings that drove me away from home and kept me away."

"All I know is, we're being hunted in three states, and we've got to get out of here. Fast! Go get your things and get us some cash. We've got to disappear. We don't want any more innocent people getting hurt." He groaned loudly. "Including us."

Fortunately, Miss Charity hadn't returned from choir practice. Lottie crept into the house and packed rapidly, mentally composing a note as she did. She dropped it off on the kitchen table under a jar of peach preserves--*Mamma, Raymond and I've had a wonderful time with you. But he wants to go down to Miami. He's never seen a Florida beach. I told him he doesn't know what he's missing. Got all my stuff in case we have to go back to work. I'll call you soon. Thanks for everything. I love you. Lottie.*

Security was extremely tight when they arrived at the Atlanta airport that evening. A bomb, sniffed out by dogs aboard an international jet earlier in the day, had everyone running scared. Lottie and Raymond had planned to fly under aliases on the first flight out to anywhere. But as they stood in line to purchase their tickets, they noticed the close scrutiny being given each passenger by the jittery airline personnel. Without proper ID, they wouldn't be able to pull off the deception.

"C'mon," Raymond said, nudging Lottie out of the line. "Let's get out of here. We don't have time for this. This is the biggest airport in the area. Clayburn's men might already have it staked out."

They descended the steep escalator to the ground transportation level in search of an alternate means of escape. On the lower level, they were greeted by a brightly lit sign, which advertised a private charter service--Eastern Shores Airline Charters. Raymond pointed to the fine print: *Specializing in flights to LaGuardia and other East Coast destinations.* "This could be our ticket out of here," he said.

"You sure we want to go back to New York?"

"Think about it, Lottie. It's a brilliant idea. Nobody'll expect us to go back where we've already been."

"If you say so."

They huddled in a secluded corner for nearly an hour until the shuttle to the charter service arrived. It took them to a small landing strip on the south end of the airport. The lot was littered with small jets and helicopters for hire.

Raymond strutted up to the counter to make the arrangements. With his impressive wad of cash, he was able to press the attendant for an immediate flight. He played the part of a harried advertising tycoon with his personal secretary in tow, a role to which Lottie was prepared to strenuously object as soon as they were safely away. They arranged to store her Lexus on the lot, and their flight to LaGuardia would land at midnight.

"Mr. Clayburn." The seasoned voice of his veteran male secretary broke through over the intercom. "Please excuse the interruption, sir, but Senator Jarrett Poteet of Alabama is on line one." John R. was in a dinner meeting with his political advisors. He excused himself to take the call.

"Poteet, you ole Scalawag," John R. said jovially. "You must be calling to check up on me, Boy? Let me guess. You want to talk to the next governor of the fair state of New York?"

"Naw. Naw. John R., you ole Scoundrel. Nothing like that. You're only winning in the polls, and we know pollsters can be bought. From what I hear, the next two weeks are going to make you or break you, Son," he slurred. "It's just I was down home to Union City today, and I got to talking 'bout you and old times, and I thought I'd give you a call."

"Talking about me?" John R. stopped short, and shooed his cronies from the room. "And just why were you talking about me, and to whom?"

"Oh, nobody, just some young writer fellow trying to make a name for himself. He wanted some color commentary on a celebrity such as yourself." Poteet chuckled spitefully. "A feature story on the new governor, I presume.

Didn't tell him much . . . not much to tell. It just reminded me that our final bet is coming due, and I thought I'd better check-in with you."

"Did you at least get the fellow's name?"

"Yeah. It was Birch . . . Burke . . . Beck . . . something like that. Don't worry. He's a nobody."

John R. switched subjects. "You know, Jarrett, I've been keeping score."

"So have I."

"We're about even in net worth. So I guess you don't owe me half of your worldly goods."

"Nope. And you got off the hook on that one, too," Poteet said. "I think we can safely declare that part of our bet a draw. I don't owe you nothing, and you don't owe me nothing. I guess we'll have to leave our full inheritance to our snot-nose kids after all." He moaned playfully. "Blast it all!"

"So then it's just down to the last silver dollar." John R. goaded. "Remember. The last man left standing with a full set, wins."

"The last silver dollar," Jarrett said tersely. "I know the rules."

"Then I want you to get down to our safety deposit box and pull out that last coin for me. My candidacy is a sure thing, and the title of *King of the World* is mine, my friend. All mine!"

"Not so fast. It ain't over 'til it's over," the senator said lamely. "Which brings me to the reason for my call. We're having a big New Year's Eve shindig at the Mansion to celebrate my victory after you come up short in the November election. But, it wouldn't be a party without you." He digressed. "Can you believe it, John R.? When the calendar rolls to 1998, it'll be 30 years since we left dear old Judson. It's only fitting that one of us ole Hound Dogs be crowned *King* to reign in this New Millennium. I can guarantee you the party will be a fitting close to our 30 years of prowess," he said enticingly. "Well, what do you say? "Will you come? Governor, or no governor?"

"You can bet your life on it," John R. said. "You throw one whale of a party. And it'll be as good a place as any for you to crown me *King*." He snarled viciously. "Rest assured. The last silver dollar is mine."

"Don't count your chickens before they hatch, Son," the senator said, and broke off the call. John R.'s patented snarl had shaken him to the marrow. It had a particularly raw edge. It crossed his mind to what lengths John R. could go to possess the final coin. *Did he say, 'last man left standing--wins?'* Naw. He convinced himself. *Not even John R. would stoop that low.*

CHAPTER 17.
▲▲▲▲▲▲▲▲▲▲▲▲

When Raymond and Lottie arrived at LaGuardia after midnight, they took a taxi to Thrush's Manhattan precinct on W. 61st and Broadway, near Central Park at Columbus Circle. Happily they found him at work in his office, sipping a foul smelling brew and scouring over his reports.

"Boo!" Raymond crept up behind him and bounced his chair.

"Wha-- What the--? Well, if it's not the fugitives from justice!" Thrush rebounded. He was working hard to conceal his relief, but his eyes gave him away. "Back to vote? Then you're early. Election's a week from Tuesday. So, why're you here?"

"Love you, too, Thrush." Raymond smiled and pulled Lottie to his side. "This is Lottie."

"Figured as much. I'm the detective around here, remember?" He brushed past her, like she was invisible, and stood toe-to-toe with Raymond. "Why did you come back here? Are you out of your mind?" He blistered him with hot breath. "If I don't have enough to worry about, now I've got to look out for you, too.

Thrush appeared to be a man suffering from too little exercise, too many donuts, and too much of that foul concoction passing itself off as coffee. It was obvious he was slightly older than Raymond, but not as old as his pouched middle and purple eyelids represented. The worry lines on his forehead ran so deep they threatened to choke off the hair on his balding head.

"We didn't have anyplace else to go," Raymond said sheepishly. "They found us in Alabama. We didn't think they'd expect us to double-back here."

"Why were you in Alabama in the first place?"

"It's my hometown." Lottie spoke up, tired of being ignored. "Union City."

"Union City, Alabama?" Thrush looked her over as though he were sizing her up for a coffin. "Never heard of it."

"That's the point," she said. "We thought no one would look for us down there. It was a good plan, but--"

"It's a long story," Raymond said. "But they did find us, and we had to get out of there in a hurry. Lottie's mother lives there and--"

Thrush raised his hand. "Say no more. I get the picture."

At that precise moment the office door edged open, and Thrush's sergeant jutted his head around the door to report for duty. Thrush waved impatiently. "Come in here, Valvino."

"Sir?" Young Sergeant Tony Valvino snapped to attention.

"I want you to go down to the Italian bakery and get us something to eat. Something light, like a loaf of bread and some prosciutto ham. Also, stop by Lenny's cart on the corner and get some of that chicken stir-fry . . . a dozen hot donuts, and some juice. And when you get back, Valvino, dump out that rot-gut over there and bring us a fresh pot of coffee."

"Yes, sir." He moved quickly to follow orders.

"Now, where were we?" Thrush resumed. "So you figured the bloodhounds wouldn't track you back here. Right?"

"Right," Raymond said. "But more than that, we wanted to be close to your investigation so we can help. We need to clear up this mess as soon as possible."

"Help? Me?" Thrush bristled pompously. "You'll do nothing of the sort. I don't need your help. And while you're here, let me lay down the ground rules for you. Are you listening?"

"Do we have a choice?"

"You will not go back to your homes!" Thrush's face glowed red-hot. "And you will not, under any circumstance, make a return visit to your blasted offices! You are not cops, and you will not go poking your noses in where they don't belong! Is that clear?"

"But you said it yourself, Thrush." Raymond countered. "You can't bring other officers in on this investigation. You said you wouldn't risk your pension by accusing the next governor of wrongdoing. Remember?"

"So how can you do it without us?" Lottie's mahogany eyes blazed. "This is not the time to: a) play the Lone Ranger; or b) be bullheaded; not when my life is on the line. You can play that macho-cop stuff--"

"Shush." Thrush snorted. "I've heard just about enough from you, Miss."

"My mother's down there alone." Lottie pressed her point. "And our lives are at stake. Who can better help you solve this case?" She swung her head away from the men, staving off tears of frustration.

"What she says is true." Raymond picked up. "No one knows we're here, and we can help you. We're not about to put ourselves in harms way," he said, turning a pleading glance toward Lottie. "Right?"

"Right." She composed herself. "Lieutenant, we won't put ourselves in jeopardy. You're the boss--the brains of this operation. You'll take all the risks, and we'll . . . we'll do your legwork. How's that sound?"

"Out of the question! Out of the question!"

Sgt. Valvino tapped lightly on the closed door and entered with an armload of food. He placed the delivery on the conference table and stepped out again. He returned with a fresh pot of coffee and handed Lt. Thrush a steaming cup before slipping out of the room and closing the door behind him.

"I feel your pain," Thrush said, attacking his donut with each sip of coffee. "But the jury's still out on whether or not I'll let you get involved in my investigation. But I will fill you in on what I've learned so far, if that's okay with you, Miss Lottie?"

"A-OK." She shrugged and took a dainty nibble from her ham sandwich. "You're the boss."

"I've made phone contact with Bradley Clayburn," Thrush said. "He admitted without any hesitation he knows Ramona Clark. They attended a class together last semester in English Lit. By his own admission, he met Ramona for coffee one evening at her request and exchanged notes for an upcoming exam. They discussed the possibility of forming a study group with some other students, but nothing ever came of it."

"So *he* says." Raymond chipped in.

Thrush poured a second cup of coffee. "According to Bradley, that's as close to a date as they ever came. It's his story that he hasn't seen or heard from Ramona since the last day of class. And he says, he has absolutely no interest in Ramona Clark, romantic or otherwise."

Thrush's metal chair squeaked when he reached for another donut. "Haven't had much luck locating Ramona, though," he said. "I checked. No one in her apartment building has seen her for over a week, and she hasn't been attending her classes at NYU. Since she's apparently missing, the judge I woke before day agreed to give me a warrant to search her locker at the university. But without an official missing persons report from her next of kin, he was reluctant to give me permission to search her apartment." Thrush snorted. "His Honor lectured me on her rights as an adult. The stubborn, pencil-pushing Fool."

Thrush stabbed a toothpick in the corner of his mouth and continued. "Did a little more digging into her family tree, too. Ramona's parents are divorced. Her mother is some sort of jet-setter fashion queen, out of the country shooting pictures God knows where. You can't talk much sense to those fashion pixies over on Madison Avenue. Too much goober dust--"

"So it's another dead end?" Raymond sagged on the edged of his seat.

"Not exactly. In a few more days, I can hit the judge up again and maybe gain access to Ramona's apartment." He tugged open the bottom drawer of his green metal desk and banged an address book on top of it. "I turned this up in her locker." He flopped it open to a marked page.

"What's this name circled in red?" Raymond said.

"Dr. A. Cooper. Ramona's shrink. I questioned the Good Doctor over the phone;

didn't have time to go over there. All I got was a recitation of the Hippocratic Oath and a fierce grip on doctor-patient privilege. Pretty much a dead end," he said grudgingly. "However, the Doc did tell me that Ramona's daddy is dead. She and her mother are completely estranged. Seems that mother and daughter haven't spoken in over ten years. Imagine that."

"I can see that," Lottie said. "What about relatives or friends?"

"Doc Cooper couldn't pinpoint a soul who would qualify to file a missing persons report on the poor kid." Thrush softened. "Aside from her mother, Ramona apparently has no immediate family, and that's what I'm gonna use on the judge next time," he said, obviously impressed with his powers of persuasion.

"It's worth a try."

"Client privilege notwithstanding, the Good Doctor did let it slip that Ramona is something of a compulsive liar with rather erratic goings and comings, and friends are hard for her to make or keep. Looks like she's a loner. Just up and vanished, and that's where my investigation hit a brick wall."

"Yet another one." Lottie scored.

Thrush clamped down on his toothpick and turned to Raymond. "And what about you?

What've you got for me? What about this missing file you've been babbling about?"

Lottie reached into her briefcase and slapped down their precious folder next to the diary. "Here," she said. "The stuff on this flap is Terry's. And these pages, here, show the information we pieced together at the Birmingham library."

"I'll hold onto this for safe keeping." Thrush mulled over the newspaper clipping. *John R.'s chauffeur sure looks familiar.* He prided himself in never forgetting a face.

"We want to work with you on this thing," Raymond said. "Cooperate fully in every way. We're a team."

"You're coming in loud and clear." Thrush scratched his head. "Against my better judgment, I may have no other choice than to let you two monkey around in this thing a bit. But I warn you both: a) do not get in my way; and b) if either of you get yourselves hurt, it won't be on my conscience." He glowered at Lottie. "Is that perfectly clear?"

"Perfectly." They chimed.

Thrush checked his watch--nearly 3:40 a.m. "It's Sunday morning, now," he said. "Not much trouble you can get into today. My advice. Get yourselves some sleep. You'll need it. First thing Monday morning, report back here and I'll give you your assignments. Got it? *I* will give you your assignments. Can you do that?"

"Of course we can, Thrush." Lottie emoted sweetly. "You're the boss."

"Valvino! Thrush shouted through the closed door. "Get in here! Make me two reservations, adjoining rooms, over at the Pimberton for my friends here."

"Pimberton?" Raymond wrinkled his nose. "That old flee bag? It's got that horrid . . . old smell. Like something out of a bad Victorian novel."

"Enough of this nonsense." Thrush fumed. "My first priority is to keep you in one piece. You'll have to put your ritzy preferences on hold for now. The Pimberton is nearby, and I've used it as a safe-house, lots of times. You can rest there and get your butts back here Monday morning. Okay by you, Mr. Executive I'm-too-cute-to-stay-at-the-Pimberton?" He scowled from Lottie to Raymond and back again. "Pick a name, any name."

"Uhh . . . Lois Givings."

"Richard Blevins." Raymond offered. "I guess I could spend the time on the Beck-mobile. I can catch most of my clients at home, or on the golf course today."

"You hear that Valvino?" Thrush blared at the timid sergeant. "Richard Blevins and Lois Givings. Get on those reservations."

Thrush hauled Raymond and Lottie out of his office by their elbows. "Young Valvino here will handle your reservations and take you over to the Pimberton. All you have to do is check in at the front desk and get your room keys. Can you handle that?"

The venetian blinds rustled noisily when Thrush slammed his office door behind them. Judging by its horribly worn appearance, rough treatment was customary.

▲▲▲▲

Unbeknownst to Raymond and Lottie, Miss Charity had bought them some breathing room before their pursuers reached Union City. She balled her face into a knot when she arrived at Mt. Zion that Sunday morning. She showed Lottie's note around to some of the biggest gossips in the congregation, counting on them to spread the news.

"My Baby done up and left again," she said. "Gone off to Miami."

Sis. Nancy McKullen, the heavy-set ringleader of the busybody society, wobbled over and returned the note. "Well, Sis. Charity," she said, "what you think the Lord gonna say 'bout your young, single daughter traipsing around the country with a Mister?"

"I don't presume to know what the Lord gonna say, Sis. Nancy," Miss Charity drawled sweetly. "But since they both grown, I'd say they can go as far and wide as they money will take 'em. What you say?"

"Hmph. It's sinful thinking like that, that's made your child turn out this way." Sis. Nancy waddled away as fast as her chunky legs would allow, spreading the unfortunate news in the most damaging manner possible.

The story spread like wildfire that Lottie and "her white man from New York" had run off to "shack up in Miami Beach for some sin in the sun." It was all over town by nightfall when the carload of thugs, who had hounded Rex at the diner, pulled into Union City.

"Them ole Boys thought they was slick." Duke clucked like a setting hen, while him and Hamp hunkered down on the side of Miss Charity's front porch.

"Northerners think every country boy's a fool." They laughed. "When me and Duke found 'em over at the *Pig*, we got 'em so spun around they probably won't never find Miami."

"Tee-hee-hee. Not unlessen they stumble over the ocean by mistake."

"Good." Miss Charity smiled contentedly. "How did y'all know they was hunting Lottie?"

"The same way we know'd Little Lottie was in town in the first place," Hamp said. "Chaney Masters."

"You remember Chaney James, for sho' Miss Charity. His Mamma died not too far back."

"Uh-huh." She rocked pensively. "I remember Miss Sadie very well. She was my good friend. We could see eye to eye."

"Chaney was always a little sweet on Lottie," Duke said, swooning dizzily. "Didn't he take her to the prom?"

"The first night Lottie showed up at your doorstep," Hamp said, "Chaney was pulling his truck up Sawmill Road. He was the first one to spot her back in Union City, and he's been keeping an eye on her ever since."

"Yeah. He still sweet on the Gal, all right." Duke's gold tooth gleamed. "You should see his eyes when he talks about her, looks like a moon-struck calf."

"Nuff to make you sick."

"Good." Miss Charity pulled her shawl close around her shoulders. "Mighty fine."

CHAPTER 18.
▲▲▲▲▲▲▲▲▲▲▲▲

Bright and early Monday morning, Raymond and Lottie reported to Thrush's office to get their respective assignments. They had taken his advice and caught up on their sleep and their business, but Thrush looked pathetic. A double homicide-suicide in the Park had kept him on duty all day Sunday. When they arrived, he was wrinkled and grumpy and making ready to go off shift.

"I'm going to say this only once." He croaked pathetically. "Raymond, you go over to NYU and take another crack at Bradley Clayburn; and Lottie, use your feminine charms to lean on Dr. Cooper. As for me, I'm outta here. Got to get some sleep. Valvino! Get in here."

"Yes, sir, Lieutenant."

Thrush handed him the yellowing clipping from Terry's file. "Get this picture down to Aiesha in the lab. Tell her I want a make on that chauffeur. ASAP-PRONTO. Got it?"

"Yes, sir, Lieutenant."

Raymond and Lottie followed closely on Thrush's heels. "Where're you going?"

"I'll be in touch." He waved limply. "Report back here; same time tomorrow."

"But Thrush." Raymond yelled. "You don't have our room numbers."

"Give 'em to Valvino. I'll call him later."

▲ ▲ ▲ ▲

"I'm Lottie Garrett." She announced to the receptionist. "Here to see Dr. Cooper."

"Do you have an appointment?"

"No. No appointment, but I was sent here by Lt. Thrush, NYPD, to speak to Dr. Cooper on a most urgent police matter."

"Urgent or not," the woman in dreadlocks bristled. "Dr. Cooper is seen by appointment, only, and you don't have one."

"If you'd do your job and let Dr. Cooper know I'm here, I'll do mine and wait right here until I see her."

Lottie took a seat alongside the psychiatric patients in the reception area and waited. Her persistence paid off sooner than she expected. In a few minutes, a woman peeked out of one of the doors along the wall. Guardedly, she scanned the waiting area, and then beckoned for Lottie to join her.

Dr. Annette Cooper was a distinguished-looking woman in her early forties, poised stiffly in her high-backed chair. Her blonde hair was curled meticulously into a bun.

Lottie hadn't expected a woman. *No wonder Thrush saddled me with this assignment.*

"Have a seat," Dr. Cooper said tersely. "My time is at a premium, and I hope you'll get to the point."

"Thank you for seeing me, Doctor," Lottie said. "I'll be as brief as possible. Lt. Thrush told me he talked with you the other day about your patient, Ramona Clark. He sent me to follow-up on that conversation."

"Let me get this straight. You're a police officer?"

"No. Not exactly. Let's just say, I'm assisting Lt. Thrush in his inquiry."

"I see. *He* couldn't get to me so he sends a woman."

"We have reason to believe your patient is a material witness in a case involving me and my business associate. We were attacked last week in our offices, and Lt. Thrush thinks Ramona might be able to give us a lead on the culprits."

Annette Cooper frowned. "Are you saying Ramona had something to do with the attack?"

Lottie scooted her chair closer to the doctor's desk, hoping to gain her trust. "No. Nothing like that. My partner and I came into possession of a file that belonged to your patient's lawyer. In the file, Ramona accused a man of . . . date rape, but apparently no formal charges were filed."

"Date rape?" Dr. Cooper stonewalled. "Is that why you need to speak to Ramona?"

"No. We simply need to talk to her about her lawyer and his file," Lottie said. "Please, Doctor. We have nothing else to go on, and we need to get in touch with Ramona right away."

"You're wasting my time, Miss Garrett." She spun her chair to stand. "I'm Ramona Clark's psychiatrist, and as such, I'm not privileged to give you any information about her or her whereabouts. I thought I made that crystal clear to Lt. Thrush last week. I cannot fathom why he'd send you here to waste my time any further. If there is nothing more, I'll bid you good day."

"Did I mention Ramona's lawyer is dead . . . murdered?"

"I beg your pardon?" The doctor's jaw dropped.

Lottie pinned her with her eyes. "Ramona's lawyer," she said slowly. "The lawyer she told about the date rape. I'm telling you, that lawyer was murdered."

"Murdered?"

"Look, Annette." Lottie entreated in a more sisterly tone. "I think it only fair to warn you that your life may be in danger, too. Everyone who's come in contact with Ramona's file has either been killed or hunted mercilessly."

"But I'm not involved. "I'm a doctor of medicine."

"And Terrence Long was an attorney-at-law. So what! That didn't prevent the people who're after that file from torturing him to death and attempting to murder me in my own home."

"I see your point." The doctor twirled her bangs adolescently. "I cannot violate privilege, but if my patient's life is in danger maybe I can help you in some way; strictly off the record, that is. What I say here, I will never repeat to anyone--especially not the police, and certainly not in a court of law. Is that understood?"

"Strictly off the record."

"Yes. Ramona Clark is a very troubled young woman, dating back to her childhood," Dr.

Cooper said clinically. "The years of abuse by her parents have, let us say, precipitated deep-seated feelings of guilt and anger that exact a high toll on her." She tight-roped skittishly. "Ramona's a compulsive liar of clinical proportions. Or in layman's terms, Miss Garrett, you can't believe a word she says. She doesn't know where fantasy ends and reality begins."

"Go on."

The doctor measured her words carefully. "She came to see me over a week ago, without an appointment, babbling about some men who'd pushed her around. If her claim about 'the bad guys' had been an isolated incident, I wouldn't have seen her. But she'd been exhibiting some serious psychotic symptoms of late, and it was my opinion she was either under some genuine duress, or on the verge of a complete break with reality."

Dr. Cooper labored. "When I placed her claim about the bad guys, alongside . . . her rape fantasy . . . against a man, who shall remain nameless, that she'd shared with me during her regular session, I became concerned and agreed to see her on the spot."

"Then you know about Bradley?"

"This is difficult enough without your interruptions, Miss Garrett. Allow me to finish.

I'll give you no more information than I absolutely must."

"Forgive me. Go right ahead."

"As I questioned Ramona more closely about her allegations, she admitted to me in a lucid moment that the rape had been a complete fabrication." Dr. Cooper mimicked her patient's coquettish manner. "'Gee Doc,' Ramona said to me. 'It's been such great fun, such high drama, you know. When I laid eyes on him, he was like all the gallant knights rolled into one. He swooped in on his white steed and had his way with me! Isn't that what knights do, Doc?'"

Dr. Cooper paused. "Honestly, Miss Garrett, I'm sure Ramona didn't intend her story to hurt anyone. She's an English Lit major, and she was playing the role of a lifetime. Unfortunately, in her warped psyche, rape is an extension of love, not the horrible act of violence it truly is." She squirmed uncomfortably. "Her father saw to that."

"Her father--?"

"Anyway. Ramona's story was very peculiar, even for her," Dr. Cooper said. "She babbled about the young man having a powerful father. She said the lawyer she consulted on the date rape charge had offered her a pay off. 'I ought to take the money,' she said, 'and get even with them for treating a princess like a peasant.'" The doctor explained. "The story didn't ring true. Besides, I had patients waiting. I told her to go home, take a hot bath and a mild sedative I prescribed, and come back the next day."

"And did she?"

"No. Ramona hasn't returned. I've been concerned, of course, but she's pulled these disappearing acts before. She likes the attention. She'll be back." The doctor rose to show Lottie to the door. "I won't repeat what I've said today; not to anyone, Miss Garrett."

"There are some very bad men mixed up in this, Doctor. Be extremely careful. You may already know more than is healthy." She followed her to the door. "Thanks again for your help. It's been very valuable. If we locate Ramona, I'll be in touch. And by the way, Annette," she said, "call me Lottie."

"Good-bye, Lottie." The doctor shook her hand warmly at the door, slipping her a business card with her home telephone number.

▲ ▲ ▲ ▲

The wind was swirling Raymond's topcoat as he prowled around the campus at NYU, attempting to locate Bradley Clayburn's dormitory. Thrush had given him directions, but somehow he'd gotten off course. Judging by the swift goings and comings when he located Allen Lane Residence Hall, classes were starting.

As he topped the second floor, Raymond nearly collided with a young man, distinguished from the rest by his stunning good looks and neatly creased khakis. His thick mane of auburn hair was neatly trimmed over his ears and a natural shock of burnished blonde fell across his forehead. The passion in his green eyes fit Senator Poteet's description.

"Bradley?" Raymond said, winded from the climb. "Bradley Clayburn?"

"Yeah. Who's asking?"

"I'm . . . Richard Blevins," Raymond said. He'd had enough of revealing his true identity. "I understand your hurry, but I'm here on some urgent police business, Son. What I have to say is a matter of . . . life and death."

"Yeah? Whose?"

"Maybe mine," Raymond said earnestly.

"Then come in." Bradley relented. "Let's get this over with. I've got class in 15 minutes."

He motioned for Raymond to sit on his neatly made bed, while he stood overlooking the courtyard. The room was a pristine page from the housing catalogue. Aside from the basics, there was nothing. No TV, no stereo, no half-empty pizza cartons, no beer bottles. Nothing. It was not what Raymond had expected. Bradley was the neatest spoiled brat he'd ever seen.

"What's this about?" Bradley said. "I talked to you people last week. Why do you keep messing with me? And what's this nonsense about 'life and death?'"

"This is about your dad." Raymond seized the element of surprise.

"I should've known." Bradley snapped his fingers. "It's this politics jazz, I'll bet."

"Maybe. That's what I'm here to find out."

"Then why bug me? Go directly to my illustrious patriarch and bug him, why don't you? He's the politician in the family. Not me."

"Has your dad questioned you about any of this already? About your relationship with Ramona Clark, I mean?"

"Certainly not. Why would he care about Ramona Clark? I haven't talked to my father in over a year, not since I moved here from Alabama. We made a four-year pact. Until I graduate, I stay out of trouble; he sends money; I spend it. It's as simple as that."

"Are you asking me to believe you haven't spoken to your daddy in over a year?"

"Yeah. Pretty rotten arrangement, I agree. But he never really understood me, and I'm done trying to explain myself. I just steer clear."

"Likely story."

"Look, I know how you guys operate. You come around sniffing me out anytime something goes wrong because I've got a record. I'm trapped in your database, and I can't break free. That's another reason I steer clear of my father and his politics. Anyway, believe what you want. I've told you the truth." He waved his arm around the room. "This is the extent of my relationship with my father. If you want to find out any more about him, I suggest you go talk to him. My checkered past notwithstanding, I've done nothing wrong."

Raymond backed off. "Let's try this again," he said. "Be straight with me, Bradley, and I'll be straight with you. This is how it stands. Ramona accused you of date rape."

"Rape?" He sagged into a chair. "You've got to be kidding. I don't even like the girl."

"Well, she accused you, and it's creating quite a stir for lots of people--me included."

"Ramona is an artsy, tattoo, black lipstick wearing, spooky woman, definitely not my type. I can assure you, I was no where near Ramona Clark on the night in question--"

"How do you know the night--?"

"Any night, okay. I was not with the girl. My woman chasing days are over--" He jammed his hands into his pockets and stared at the floor. His indecision hung in the air.

"Over? Why over?" Raymond pressed. "Talk to me, Man. Don't hold back. I believe what you've told me, but we need everything. People are getting hurt, Bradley. Please."

"I'm married!" He blurted "Okay. Okay. I'm married." His eyes glowed softly. "When I was at Judson, I met the sweetest little Southern Belle you'd ever want to meet. Her parents didn't know about me. When I got drummed out of there, she talked them into letting her spend a year as an exchange student at Columbia to study fashion design. It was an excuse so we could be married and spend some time together before we have to face the music, on both sides of the family tree."

"From what I hear, that's not your style."

"She taught me how to love. I'm doing better, now. Mended my boozing ways, and my wife and I are doing fine. But I haven't broken the news to Dear Old Dad." He huffed. "I don't like sneaking around. I'm proud of my bride. But we don't need any added pressure from him just now, thank you very much. He pays the bills, and I'll take it until we can get on our feet. Anyway. He owes me." His eyes glazed. "Are you gonna ruin our secret?"

"Not on your life." Raymond grinned. "I love young love. So the night you were supposedly raping Ramona Clark--"

"I was at home with my wife. We have a neat little efficiency over near Columbia. It's the closest thing to a home I've ever had. Why on earth would I be interested in weird Ramona? And rape her? Out of the question, not even in my wildest days. Anybody who knows me knows that."

"I wouldn't mention our little conversation to your daddy." Raymond warned on his way out. The naked dorm room made more sense.

"Mums the word." Bradley pledged.

▲▲▲▲

Raymond wasn't the only one who uncovered new evidence that Monday morning. Although barely able to drag his tired carcass from the precinct, Thrush cut a beeline to Ramona Clark's apartment on his way home. The feeling in his gut wouldn't wait until the judge wised-up.

"You say you're from the police, but where's your warrant?" The hard-nosed building superintendent objected. "I know about these things. Police or no police, you got no right to go in Ms. Clark's apartment without a warrant."

"Well, I could go back and get a warrant." Thrush swaggered. "But I'm tired. And when I'm tired, I stop off and shoot the breeze with my drinking buddy, Inspector Fields. You know Inspector Fields, don't you, Mr. Feisty-Super?"

"Huh?"

Thrush reached up and poked the test button on the smoke alarm. It didn't work. "Yep," he said, "this is Fields' district, all right. And when I see him, we get to talking about code violations, like dead batteries in smoke detectors. He's a pretty hard-nosed guy, too."

Thrush shadowed the super's doorway menacingly. "On the other hand, I could spend the time taking a little look-see around Ms. Clark's apartment; just to be sure the young lady's safe. And then I'm outta here, on my way home to my bed; and I don't see Fields—"

"Sure. Sure thing." The nervous super sputtered. "It's your job to be sure Ms. Clark is safe. Just follow me up to the third floor."

The super tapped repeatedly on Ramona's door. When there was no response, he opened it with his passkey. "Lock up on your way out," he said, and shrunk back down the stairwell.

Thrush fumbled for the overhead light and switched it on. He was startled by the mess that greeted him. Drawers flung open. Pictures askew. Dirty dishes strewn from the dining room to the kitchen sink.

At first glance, he couldn't decide if the apartment had been ransacked, or was the victim of careless housekeeping. Careful to touch nothing, he pulled on a pair of latex gloves from his kit. He'd have a fingerprint expert come by later, after he obtained a warrant, and he didn't want his prints to be among them.

Thrush wandered from room to room, looking for signs of foul play. His initial walk through failed to turn up either blood or body, two possibilities for which he had braced himself. In the bathroom, however, he discovered something peculiar. The bathtub was brimming full of cold, murky water and an empty syringe floated on the top. Cautiously, he picked up the syringe with his tweezers and sealed it securely in an evidence bag. No one had told him Ramona was a druggy.

He retraced his steps to the kitchen and carefully retrieved a half-empty mayonnaise jar from the refrigerator. He bagged it for fingerprint comparison and slammed the door on the moldy remains. He took extra precaution to leave the apartment unnoticed. Locking the door securely behind him, Thrush headed home to get some sleep.

CHAPTER 19.
▲▲▲▲▲▲▲▲▲▲▲▲

It was a cold wind that blew Raymond back to the Pimberton. His visit with Bradley Clayburn had heightened his foreboding, and the crowded subway ride at rush hour hadn't improved his mood. He was itching to dive straight for the hotel bar, but didn't want to chance missing Lottie when she returned.

He beat a hasty path through the threadbare lobby when the manager, who had been on duty when they checked in the night before, slid narrow lips over yellowing teeth into a meaningless smile. Raymond found a spot near the bar on the mezzanine level, shielded by a sadly chipped Steinway piano. *This place smells like financial ruin. The same smell that'll be hovering over Beck, if I don't get my mind back in the game . . . and soon.*

From his vantage point, Raymond spotted Lottie when she swung through the revolving door at the side entrance. He signaled her to meet him in the bar and accidentally banged his *football* knee on a rusted urn of pink feathers. "Blast this flea-bag hotel," he cursed under his breath and hobbled off to join her.

Lottie was ravenously hungry, and she nabbed a stool at the bar for quick service. "Be a good chap." She joshed with the bartender. "Bring me an extra greasy cheeseburger and a tall cola with a cherry on top."

Raymond ordered a shot of bourbon, neat. No food. And they settled in at the long oak bar in an animated whisper, careful not to let the bartender overhear. "So where does it leave us?" Raymond said. "Bradley says he didn't rape Ramona Clark—"

"And Dr. Cooper says Ramona's a liar."

"So why is Long dead? And why are we running for our lives? None of it makes any sense!"

Lottie waited until the bartender dropped off her burger. "It just means we've gotta find Ramona—and fast. She's the missing link in this mess. She's the only one with hard facts about her case and the supposed bad guys that attacked her. We need to talk to her right away."

"But--" The bartender returned with the pint of bourbon Raymond ordered. "Eat up, Lottie," he said. "We can talk more freely upstairs."

It was a quick trip to the fifth floor by elevator. Lottie went to her room to freshen up, while Raymond went down the hall to fill his ice bucket. He poured drinks for him and Lottie and pecked on her adjoining door.

"No thanks." She waved off the bourbon and took a seat at his table. "So Bradley's a newly-wed?" she said. "Hmph. Shoots giant holes in Ramona's rape claim. Is it possible this is all one big lie gone south?"

"But if Ramona's lying, why is John R. involved?" Raymond drained the glass of bourbon Lottie left unattended. "It's got to be more than--" Raymond shook visibly when the telephone blared.

"Who?" Lottie breathed unevenly.

"Must be Thrush. He got our numbers from Valvino." Raymond answered on the third ring. "Hullo. Hullo." The dial tone hummed loudly in his ear. "Wrong number."

"If you say so." Lottie reeled wearily to her feet. "It's late. I'll be in my room. We can pick this up tomorrow. Good night."

KNOCK--KNOCK--KNOCK
"ATTENTION! THERE HAS BEEN A GENERAL POWER FAILURE. NO NEED TO PANIC. BUT EVERYONE MUST EVACUATE THIS FLOOR. IMMEDIATELY!"

Lottie bolted upright in her bed, awakened by the frantic pounding on her door and the commotion in the hallway. The clock on the nightstand was swallowed up in darkness. She checked the time on the lighted dial of her wristwatch--3:49 a.m.

"We've had a complete power outage on the first five floors!" the voice bellowed in the hallway. "A problem with the main breaker. No need for panic! But we need to evacuate everyone off this floor. Immediately!" the voice repeated. "Get your things, and hotel personnel will be back in ten minutes to escort everyone to the lobby. Ten minutes! Be ready!" The voice trailed off down the hallway. "The front desk will help make other arrangements."

Raymond thundered on the adjoining door to Lottie's room and barged in when she opened it. "Did you hear that? His breath reeked of stale bourbon, and even the darkness was unable to camouflage his panic. He pushed past Lottie and groped for the telephone on her bedside table.

"What're you doing?"

"Shh-hh." His fingers stumbled through Lt. Thrush's number in the dark, and he pressed the receiver to his ear. "No dial tone," he whispered. "Phone's dead, too? Lottie, this is too weird. A brown-out, I can believe, but the phones, too? We need to get outta here. I'll grab my things and be right back."

When Raymond returned to her room, he was fully dressed and his belongings were stuffed haphazardly into his bags. She had followed suit. They eased open the door to her room and peeked out into the hallway. A few of the guests had been supplied with flashlights, which formed an eerie haze in the pitch-black void. They huddled together, some clad in robes and pajamas.

Raymond tugged on Lottie's arm and stole her away from the group. Little by little, they inched away from the glow of the flashlights. Raymond guided her toward the opposite end of the hallway to a laundry room he'd spotted when he filled his ice bucket. He pushed against the door of the small enclosure, and Lottie sneaked in behind him, leaving the door slightly ajar. As their eyes grew accustomed to the darkness, they hid behind a shelf of folded linen.

"Why're we here?" She breathed.

"Shh-shh." Raymond shook her arm sternly. "Something about this whole thing just doesn't feel right. I don't want to be with the herd when they get down to the lobby. Keep quiet. We'll wait right here."

The complaining voices of the guests grew more and more distant as the hotel personnel led them down the stairwell at the opposite end of the hallway. After it had been quiet for a while, Raymond crawled to the laundry room door and poked his head into the empty blackness. He touched Lottie's knee and motioned for her to follow him out.

They felt their way along the wall, guided by the dim glow of the exit sign at their end of the hallway. When they reached the stairwell, the heavy emergency door gave way to their persistent tugs. They clung to the cold metal handrail and carefully descended the concrete service stairs. Fourth Floor. Third Floor.

Suddenly a beam of light from the bottom of the stairwell penetrated the darkness, coiling toward them like an eel. "Oh my God!" Lottie gasped nauseously, her blood gushed in violent jolts, pounding the base of her skull. "Lord, please have mercy on us," she voiced through trembling lips. She squeezed her eyes shut and prepared to die.

As the shadowy light slithered closer and closer toward them, Raymond squeezed her hand like a vise grip. His mind went blank and his knees gave way. Side by side they jammed their backs to the wall, frozen. Within moments, the light from the taunting beam swallowed them up.

"Aye, Dios mio!" exclaimed a young Spanish-speaking woman dressed in a maid's uniform and carrying a flashlight. Her bundles of dirty linen went one way, and she went the other. She lost her footing and threatened to tumble backwards on the stairs, until Raymond rallied his senses and grabbed her arm to break her fall. The trio slumped to the stairs, limp with relief.

"My God!" the maid cried in broken English. "Me was but frightened to death, Senor. I'm on my way to the laundry room on floor number six, where the lights did not go out. Who are you?"

"It's okay." Raymond gurgled; his heart began to beat again. "We're guests on this floor." He fibbed cagily. "Somehow we got lost from the group."

"Well, Senor," the maid said. "I'll be glad to leave my bundles and take you down to the lobby with my flashlight. Me, myself, I'm not supposed to be here, neither. But I did not want to get behind on my work and have to work the overtime. No. Not today," she said, crossing her heart reverently. "My baby girl, she gets the christening at church today."

"No . . . no thank you," Raymond said. "Don't bother. We'll find our own way down just fine. You just be careful on your way up."

"Thank you," Lottie called out softly. "Enjoy the christening."

Carefully, they measured the remaining steps on their descent. When they reached the first floor landing, they could hear the disgruntled guests milling in the lobby. "It could be very unhealthy for us to open that door," Raymond whispered.

"I don't know," Lottie said quietly. "You could be right; you could be wrong. But it won't hurt us to do it your way."

"C'mon." He led the way downstairs. "We'll go to the garage and get out of here." Slowly, he eased open the garage door. Everything looked normal in the dimly lit cavern, labeled with a giant yellow *P1*. They proceeded cautiously, following the exit arrows to the street level.

Over in a far corner, a pair of headlights flashed on like blazing tiger's eyes. Lottie and Raymond quickened their pace and hugged the parked cars as they hurried toward the exit. The

car with the headlights squealed out of its space and peeled around the curve toward them. They picked up the pace and jogged toward the exit. The car gunned over the speed bumps to overtake them.
"Lottie! Lottie! Get out of here!" Raymond yelled over the screeching tires, pushing her out of the path of the rampaging vehicle. "Get out of here and meet me back at Thrush's office! Go!"
Raymond galloped around the curve, and the car chased after him. Recklessly, it sideswiped a row of parked cars and skidded out of control. When Raymond rounded the corner ahead of it, he ducked down behind a parked truck and out of sight. When the car barreled pass him, he scrambled atop the truck bed and grabbed hold of the guardrail on the deck above. For a split second, he doubted his fitness to chin-up to the next level, but limited options furnished uncommon strength.
He scuffled up and over the guardrail to *P2*, sliding spread-eagle on his belly underneath a late model Lincoln. From his concealed vantage point on the ice-cold floor, Raymond watched as the blazing eyes skulked along and searched for him--slowly, methodically. His

nerves drummed in his temples. He fought the urge to balk and run from his hiding place.

"Wait! Wait!" Raymond commanded his twitching muscles. "Just a few more seconds . . . a few more seconds. Then make your move."

When the fiery-eyed car cruised slowly pass him and up the ramp to *P3*, Raymond slithered back down to *P1*, scrubbing his belly raw against the concrete. Like one of his football drills, he dropped down and tucked into a forward roll that propelled him off the truck. Without breaking stride, he raced full speed up the exit ramp to the street. The tires on the menacing car spun out of control in pursuit.

When he reached the sidewalk, Raymond sprinted faster and faster. The wind cut into his broken skin like a blade of steel. He gripped his tattered coat and raced the twelve blocks to Columbus Circle. By the time Thrush's precinct was in clear view, his bad knee was screaming, and his lungs were pleading in pain.

CHAPTER 20.
▲▲▲▲▲▲▲▲▲▲▲▲

Neither Lt. Thrush nor Lottie was at the precinct when Raymond arrived. It was just as well. He was in no condition to face them. His hands were trembling so violently it took both of them to steady the steaming cup of black coffee that dropped from the machine. He crouched into a near-fetal position on the hardwood bench in the hallway and waited.

After a few tortured minutes, Thrush's black fedora rounded the corner, and Raymond staggered into his office behind a wobbly knock. Thrush was shocked at the sight. "Man!" He gasped, assisting Raymond into a nearby chair. "You look like you've been struck by lightening? What happened?"

"I--" Raymond stammered weakly. "We--"

"Praise God!" Lottie stormed through Thrush's door, gasping for air. "You made it, too, huh Raymond!" She pounded his back approvingly. "Am I glad to see you. How'd you get away from that killer car?"

"Killer car?" Thrush yelped. "What killer car?"

"Didn't Raymond tell you?" she said. "He saved my life, and with no small risk to his own. He's a regular hero."

"Will somebody tell me something?" Thrush turned to Raymond, but he refused to speak. He was as tight-lipped as a juvenile in lock-up. Thrush pounded his desk. "Somebody had better tell me! And tell me quick!"

Lottie spoke up. "Our floor at the hotel went totally black before day this morning. Power outage . . . or something . . . and everyone was ushered to the lobby. But Raymond--" She paused for him to elaborate, but he continued to sulk. "Raymond decided it wouldn't be safe for us to stay with the group, 'cause the killers could be trying to smoke us out."

"And?" Thrush pushed. "Get on with it."

"So we slipped down to the garage, and when we got there a car tried to run us down. But Raymond pushed me aside and played decoy for the maniac while I got away."

"Got away? How?" Thrush bristled

"I didn't go up the exit ramp like we planned," she said. "I was afraid I might run headlong into more thugs on the street. So while the car sped after Raymond, I doubled back to the hotel, all the time praying for a better way out than the lobby. So I snuck back up the service stairs, and about that time an emergency generator kicked in and some auxiliary lights came on."

"Lights?" Thrush drummed his temples. "Anyone see you?"

"I bumped into a maid coming on shift." Lottie twinkled mischievously. "She was a new employee, and thought I was, too. She was lost, and I helped her find the uniform closet on the second floor. We took what we needed."

Lottie swung open her coat and modeled her maid get-up, complete with white apron. "With a load of paper towels in one arm and my stuff in the other, I shuffled through the lobby." She demonstrated. "This uniform made me invisible."

"Was anybody looking for you in the lobby?" Thrush said.

"I saw two guys with ponytails and long overcoats hovering over the front desk," she said breathlessly. "But none of the other guests had

on coats. No one had been outside. The *ponytails* were looking for us, all right. When I got close to the revolving door, I ditched the towels and made a run for it. And I didn't stop running until I saw your precinct door."
"Anybody follow you?" Thrush pressed.
"Dunno." She collapsed into a vacant chair. "Don't think so. But I know it's a miracle we got outta there in one piece. How'd you shake that crazy car, Raymond?"
"I managed." He stiffened, draping his tattered coat about him like a badge of honor. "But unlike you, Lottie, I don't turn it into a praise party when I nearly get myself killed!"
"No need to get testy." She poked fun at his mean streak. "If our roles had been reversed, you'd be just as cute me in this uniform."
"I'm not amused." Thrush blared. "Someone tried to kill you on my watch--"
Just then Sgt. Valvino broke in with papers for him to sign. "Begging the Lieutenant's pardon," he said timidly, "these are urgent--"
"Get outta here, Valvino!" Thrush said. "Set 'em on the desk and get out!"
Raymond thawed when the door closed. "What's with you, Thrush? Why do you treat that poor guy like a clown?"

His words sucked the air from the room, and Thrush's jaw crackled in the vacuum. "Don't you dare question me about police business," he said. "Must I remind you? With the exception of those of us in this room, Valvino is the only other soul that knew you were at the Pimberton." He banged his fist on the desk. "I knew I had a mole in my department, and now I've found him. I'll deal with him later. The right place for a snitch like Valvino is on the front lines of a drug bust."

"But you don't know--"

"Enough!" Thrush snapped. "You may be interested in the call I'm about to make." He dialed a sequence of numbers on his speakerphone. "Dr. Cooper? Lt. Thrush of the 61st Precinct, here. You remember me?"

"Of course. How could I forget?"

"I've got one more question for you, Doc." Thrush bullied for the benefit of his guests. "And I don't want to have to bring you downtown to get it."

"What is it, now, Lieutenant? Make it quick. I'm in session."

"I'll come straight to the point, Doc. Was Ramona Clark an intravenous drug user?"

"A junkie? Absolutely not! Ramona has many frailties, but drug and alcohol addiction are not among them," she said. "She witnessed her father die from substance abuse, and she knows she's prone to repeat the cycle. She's determined not to. This is a troubled kid we're talking about, Lieutenant, not a stupid junkie." She heaved a long sigh. "Now, if there's nothing more . . ."

"Ahem." Thrush attempted to conceal his embarrassment at being bested by a civilian. "Nothing more at this time. But I'll be in touch."

He stabbed the red release button and pressed a number on his speed dial. No speakerphone this time. "What was it?" Thrush badgered. He listened closely before fumbling the receiver back into its place. "That was my lab on the phone," he explained. "I found a used syringe in Ramona Clark's bathroom. The needle has traces of morphine on it." His flabby face creased with concern. "If that Ramona girl is still alive, we've got to find her. ASAP-PRONTO."

"If?" Lottie cringed.

Thrush hurled out assignments. "Lottie, I want you to lean on that smart-mouthed Cooper woman." She snuck a wink in Raymond's direction. It was obvious that Dr. Cooper was under Thrush's skin. "I want you to contact all the nut houses and hospitals in the area until you turn up something on Ramona," he said. "And Raymond, you're coming with me."

"Where're we going?"

Thrush grabbed his overcoat from the rack and tossed Raymond his spare. "Here," he said. "Wear my back-up. Where we're going, you've got to look your best."

▲ ▲ ▲ ▲

When Lt. Thrush and Raymond arrived on Wall Street, it was nearly noon. Thrush circled twice around the congested block in search of a parking space at the Pinnacle Towers. Frustrated, he jammed his portable flashing light atop his unmarked police issue, and pulled into the *No Parking Zone* at the side entrance. He hopped out of the car, and Raymond followed him toward the building.

They arrived in time to see John R. Clayburn climbing into the back of his sleek, pearlescent limousine, assisted by his uniformed chauffeur, the man from the newspaper clipping. Raymond locked eyes with the chauffeur, and he caught a glint of recognition. He remembered his mother saying, "You can tell by a man's eyes if your name has been in his mouth." If that were the case, Raymond knew the chauffeur had spoken of him many times.

Lt. Thrush mumbled as he trotted back to his car. "R . . . G . . . J . . . J--essup. He snapped his fingers loudly. "Geoffrey Jessup! That's the chauffeur's name. I knew I recognized him. I never forget a face, or a rap sheet a mile long." He yelled back at Raymond, "C'mon! Hustle up! We've got to get back to the precinct. I need my computer. ASAP- PRONTO."

▲ ▲ ▲ ▲

"Doc, I see you traded your pit bull at the front desk for a chihuahua. Nice change," Lottie said. "Thanks for seeing me on short notice."

"Sit down, Lottie," Dr. Cooper said. "After your phone call, I contacted Ramona's former roommates."

"Have they seen her?"

"No. Not in several weeks. They think it's strange, and I'm starting to get worried. It's impossible for Ramona to go this long without crying on somebody's shoulder."

"Like I said on the phone, Annette. She's in real danger, and it's up to us to help her."

"I also started checking the psychiatric hospitals to see if Ramona, or a Jane Doe meeting her description, has checked in."

"Great idea! Any luck?"

"Not yet. I'm faxing her photo to all the hospitals within a three state area."

"Won't that raise a red flag?"

"Not really. We lose patients from time to time, and this is a common method for getting them back, albeit, it's usually not a tri-state hunt.

But the hospitals aren't networked, so nobody'll be the wiser."

"Let's send your nurse home for the afternoon." Lottie said. "I'll man the phones out front and check with the local emergency rooms. The fewer people that know about our little woman-hunt, the better, don't you agree?"

"You're right, of course. Carla, my pit-bull as you put it, quit on me suddenly. In fact, the day after your last visit. She left me at loose ends, and I was very fortunate to find Joyce. She's been great, and I don't want to upset her."

▲ ▲ ▲ ▲

When they returned to the precinct from Pinnacle Towers, Lt. Thrush stuffed his messages into his shirt pocket to attend to later. The Clayburn case had become his number one priority. He didn't have enough hard evidence to take to his superiors, but he was convinced this case had the makings of a conspiracy that reached all the way to the top.

He accessed his computer for one, Geoffrey Jessup. The printer churned for several minutes, spitting out his complete rap sheet and his varied aliases. Jessup's juvenile days were peppered with one incident of gang violence after another. His criminal record had matured along with the man, resulting in numerous arrests, but a limited number of convictions. No matter the severity of the crime--ranging from pandering for prostitution, to armed robbery, to manslaughter--most of the charges had either been dropped, or punished with time served.

Thrush brought himself up to speed on the file, while Raymond fingered Jessup's picture in the clipping, feverishly scrolling his mental index. *I've seen this face before. The sneer looks so familiar. But where? When?*

"What's Clayburn doing mixed up with a two-bit hoodlum like Geoffrey Jessup?" Thrush mumbled. "His mob connections go way back. I'm gonna get to the bottom of this unholy alliance--if I have to call in all my markers."

"Useless!" Raymond pushed the clipping to the floor and stormed out.

Thrush rounded the table to catch him. "Wait a minute." He dogged his steps. "Where do you think you're going?"

"Back off, Thrush! Raymond stiff-armed him at the rear exit. "Need some air."

▲▲▲▲

While Dr. Cooper faxed Ramona's picture to the psychiatric facilities in the tri-state area, Lottie kept vigil at the reception desk. The phone rang incessantly, but she kept the lines open. "Dr. Cooper's Office," she greeted patently. "If this is not an emergency, please call back tomorrow."

"Dr. Cooper?" The attending nurse at Yonker's Crisis Center inquired.

"Yes." Lottie fibbed. "This is Dr. Cooper."

"It appears we have a Jane Doe fitting your description."

"Is that so?" Lottie reigned in her excitement.

"Mind you," the nurse said. "The patient can't or won't supply her name, and the picture you faxed is rather hazy. We can't be absolutely sure, but you can come by and make a positive I.D. The patient is not responding to treatment. Without her history, we can't help her."

"Yes. I understand." Lottie said. "My nurse and I will be there as soon as possible. We'll do everything we can to assist in her care."

"No hurry," the nurse said crudely. "She ain't going nowhere."

Each time Lottie sprinted away from the desk to give Annette the good news, the phone rang again. Twice she raced back to grab it, and twice the line went dead. The third time, the caller identified himself.

"Dr. Cooper?" A soothing male voice inquired.

"Why, yes," Lottie said.

"This is Dr. Lawrence Crandall at the White Lily Sanitarium," he crooned smoothly. "We're a private facility on the outskirts of Newark, and I think we just might have your missing patient with us. We have a young woman who looks identical to your photograph. She arrived by private ambulance four or five days ago."

"Is that so?" Lottie breathed slowly.

"Highly irregular." Dr. Crandall admitted cautiously. "The patient was not checked in by anyone, nor has anyone come to visit since she was admitted. According to the ambulance attendant, her name is Rachel Cross." He lowered his voice and spoke uneasily. "The driver said he was paid in cash by courier to transport her here. He said the caller let it slip that her rich, older lover had found her in the midst of a drug overdose, and her benefactor wished to remain anonymous. We took this explanation at face value," he said, "but now I'm not so sure."

"Why's that?" Lottie consoled. "What made you change your mind?"

"As far as treatment goes." He steered the conversation toward his clinical observations. "Rachael Cross is heavily sedated to keep her calm and resting, but she should come out of it soon. And when she does, we'll need her complete medical history to develop an adequate treatment plan. That's why I'm calling, Dr. Cooper. Can you help us in that regard?"

"We'll be happy to help you, Doctor. Would it be possible for me to see the patient and make a positive identification? I'll bring along her medical records."

"By all means, Doctor; the sooner, the better. Rachel's . . . Ramona's care hangs in the balance."

"By the way," Lottie said, not wanting to spook him. "May I inquire as to who is paying your bill? I only ask because it has come to my attention that Ramona recently lost her job and her medical insurance right along with it."

"Why, her benefactor, I presume," Dr. Crandall said uncertainly, obviously embarrassed by his lack of information. "A messenger also dropped off a six-month cash advance for her care. It's all a bit odd."

"Very well, Dr. Crandall. "Give me the address of your facility, and my nurse and I will be there as soon as possible. By the way, we don't want to upset the continuity of Ramona's care, so it may be a good idea not to mention this conversation to anyone."

"Well . . . yes. I guess you're right. We'll keep it between ourselves for the time being. I look forward to meeting you this afternoon. Must go now. I have a visitor," he said, ending the call. "Come in, Nurse Jamison. Come in."

"Hello, Doctor. You're looking well."

"What a pleasant surprise!" Dr. Crandall said. "Back so soon from your leave of absence? Couldn't stay away, huh? Well, you've been sorely missed. We'll put you back to work right away."

"Annette! Annette!" Lottie bounded from the receptionist desk. "We got a lead on a Jane Doe from Yonkers, but I'm certain we've found Ramona in Jersey."

Dr. Cooper fumbled her papers to the floor, and Lottie reported her conversation with Dr. Crandall. "Great news!" Annette smiled happily. "Let's not waste any time. I'll gather up Ramona's files, and we can be on our way. It'll probably be more convincing if you wear a uniform, Lottie. I'm pretty sure you'll find your size in the staff lounge."

On her way to the locker room, Lottie sneaked back to the reception desk. She wanted to bring Thrush and Raymond up to speed, but she didn't want to upset her tenuous rapport with Annette by mentioning Thrush's name.

"What?" She fumed at the haughty duty clerk. "Lt. Thrush is not there? Then you call him and tell him it's an emergency. He needs to meet us at the White Lily Sanitarium in Newark right away."

In the staff lounge, Lottie located a size 8 uniform in locker No. 3. When she removed it from the hanger, she made a startling discovery. "Annette! Annette!" she shrieked. "Come here! Take a look!"

"Joyce Jamison, R.N." Dr. Cooper read the badge pinned to the lapel. "So what? I told you my nurse's name is Joyce--Joyce Jamison."

"Look closer." Lottie pointed. A white lily was etched into the right corner of the badge.

Dr. Cooper's mouth flew open. "I didn't have time to check her references. Do you think Joyce is a spy?"

"At the risk of sounding paranoid, Doc, what else could it be?"

Annette's bottom lip quivered. "And to think I trusted her. What do we do now?"

"We follow through with our plan," Lottie said. "That's what we do. We must. Ramona needs us."

CHAPTER 21.
▲▲▲▲▲▲▲▲▲▲▲

Meanwhile, Raymond wandered the streets outside Thrush's precinct fighting the cobwebs in his brain. Returning to his office would be dangerous, especially since Geoffrey Jessup had spotted him. *But if I don't go back, how will I ever remember where I saw Jessup before? My entire past is squirreled away in my office.*

On foot, Raymond was able to sneak past the garage attendant when he reached 1000 Liberty Place. The youngster was sound asleep in the booth, and it went unnoticed when he ducked into the elevator.

When the door glided open on his penthouse floor, Raymond cautiously poked his head into the hallway. Soft lighting had been all the rage when his interior designer talked him into the wall sconces, but given his limited sight line, he scorned his decision.

He locked the elevator door behind him and jogged softly on the thick pile carpet to his office. His key fit smoothly into the lock and he edged through the doorway. The incandescent glow from the floor lamp confirmed the visit by Thrush's clean-up crew--a welcomed sight. Raymond had absolutely no desire to re-visit the scary scene that had sent him running for his life.

He clicked on the reading lamp on his desk and sat down. It felt good. It felt like home. He used the small key he'd hidden under the lamp to unlock the bottom drawer of his credenza. He felt around for the yellow box in which he had neatly packed away his past. He braced himself for the memories he was about to uncork, many of which he'd spent the better part of a lifetime trying to forget. He opened the box.

Suddenly, there was a noise. Raymond halted. He tried to convince himself it was the plumbing, expanding in the distance. But there it was again. He couldn't deny it, or the queasy feeling tumbling through his gut. He slunk to the floor, telephone in hand, and dialed Thrush's number.

"Hullo." Thrush answered.

"It's me," Raymond whispered.

"Well, it's about time. Have I got news for you? Lottie and the Good Doctor--"

"Sh-hh!" Raymond hissed. "Later. Okay."

"What's wrong?"

"Sh-hh. Just listen. I don't have much time. I'm in my office--"

"Your office? What the--"

"Not now, Thrush. There it goes again, that grinding noise. What do I do?"

"Is there a back way out of there?"

"No." Raymond panted. "Only the elevator and a locked stairwell at the other end of the hall. I can open it with my passkey."

"Get out of there! I'm on my way."

Raymond knocked over the lamp as he fumbled for his yellow box and bolted for the door. When he cracked it open, he noticed two small holes on either side of the door jam. He hadn't noticed them before. *Blast it all. I must've triggered a silent alarm.*

He scrambled for the stairwell. When he got there, he realized the grinding noise was coming from that direction. Someone was cutting through the metal door! He skidded back to the elevator and hopped on, releasing the lock. His mind was spinning.

He pressed *10* on the control panel. The 10th floor was under renovations. When the elevator stopped there, he held the doors open until the *down* arrow recycled. Then he pressed *1* and jumped out of the empty elevator. He hoped the decoy would throw off anyone tracking the car from the lobby.

Unlike the penthouse floor, the 10th floor had two sets of elevators and stairwells. Raymond sped across to the opposite set of stairs and lodged his ear to the door. Nothing. He jerked open the door, and his heels clicked against the metal stairs as he raced down two flights.

Exploding onto the 8th floor, he scrambled to the second bank of elevators. "Next car!" he shouted at the threesome attempting to board with him. He jabbed *4* and *Close Door*, speeding the car on its way.

On the 4th floor, Raymond pushed pass the press of people waiting to board the elevator. He galloped toward the stairwell on the penthouse side. *They probably didn't post a guard. Didn't think I'd live this long.*

Raymond charged the stairs, taking them two-by-two, his yellow box clutched under his

elbow. He bounded into the garage at full speed. As he ran pass the attendant's booth, he pounded on the bulletproof glass, warning the sleepy-eyed youngster.
 The sound of fast feet closed in behind him. Raymond sprinted faster still. A blast of gunfire from an automatic weapon rang out in the cavern. Bullets whizzed pass his right ear, ricocheting off the wall. He bobbed and weaved, and before the next round of shots, he blazed out of the garage onto Liberty Street.
 Horns blared as Raymond dodged in and out of on-coming traffic. Racing to the opposite side of the street, he fell in lock step with the throng of pedestrians on the sidewalk, using their breadth as a shield from the relentless gunmen.
 Raymond caught sight of what appeared to be Thrush's police cruiser crawling along the street. Eluding the gunmen, he pushed upstream and edged street-side to risk a closer look. It was Thrush. Raymond glued himself to the passenger side of the moving vehicle, banging wildly on the locked door. Thrush flung it open, and Raymond lunged inside.
 "Whatever possessed you to pull an idiotic stunt like this? Thrush blasted as they sped away to the precinct. "Going back to your office? When Clayburn's men know you're in town?

Never in all my years on the force have I ever seen anything so utterly stupid."

"I just had to know more about Geoffrey Jessup." Raymond squirmed "He's an important piece to this puzzle, right? It's been driving me crazy. I know I've seen him before." He slid his yellow box toward Thrush. "It's all in here."

▲ ▲ ▲ ▲

Meanwhile, Dr. Cooper and Lottie arrived at the White Lily Sanitarium to meet with Dr. Crandall late in the afternoon. The facility was tucked away on sprawling wooded acreage. A slender ribbon of graveled road delivered them from the asphalt highway to the main gate.

"This looks like a ranch out of one of those old western movies," Lottie remarked as they followed the crude arrows from the highway.

"Yep, Partner." Annette said. "But once you're back here, it'll be tough getting out."

When they arrived, Dr. Crandall was out on his afternoon rounds. Uncomfortable with deception, Annette paced like a caged tiger. She collided head-on with Dr. Crandall when he entered the door.

The senior Crandall, dressed in a white smock, avoided her with a lively two-step. "Dr. Cooper, I presume?" He smiled.

"Uh... yes." She blushed brightly.

"Then that makes me, Dr. Crandall." He placed her cold hand into his warm one. "I'm glad you could make it."

"We're happy to help. Ramona's made us more than a little nervous," she said, attempting to explain away her moist handshake. "This is my assistant. Nurse Denise Stewart."

"Pleased to meet you, Nurse Stewart." Dr. Crandall led the way to his desk. "Let's sit here and review Ramona's case files, shall we?"

In no time, Annette grew more relaxed. It was obvious that Dr. Crandall was a highly skilled professional, seasoned from many years of practice in helping troubled patients. "I'm very impressed with the size of your campus," she said. "Is Ramona on this ward, or in one of your other buildings?"

"Since I knew you were coming, we moved her just down the hall in room 112. When we've finished here, I'll take you down for a closer look. If she's awake, she'll probably be very happy to see you."

Annette whispered something to Lottie, and she excused herself. "I left an important file in the car," she explained. Nurse Stewart will get it while we continue."

Once outside the office door, Lottie surveyed the hallway to get her bearings. It was deathly quiet. She skimmed along the white wall toward the patient rooms. In the distance, she glimpsed someone manning the nurse's station and stopped in her tracks. It was Joyce Jamison. Lottie ducked behind a metal gurney in the hallway and waited.

When Nurse Jamison moved away from the front counter to answer the phone, Lottie crawled past it on hands and knees. She ducked into the first open door and closed it softly behind her. In the musty darkness, she groped around the doorframe for the light switch. Nothing. She waved her hand furiously until she collided with a pull string and jerked on the light.

It was an orderly's closet filled with stale mops and assorted items for repair. An orange jumpsuit was flung across a rollaway bed, which had an ugly bloodstain on the mattress. A portable wheelchair with a rip on the back flap was propped against the wall.

Lottie climbed into the jumpsuit to camouflage her nurse's uniform. A grimy baseball cap was stuffed inside the pocket. Her white shoes stuck out like sore thumbs. She located a pair of brogans in a mop bucket on wheels, with a pair of smelly socks. She gritted her teeth as she pulled on the socks. *Get over it, Girl! Get on with it!*

Lottie flung her nurse's shoes into the bucket and guided it with the mop, while she clutched the folded wheelchair tightly under her armpit. She pulled the baseball cap down low over her forehead and turned out the light. Careful not to look back at the nurse's station, she steered the mop bucket slowly up the hallway. She spotted room 112, but kept a steady pace pass it.

When she reached the next wing, Lottie scooted the bucket into room 135, the first empty room she could find. She tiptoed next door where a patient was snoring softly. She tipped the contents of the bedpan onto the floor, rang the nurse's call button, and ducked back into the empty room. When Nurse Jamison answered the call, Lottie grabbed her shoes and the wheelchair and sprinted back to Ramona's room.

Ramona was struggling to lift her head when Lottie entered room 112. When she saw her, Ramona froze and squeezed her eyelids shut. In her faulty mental state, she thought she could hide behind her eyes.

"Don't be afraid," Lottie whispered. "Dr. Cooper sent me to get you."

Ramona cracked open one eye and attempted a fleeting smile. "Y-e-s." She nodded.

Lottie released her from the I.V. tube that was dripping something into her veins. The bag was nearly empty. She removed it from its perch to take to Dr. Cooper. Assisting Ramona into the wheelchair, she arranged her mane of dyed jet-black hair to conceal her face.

Ramona was as weak as a noodle, too limp to sit up straight. Her head drooped like a wilted lily, and her smile waned pitifully. Lottie propped her with pillows and swaddled a blanket to keep her from slipping onto the floor.

She peeled away the jumpsuit down to her nurse's uniform, and jammed the orange mass under the bed covers in the shape of a sleeping form. Lottie kicked the shoes and socks underneath the bed and stamped back into her nurse's shoes, all the while wielding Ramona's wheelchair into the hallway. She sped past the empty nurse's station and out the front exit.

Lottie inhaled in gasps as she rumbled across the graveled surface of the parking lot. The crisp country air was a sharp contrast to the medicinal scent in the ward. Ramona's head bobbed loosely.

At the car, Lottie hoisted Ramona's dead weight onto the floor of the back seat. She covered her over with the blanket amid her incoherent groans. Afterwards, Lottie crawled into the front seat and locked the doors. She paged Dr. Cooper with their prearranged code, *911*.

Dr. Cooper welcomed the blare of her pager. She was running out of ways to occupy Dr. Crandall without creating suspicion. She checked the message and snapped up from the table. The *911* alerted her that Lottie was calling from the car, and Ramona was with her.

"I'm very sorry, Dr. Crandall," she said. "I'm being called away on another emergency. This is very awkward, I know, but it can't be helped. I'll come back tomorrow and bring the missing file." She cranked his hand and backed out the door. "Thanks, again, Doctor. Thanks."

"Doctor Crandall!" Nurse Jamison burst into his office, only moments after Annette's exit. "Ramona Clark, room 112, she's missing! Not in her room! Nowhere to be found!"

"How did you know?" Dr. Crandall knitted his eyebrows suspiciously. "How did you know her name is Ramona Clark?"

Nurse Jamison pulled a small caliber revolver from her smock pocket and pushed Dr. Crandall into a chair. "Sit down, Old Man!" She commanded gruffly, training the gun on him while she used his phone. "Sit there!" She warned. "And don't get in my way!"

▲ ▲ ▲ ▲

Back at the precinct, Thrush yanked open the sticky bottom drawer in his metal desk. He pulled out the flask of bourbon he kept hidden there and poured him and Raymond a shot, disguised in paper cups from the water cooler. He had no doubt Raymond would accept it; after all, it was their mutual fondness for the therapeutic elixir that had brought them together in the first place.

They examined the contents of Raymond's yellow box. "I just can't believe it," Thrush said. "I cannot believe you'd be foolish enough to return to your office, knowing that Jessup--"

"You'll see." Raymond carped confidently. He removed a bundle of envelopes, secured with rubber bands and placed them close at his side. He scattered the remaining yearbooks and scrapbooks onto the table.

"What's all this?" Thrush grumbled, pretending not to notice Raymond's maneuver with the envelopes.

"Here." Raymond slid him the scrapbooks. "Make yourself useful. Let's take a stroll down memory lane."

"All these years, and I didn't know you were a quarterback at Arizona State," Thrush said. He thumbed through the scrapbooks until

Raymond began swirling pages in his senior yearbook. Thrush moved over for a closer look.

"See this guy." Raymond pointed out Willy Hawkins, right tackle. "He was a 6'7", 300-pound mountain of a man, but equally naïve," he said fondly. "The fellows would set such a fire under him on big game days, he'd nearly kill the nearest opponent when we hit the field. Poor Willy never caught on."

"Big, Dumb Jock, heh?" Thrush laughed.

Raymond cleared his tight throat. "One day, late, after everyone had left practice, I came upon this guy pistol whipping Willy in the locker room. Willy was putting up no defense. The guy was killing him, so I stepped in."

"What happened?"

"I got pretty banged up for my trouble. The guy stomped my right leg, over and over, as he sneered down at me. Finally, Willy came to himself, pulled the guy off me and tossed him out on his ear."

"Did he stomp him, too?"

Raymond scrubbed the crown of his head with both hands. "I don't know if it was the beating I took that day or what, but at the game the next day when I set up to throw a big bomb for the touchdown, my right leg buckled under me. I had to be carried off the field on a stretcher. It was the final game of the regular season. I missed the pass. We lost the game. That play cost us a bowl berth and me the Heisman."

"Wow, Raymond. I never knew."

Raymond reached for his stack of letters and clutched them close to his heart. "I had so wanted my Mom to be at the big game. But she died the month before. Struck down by an aneurysm, while waiting tables." He raked away a tear. "I rushed to her side, but she didn't last the night. Never talked to her again."

"Did your dad come--"

"He didn't dare come to the game." Raymond flared. "It was off limits to him. He knew he wasn't welcomed."

"I bet there were lots of pro scouts out that day, hey, Raymond?" Thrush sidestepped.

"Yep." Raymond fished through his painful memories. "Scouts were out in droves. I healed up enough to be picked in the first round, and I landed a five-year, no-cut contract, too. But things were never the same." He rubbed his right knee. "My knee snapped again in my first outing as a NFL quarterback, and I never saw any real action after that."

"Too bad, Man."

"Anyway." Raymond regrouped. "The guy that beat up Willy in the locker room is the same guy I saw opening John R. Clayburn's limousine door today."

"No! You sure? Jessup?"

"It's Jessup, all right." Raymond nodded. "I couldn't put my finger on it at first. His face is a little different now, older, but I'll never forget that *hate-your-guts* look while he stomped my leg. The same wise-guy smirk in Long's file, and the same look that Bozo gave me today."

"Jessup's rap sheet did mention him being extradited to Arizona once on some racketeering charges that were later dropped."

"I found out Willy had gotten crosswise with the mob because of his gambling debts."

"Gambling? On your games?"

"Yeah. But Willy was a simple-minded teddy bear. He had no clue that betting on our games was wrong, or illegal. He bet us to win."

"So that's the tie." Thrush snapped his fingers. "I had Aiesha over there doing some research, and it's all starting to come together."

"I see," Raymond said, following Thrush's eyes to the woman sitting at the computer on the other side of the glass wall. She was trying to disguise her beauty, albeit unsuccessfully, behind big glasses and her mind; but her shapely legs that never quit gave her away.

Thrush winked at Raymond when he caught him staring. "She's a whiz at that computer, too." He snickered. "Anyway, Aiesha did some background checks on Clayburn's campaign. He's connected to all the right causes and the big money boys, but his connections don't stop there. Seems he's getting some heavy backing through some dummy corporations that can be traced to organized crime; although, we haven't confirmed that yet. She's still digging."

"The mob?"

"Yep. The connection between Clayburn and Jessup is coming into focus. Maybe he's not so much Clayburn's chauffeur as he is the eyes-and-ears for the mob, protecting their investment in their handpicked politician. After all, what better plumb than the governor of New York State?"

"So what's our next step?"

Thrush put his feet up on his desk and his hands behind his head. "We'll shake every tree until we see what falls out," he said. "Jessup is getting a little long in the tooth to spend time on death row for a murder rap all by his lonesome. We'll see who he wants to take down with him."

"Murder?" Raymond paled.

"Our man, Long, didn't get those burns by accident." Thrush reminded him. "Don't you get it, Boy? This is high stakes poker. These guys play for keeps--maybe they did-in our friend, Long, and maybe the Clark girl, too. With what we know, I can leverage the rest when I get my hands on Jessup." He gestured. "I'm gonna squeeze him 'til he sings like a bird."

"Ramona?" Raymond shook. "Where's Lottie?

"Calm down," Thrush said. "They should be all right. I sent out the cavalry."

"Cavalry? For what?"

Thrush filled Raymond in on Lottie's call about the White Lily. "In the excitement of rescuing you from your office, Smart Guy, I forgot to tell you. They wanted us to join them, but then you got your bright idea, and I couldn't be in two places at once, could I?"

"Forgot? How could you forget something so important? If something's happened to Lottie, Thrush, I'll never forgive you."

"I sent Captain Ruppert, my buddy in Newark, to look for the ladies. I haven't heard back from him, but he's very reliable. We can call him now, if it'll make you feel better."

CHAPTER 22.
▲▲▲▲▲▲▲▲▲▲▲

No sooner than Thrush picked up the phone to call Capt. Ruppert, Lottie burst through his door with an officer from the Newark Police Department trailing her. "Thrush!" she shrilled. "You nearly got us killed! Annette and me, we trusted you, and you fed us to the wolves. Where were you?"

"Looks like you made it in one piece." Thrush countered. "At least your mouth did."

Lottie lunged for his throat, and Raymond stepped between them. "No thanks to you!" She knotted her tiny fists in rage. "If it weren't for this nice officer here, we'd both be dead."

"Sit." Raymond commanded, forcing her into a chair. "What happened?

"And your name, Sergeant?" Thrush brandished his superiority.

"Sgt. J.T. Shorter, sir," he replied, snapping to attention. "Capt. Ruppert put me on detail to look out for these lovely ladies."

"So then where's the Cooper woman?"

"I must decline to say at this time, sir. Got strict orders from my Captain to leave Miss Garrett in your custody and return to the station."

"Decline? But surely you can give me a full report?"

"Sorry, sir. Have my orders," Sgt. Shorter said, while slipping Thrush a note. "Captain says, better get somebody over there right away." He tipped his hat respectfully and closed the door on his way out.

Thrush turned his gaze on Lottie. "Then you tell me what happened."

"For your information, *Raymond*." She turned her back to Thrush. "Annette and I managed to sneak Ramona out of the White Lily. We were scared to death. When we got to the exit gate, the wooden arm was down, and we waited for the parking attendant to open it. He was on the phone. And then all of a sudden, he dropped it and came after us. Annette panicked and broke the gate down getting out of there."

"Were you followed?" Thrush pressed.

Lottie rolled her eyes in his direction and returned her attention to Raymond. "By the time we got back to the main road, a red Volvo was laying down dust behind us. Annette sped up to the challenge, and we made it to the highway. But the Volvo didn't quit. It tried to force us off the road, ramming us from behind, time and time again. Annette was screaming and swinging her car from side to side, but somehow she was able to maintain control." Lottie rotated her neck.

"What happened? What happened?"

"The Volvo slammed into my side, forcing us into the path of an oncoming Mack truck."

"Mack truck!"

"The truck driver swerved just in time to avoid a head-on collision." She stroked her arms to warm them. "Then out of nowhere, a black car barreled in--flashing lights, sirens, the works. Sgt. Shorter to the rescue! When the red Volvo saw him, it made a screeching U-turn and fled in the opposite direction. He saved our lives, Raymond." She shot a convicting glance over her shoulder. "No thanks to your friend, here."

"Well, don't make me ask." Thrush cracked. "Where's the Good Doctor now?"

"You're the detective," she said. "What's that in your hand? I suspect the piece of paper Sgt. Shorter sneaked you has the answer. He tucked Annette and Ramona away at some safehouse somewhere."

Thrush uncrumpled the wad of paper. It was the newspaper clipping of Clayburn and Jessup he'd faxed to Capt. Ruppert earlier in the day. Jessup's picture was circled on the front, with a Newark address and a note scribbled on the back. "Miss Clark says he's your man."

"Did he tell you?" Lottie said.

Thrush rammed the note into his pocket for safekeeping. "Lottie, it may interest you to know," he said, "Sgt. Shorter's commanding officer is my poker buddy. And when I couldn't meet you on time, I sent him to get you."

"Sure," Lottie said dubiously.

"If you two'll quit sparring for a minute," Raymond said, "I'd like to know our next move?"

Thrush propped his feet up on his desk and clasped his hands behind his head. "I'd say you two have outstayed your welcome," he said. "With Ramona's eyewitness testimony, this is now an *official* police matter. And with the election next Tuesday, it gives me less than a week to bring Clayburn and his mob buddies down." He glowered. "You two are getting in my way."

"So what're we suppose to do?" Raymond said. "Evaporate?"

"Capital idea!" Thrush hammered his desk. "I want you out of my town. And if we're lucky, you can come back next week and vote. We'll have to walk the gauntlet to get John R. But get him, I will. I assure you. It's gonna be a madhouse, and I don't have time to baby-sit. And thanks to you, Lottie, I'm all outta markers."

"But--"

"But-nothing." Thrush dug in his heels. "I don't even want to know where you're going; just call me when you get there. A word of caution," he said, "don't travel by plane. I'm pretty sure they're all over the airports. Buses to Philly and Baltimore run every hour on the hour from places not so easy to pin down."

"Bus? But--"

Thrush waved off Raymond's objections. "I don't want to see you back here until I've made my case against Clayburn. Got it?"

"But how will we know when it's over?" Raymond said.

"Not to worry. When this story breaks, it'll rock the nation. Bigger than . . . Watergate."

"But--"

"That's it!" Thrush stamped his hands on his desk. "I'll send one of my men with you as far as the subway--"

"No!" Lottie and Raymond united in their objection. "No more police escorts, and no more subways. We'll handle this ourselves."

In the evening shadows outside the precinct, Lottie and Raymond nearly collided into a passerby couple that were kissing and holding hands. They shared a common space, but their realities were worlds apart.

▲▲▲▲

"C'mon, Lottie. Hurry!" Raymond yelled as they hot-footed it across the platform at the Market East Terminal in Philadelphia. "Our ride to the airport is pulling out of the station. Hurry!"

"You know, Raymond," she said, once they settled aboard the R1 train. "Clayburn's goons expect us to be together."

"Are you saying we should split up?"

"May not be a bad idea."

"Since Clayburn's goons have turned Tucson upside-down, maybe it's safe to go there for awhile. Besides I need to check on Rex."

"All right . . . but we've got to get back to Union City before too long. I don't like leaving Mamma alone like this."

"Deal." He squinted as the train pitched and swayed under the cover of darkness. "Just give me a few minute to rest my eyes."

By agreement, when they de-boarded the train at Philadelphia International Airport, Lottie purchased a one-way ticket to Tucson on Western Airlines under the name Mae Garrett. Raymond ticketed himself with Pacific Coast Airways as Earl Beck. They used the middle name on their driver's license, and the busy ticket agents didn't quibble over the minor deviation.

▲▲▲▲

"What fool is this?" A voice garbled angrily over the telephone. "It's nearly 2:00 a.m. Are you out of your mind?"
"Rex." Raymond hissed. "Just listen."
"Ray--?"
"Meet me at Raoul's . . . noon tomorrow. Wait till I get there."
"Sure thing, Good Buddy. See ya--"
Raymond cradled the phone and tossed fitfully in his rented bed near the Tucson Airport. Lottie sobbed quietly in the next room.

▲▲▲▲

"Where're we going?" Lottie pouted as she climbed into their rental car at the Renegade Motel. "I'm sleepy. Why so early?"
"Time's wasting." Raymond clipped.
"You look as bad as you did last night at the airport. Aren't you happy to be home?"

"Just get in, Lottie. We need to go."

"Wow, it's breathtaking!" She remarked as they drove toward town. "I thought *desert* meant *ugly*."

"No. Not at all. It's beautiful."

"How can anyone see these colors and not believe in God?"

"Humph." He circled the block for the third time.

"Lost?"

"No." He checked and rechecked his rearview mirror. "Just making sure we're not being followed. We're going in over there." He pointed to a strip shopping center. "Keep your eyes peeled while I find a parking spot."

It was a little early for the bar devotees when they arrived at the Las Cabos Bar and Grill. A few locals were sprinkled about, sharing coffee and swapping gossip. Raymond led Lottie to the far end of the bar, unnoticed by the bartender who was engaged in a heated dispute with a liquor vendor over the cases in his last shipment.

After a few minutes, Raymond climbed off his stool and slipped behind the bar. His proximity alarmed the bartender, and he reached under the counter for his shotgun. Before he could locate it, Raymond rushed him and smothered him in a tight bear hug.

The startled bartender gasped for air and wrenched his body to face his attacker. His laughter erupted like claps of thunder. Raymond loosed his grip, and the two men leapt round and round in a tight spiral, prancing and guffawing like a pair of playmates.

"Raymon', you ole' Sidewinder," the bartender said in a Spanish accent. "Man, you're a sight for sore eyes to see!"

Raymond hugged his friend and led him to the end of the bar. "Raoul," he said, "I'd like you to meet Lottie."

The strangers stared at each other incredulously. Raoul Gonzalez was the first to find his manners. "I am very pleased to meet you, Senorita," he said, bowing politely from his waist. "My friend Raymon' and me, we go way back, you see . . . back to our days of touch football in the school yard. It is good to have you here with him."

"I'm happy to be here, too," Lottie said. "And it's an honor to meet Raymond's friend."

"The honor, Senorita, it is all mine."

Lottie sat on the sidelines while Raoul and Raymond animatedly relived old times. She was the first to notice when a broad figure skulked in through the side door. Instinctively, she knew this brute of a man with the crimson beard could be none other than Rex from the Last Chance Diner. His kind eyes gave him away. They matched the compassion in his voice.

Lottie met him at the door. "You must be Rex?" she said brightly. "I'm Lottie."

Rex tipped his sweat stained, 10-gallon hat in a gentlemanly manner. If he was surprised, he didn't let on. "Howdy, Little Lady, so you're Miss Lottie."

His booming voice seized the room and the attention of Raymond and Raoul. The three men grinned from ear to ear, and before long they were reenacting the ritual friendship dance that reduces grown men into mere boys.

Rex grabbed Raymond's shoulders in two giant hands. "You're a sight for sore eye, Son," he said. "With all that's been going on, I didn't know if I'd seen the last of you or what."

"With all that's been going on?" Raoul scowled. "What have you two ole Geezers been hiding behind my back?"

"Oh, nothing. Nothing," Rex said. "Just business. You know they play cut-throat in the big city."

CHAPTER 23.
▲▲▲▲▲▲▲▲▲▲▲▲

Lottie gave way for the old friends to visit at the bar. She found a secluded spot near a window flooded with brilliant sunlight. Before long, however, the solitude ushered in the nagging concerns for Miss Charity that had tortured her through the night. She had abandoned her mother for a second time, and this time her life could be in danger.

Despite the warmth in her little corner, the cold stole back into her bones. The thought of losing her mother stampeded her mind, like a herd of wild horses. Amid the smell of beer and honky-tonk music, she bowed her head and prayed; something she hadn't done since she left Mt. Zion.

"Lord Jesus," she whispered reverently. "I'm sorry I stayed away so long. But after *the incident* in the barn, I thought you wanted me to make my own way." She sniffed. "What am I saying? That's not true. The truth is . . . I blamed you. I turned my back on you." Her silent tears flowed freely. "But you never stopped loving me. Just like Mamma. I know that now. And no matter what happens, we have eternal life in you. And someday, Lord, I hope Raymond will come to know you, too. Amen."

In that moment, the burden of years fell away from Lottie like dead weight. Her wandering had come full circle, ending where it began--not in her performance, but in her faith. "Hmm-mm!" She groaned nosily. "It's so good to be home."

"Lottie, you okay over there?" Raymond flushed, suddenly embarrassed they had totally abandoned her.

"Come over here and join us, Little Lady." Rex said.

"No. No, thanks." She waved them off with a smile.

"Then we'll join you." Rex rebutted. "It's about time for Raoul, here, to get back to work."

Raoul greeted an arriving customer, and Rex and Raymond joined Lottie at her table.

"I've known this Boy, here, a long time." Rex glimmered. "He's like the son I never had."

"So I gathered." She smiled wryly.

"I imagine you know him pretty well yourself." He removed his hat and scratched his balding head. "What I can't figure, though, is why I can't get it through his thick skull to let bygones be bygones and go visit his daddy while he's in town? I thought I taught him better than that, but he's being bull-head stubborn about it." He appealed to Lottie for support.

The internal struggle registered on Raymond's face, and Lottie peeked at Rex through knitted fingers to signal him to back off, but he persisted. "I can't even talk sense to the Boy about it," he said. "It ain't good for him. Is it, Lottie? Tell him."

"Stop right there!" Raymond blew like a volcano. "That man has been like an evil dust devil all my life. He was when by Mom was alive, and he is now." He ranted out of control. "But I've proved him wrong. Mom and me didn't deserve the hateful things he did. He was wrong, not us. He's the 'poor-white-trailer-trash,' not us. I give more to charity than he gave us his whole life. And now you want me to go crawling back to him? Ha! Not on your life!"

Raymond poked his finger in Lottie's face. "And why should I listen to her? She's nothing more than hired help." Rex flushed blood red, but Raymond didn't back down. "I'm not going near the man," he said. "Forget it! Forget it!" He lurched from his chair, flung it to the floor, and stormed outside.

From his place at the bar, Raoul strained at the commotion, but Rex waved him off, stammering an apology to Lottie. "He just doesn't know his daddy's dying, is all."

Lottie sat stunned, Raymond's explosion resounding in her ears. *He thinks putting others down will put him back on top. Just like my sister, Rose, and her sorry seesaw approach to life--me up, you down.* She smirked knowingly. *But trouble's the great equalizer. Not even Raymond can put this Genie back in the bottle.*

From behind the bar, Raoul kept a careful eye on Lottie. He noticed when Raymond returned to the doorway and beckoned her to leave with him. He saw Lottie's eyes turn the color of hot molasses as she stared him down. Raymond stabbed at his watch, and then threw up his hands in defeat. In her own good time, Lottie ambled to the door, and Raoul blew her a kiss. Rex was nowhere in sight.

Raymond was steaming when she finally reached the car. "Do you want to talk about it or not?"

"Only if you do." She slammed the door.

"I don't." He turned the key violently in the ignition and pealed out of the parking lot toward the main highway.

"Where're we going?" Lottie said evenly.

Raymond hunched his shoulders and refused to speak. He pointed to a highway sign that flashed by--Tucson Airport, 22 miles. Since he'd arranged to return the rental with a full tank, he skidded into a service station near the airport and parked at the pump. He went inside the convenience store to pay and came out with a quart of beer and a day-old edition of the *New York Times*. He passed Lottie's open window and flopped the paper into her lap.

She pounced out the car and confronted him at the pump. "You've made our relationship plain, Mr. Beck." She pulsated, hands on hip. "But don't you think for one minute you can disrespect me."

"Wh--?" His eyes went wide.

"That's your problem, Raymond. You're just plain mean. Look how you treated Rex and Raoul. I've tried for ten years to please you, but all that ends today. You're impossible!"

"How dare you—"

"You're just like . . . Charley Poteet." She brandished her hips. "But then I guess you Big-Shot-White-Boys are all alike. You act all liberal when it suits you, but when the chips are down you want to roll over people you think are beneath you. Well, Mister, let me put you on notice." She bobbed her finger. "I am not the dirt under your feet. And I will not tippy-toe around your little petulant feelings any more. You can take your nasty ways and shove 'em." She stamped her foot resolutely. "I wash my hands of you, Bubba. You're in the hands of the Almighty."

"You--" Raymond charged her.

"Poof!" She flashed him her palm. "Be gone! I suggest you channel your hostilities where they belong, and leave me alone." She spun on her heels and sashayed to the car. Landing gracefully in her seat, she gently closed the door behind her.

As they drove toward the airport, the electricity between them was like a downed power line. Raymond kept his eyes glued on the road, and Lottie scoured the paper for any news about Clayburn. She came across a short item tucked away in an obscure column, and her voice penetrated the silence as she read aloud.

Tuesday, October 26 – *Chauffeur Questioned*. "Geoffrey Jessup, chauffeur to gubernatorial candidate John R. Clayburn, was brought in for questioning in connection with the beating death of Attorney Terrence Long and the disappearance of coed Ramona Clark. Mr. Clayburn was not available for comment and the detective in charge, Lt. Leland Thrush, declined to make a statement."

"Is that all?" Raymond said.

"That's it."

When they arrived at the Tucson Airport, Raymond dropped Lottie at the curb to buy their tickets and the latest edition of the *New York Times*. She sprinted back to the terminal to meet Raymond when she read the headlines.

"Now, that's more like it." He read the account over her shoulder.

Wednesday, October 27 – *Candidate's Aide Confesses in Lawyer's Death*. "After being questioned for several hours by police, Geoffrey Jessup, gubernatorial candidate John R. Clayburn's personal chauffeur, admitted complicity in the beating death of Attorney Terrence Long. In his statement, Jessup admitted having interrogated Long on an 'undisclosed matter,' and that the attorney had a heart attack in the process."

"Jessup is quoted as saying, 'I never intended to hurt that lawyer fellow. How was I to know the man had a weak heart?' Jessup confessed to having left the scene without rendering aid, but denied any wrongdoing. He could not, however, give an explanation for the burn marks on Long's extremities.

"When asked about his connection with the kidnapped coed Ramona Clark, Jessup had 'no comment.' With next Tuesday's election hanging in the balance, it is reported that John R. Clayburn is on the campaign trail and cannot be reached for comment."

"That's it?" Raymond said. "The election's next week, and Thrush's no closer to canning Clayburn than this?"

"There's gotta be more." Lottie fumed. "We need to talk to Thrush ourselves."

When the *last-call* announcement rang out for their flight to Atlanta, Raymond and Lottie sprinted for the gate. The plane was full, and the agitated flight attendants directed them to the remaining middle seats on alternate rows. Lottie was happy not to sit with Raymond for the duration of the flight. She found his company less than desirable.

CHAPTER 24.
▲▲▲▲▲▲▲▲▲▲▲▲

When they arrived in Atlanta, Raymond trotted through the airport to catch up with Lottie in the ground transportation lobby. She'd left him standing flatfooted at the arrival gate, and he had to hustle to open the door for her to board the shuttle to Eastern Shores Airline Charters.

"I'll drive." Raymond offered when they reclaimed the Lexus from the remote parking lot.

"Sure thing." She tossed him her keys. *Humph . . . had time to cool his heels. But he never changes. Fortunately, I don't care about his miserly opinion of me any longer.*

"Buckle up." He coaxed. "I'll get us back to Union City before nightfall."

Lottie and Raymond slipped back into Union City around dusk. When they pulled into Miss Charity's front gate, the dogs were romping playfully, but the house was pitch black.

"That's odd." Lottie's voice cracked. "Mamma's usually home by now." She lowered her window and listened for signs of life, but with the exception of nightingales exchanging calls in the distance, all was deathly still.

Raymond considered honking, but it didn't seem quite right in Miss Charity's front yard. "Maybe she's out back," he said, pulling around to the makeshift shed at the rear of the house.

Lottie jumped out of the moving car and bounded the steps to the front door. "Mamma! Mamma!" She yelled, but her repeated knocks brought no response. She spun across the wrap-around porch to the side entrance. Miss Charity's mud-caked boots were stationed like faithful sentries, but their mistress was nowhere in sight.

About that time, Lottie spotted her lopping strides emerging from the dense stand of pines. Her heart did somersaults. She tore across the open field. "Mamma! Mamma!" she cried, her feelings lapping the circuit from joy to relief and back again. She collected her mother's slight frame in her arms and smothered her face with kisses.

"Why you gone all mushy on me, Gal?" Miss Charity held her at arm's length and frisked her with her eyes. "What y'all been up to?"

Lottie's emotions flattened like a pancake. "Told you in my note, Mamma. Remember? Anyway, how've you been?"

"I been fine, Miss Lottie," she said, rebuffing her lack of candor. "Jest like always. 'Xcuse me, Chile; we got company. Talk to me when you ready to speak the truth." Miss Charity moved toward Raymond and wiped her hand on her apron before extending it to him. "How are you today, sir," she said with a twinkle. "I hate you find yourself the lone rooster amongst a pair of prattling hens, but I'm mighty grateful you brought my daughter home in one piece."

"I'm fine, Miss Charity. Mighty fine." Raymond squeezed her hand respectfully. He couldn't have felt more special if it were royalty recognizing him.

Lottie grimaced. *Mighty fine? What's he up to, now?*

Miss Charity gripped the handrail and steadied herself up the steps to the porch. "Y'all just in time," she said. "I put my supper on a little earlier, and y'all are welcome to join me."

"Let's eat!" Raymond said. It was the invitation for which he had hoped.

When they entered the side door, Lottie knocked over an object propped against the opening. She reached out to grab it before it hit the floor and realized it was a double-barreled shotgun; no doubt the one Hamp and Duke had told her about. *When Daddy was alive, he wouldn't have allowed this gun in the house. Mamma knows that. He hated weapons and the violence they represent.*

"Yo' Daddy's dead, now," Miss Charity said, chastening her look of censure. "But don't fret yourself none, Daughter. The thing ain't loaded. I ain't had no more trouble since the two of y'all been gone."

Lottie's face registered guilt for the trouble she'd caused. "Good to hear, Mamma. I'll just set your shotgun over here in the corner. Need any help with dinner?"

"No, Baby." Miss Charity smiled the smile of a mother who knows her child. "Jest sit yourself down, and let's bless the food." She joined hands with each of them and bowed her head in prayer. "Dear Lord," she said, like she was chatting with a long-time friend. "Thank you for bringing us together safely, once more and again, and for this our daily bread." They joined in unison, "Amen."

For a split second, Miss Charity's mellow expression locked onto Raymond's somber one, but he swiftly retreated. "Pass me those collard greens, Lottie," he said, piling his plate high.

Although she wisely dropped the subject of the shotgun, Lottie couldn't dismiss it. It lingered with her through dessert. "I sure do miss Daddy," she spouted impetuously. "Don't you, Mamma?"

Miss Charity shot her a *not-now* glance to remind her of Raymond's presence, but Lottie's pitiful expression softened her response. "Of course, Daughter," she said. "Your Daddy is sorely missed."

"And then there're those fathers who aren't worth missing," Raymond said. And as soon as the words slipped his lips, he wanted to retract them.

"How about another piece of cake, Son?" Miss Charity passed the plate.

Raymond gladly stuffed his mouth, while Miss Charity finished up the dishes. "Lottie," she said, "go look at the *Montgomery Chronicle* in there on my bed. I think you'll find something real interesting." As soon as she was out of earshot, Miss Charity turned to Raymond. "And you, Young Man," she said, "I want you to sit with me on my porch for a little while."

"Yes, ma'am." He followed like a lad being coaxed by his ear.

All of nature had settled down for the night. Miss Charity eased into her rocker and parted the still of the evening with her rich soprano. "I've been looking at you, Son, and there's a few things I've been led to say." She raised her hand against his objections. "Wait, now. Before you interrupt me, I already knows it's none of my business. But I just hope you'll grant an old lady her prerogative and hold your peace 'til I'm done. Is that all right with you?"

"Where're you going with this?" Raymond squirmed, wishing Lottie would join them and provide some distraction.

Miss Charity rocked smoothly. "I can tell you're carrying around some long-ago stuff--"

"You don't know—"

"Whoa!" Miss Charity teased. "Hold your horses, Baby. Don't go getting your back up. Just give me a chance to say my piece, and when I'm finished you can do what you will with it. We got ourselves a deal?"

Raymond's silence gave consent, and she proceeded uninterrupted, her words borne up on the even tempo of her rocker. "Life is lived in your mind, Baby," she said. "Get your thinking right, and it's amazing how life kind o' falls into place. Whatever mistakes your daddy made, them are his orphans. They can only hurt you if you let 'em take up residence in your mind."

She paused her rocker and drew closer to Raymond. "Now if you was to forgive him," she said, "you can evict his orphans--kick 'em out. Clear out your daddy's choices and make room for your own. You don't have to let his mistakes be a fall back for your failure."

Miss Charity stopped rocking and allowed her words to settle. Carefully, she weighed the merits of delving deeper. "I'm gonna tell you a little secret," she said. "Something I never told another living soul, and I hope you don't neither."

The porch creaked as she pounded her rocker. "Way back when, when Lottie and her sister wasn't much more than babies, their daddy lost his job, and he'd just about give up looking. In fact, when he should o' been looking, he was out carousing and drinking, night and day. He'd drag home most nights after the girls was in bed and make sport o' cussing and low-rating me."

"Lottie's daddy?"

"If I tried to speak up in my own defense, he'd shove me . . . and even knock me around some, too. I got so I learned how to make myself real small when he was around, so he wouldn't hurt me ... or my babies."

She slowed her rocker to a more deliberate pace, and Raymond listened with increased interest. "One night he came home real drunk, wanting to see 'his girls,'" she recounted. "Rose and Lottie was sound asleep, but he pulled Rose, the oldest one, outta the bed they shared and began jostling her around and tossing her high in the air. I think he called hisself playing, but he tripped over the rug while she was in mid-air, and I saw my baby falling to the floor."

Miss Charity's rocker stopped and she gasped for air. "It was like it was in slow motion. It was just a blessing I was near enough to throw myself on the floor before Rose came crashing down on me. It scared her real bad, but wasn't nothing broke." She wheezed. "I rocked her back to sleep and laid her in the bed with Lottie. Her daddy passed out drunk in his chair."

Miss Charity folded her hands across her lap, and Raymond rolled up on the edge of his chair. "That same night," she said, "I came out here on this porch. I was so scared I was trembling. I got down on my knees beside that chair you sitting in now, and I prayed out loud. I said, 'Lord, you promised you'd never leave me nor forsake me, and I believe you. But Father, I don't know how much more of this I can stand. I've tried to do it your way, but nothing reaches this man's heart. He's getting worse instead of better, and now I fear for my life and for my babies, too. I'm getting scared . . . scared I might hurt that man in his sleep. Please, Sir.' I cried out loud. 'Help us! I've got no one to turn to but you, and you've got all power in your hands.'"

Miss Charity slowed her rocker to a steady cadence, back and forth, and Raymond hung on her every word. "I got up, then, and sat in that chair you in. I cried 'til I poured out all the hurt I had bottled up inside me. I cried 'til I was limp. After that I wasn't scared no mo. I wasn't mad no mo. I was just through. My husband know'd it, too, 'cause from then on when he cussed me, I looked him straight in the eye. When he swung at me, I didn't back off; and I wouldn't say a mumbling word in my own defense. I'd catch him looking at me real strange out the corner of his eye when he didn't think I was looking."

She swayed her body to and fro in her stilled rocker, and Raymond's heart pumped like a jackrabbit's. "Then one night, that man came home sloppy drunk and he swung on me," she said quietly. "When I stepped into it, he missed me and swung hisself to the floor. The next thing I know'd his arms was wrapped around my ankles, begging my pardon. He was crying like a baby. 'Please, Lord. Please.' He wailed. 'Forgive me for how I been treating my wife and my babies.'" Miss Charity threw her arms in the air. "'Oh, Glory! I looked up to heaven and praised my Jesus for doing something only He could do--change a man's heart!"

"I'm so sorry for your pain, Miss Charity." Raymond blubbered consolingly. "That's the same hateful way my Daddy treated me and my Mom; so you can understand why I hate him so."

Miss Charity rocked thoughtfully. She hadn't bared her soul to earn Raymond's pity, or justify his malice. "From that night 'til the day he died," she said quietly, "Lottie's daddy was a changed man. The main thing in his life was taking care of his family. He even started going to church with the girls and me; became a deacon, too. That's the daddy his children know'd. They don't even remember the other."

"Are you trying to say my Daddy can change? Fat chance!"

She scooted her rocker closer to Raymond, until their knees touched, and buzzed her closely held secret in his ear. "That's not all. Lottie probably don't know to this day why it seemed like her daddy favored Rose the best, and I ain't never told her. I only hope she's got enough Jesus in her to forgive him without knowing why he treated her with partiality. I didn't want to lay his mistakes at her feet. It wasn't that he loved Rose better. Naw. That wasn't it at all. It was just he almost killed Rose when he dropped her that time, and he know'd it. His heart bled every time he looked at the child." She sighed heavily. "Lottie's daddy was a man, with the same frailties and failings that besets us all. Just like your daddy, I 'magine, Raymond."

"No comparison."

Miss Charity patted his hand tenderly. "Son, we can't change people, but they can be changed; unlessen we hold 'em back. We can bind 'em so tight to their past mistakes, they can't never break free. Just think if I had o' kept my husband bound to his faults, he could o' never become the daddy his girls loved and respected. That's why forgiveness is so important. It's important for the one that's wronged you . . . and it's important for you, too."

"For me? But he killed my Mom."

"Really?"

"Well, he just as good as killed her. He sapped all the life out of her. And I can't forgive him for that. Never. The feelings run too deep."

Rocking at an easy pace, Miss Charity patiently stayed her course. "Forgiveness ain't about feelings, Baby. It's an act of your will, and it's mostly for you."

"For me? But I didn't--"

"Yes," she said firmly. "It's mostly for you. 'Cause forgiveness is the only power you got to set the captive free. The jailer's behind bars, too, ain't he, Baby? Your daddy may be guilty, but being a jailer ain't much fun neither; now is it, Raymond?"

The decades he'd hated his daddy played back for Raymond. For the first time he recognized the peace forfeited and the time misspent. "No, ma'am, Miss Charity," he said. "It's not much fun for the jailer, neither. Why did you tell me your secret?"

She rocked at a sprightlier pace. "I heard what you said bout yo' daddy tonight, and you heard what Lottie said bout hers. Something told me it might help you knowing sugar-coated things ain't always what they seems. Lottie's childish recollections ain't all there is. Just like you don't know what caused your mamma and daddy to act the way they did. It just so happened Lottie caught her daddy on the upswing, and unfortunately you caught yours on the down. You froze his bad behavior, just like Lottie froze the good."

"But you don't know how he hurt us--"

"And you don't know nothing bout your daddy before you came along, nor since you left." Miss Charity smiled coyly under the harvest moon that peeked from behind the clouds. "Your mamma saw something in the man to stay with him all them years. But that was grown-folks' business and you don't know nothing bout that, and maybe you never will. But I'm a living witness, people can change if you let 'em."

"But he did horrible things--"

"Whenever things get really bad," Miss Charity commented plaintively, "I remembers two things: One--I could be dead, but I ain't. And two--I could o' never been born, but I was. So between them two points, everything is a blessing if I grow from it. Everything."

"But he's never asked for my forgiveness."

"Your picks don't have to be your daddy's picks." Her voice smiled. "And now that you know better than to trust a man, you can put your faith where it truly belongs."

"I know exactly where it belongs--in me. There's no one else I can trust."

"And look where it's got ya. You're like that mare o' mine that gets bogged down in the mud. Hard as she tries, she can't pull herself out by herself. The more she tries, the deeper she sinks. That's why she needs my help. 'Cause I got power she ain't got. You see, Raymond? None of us can make it out of the mire on our own. We need somebody bigger than us to save us." Her aging eyes glistened. "And Jesus is a mighty good Savior! Mighty good! He's pulled me out o' many-a-muddy-mess, just like He promised."

"I don't know about all that, Miss Charity, but I must admit, there is something quite special about you."

"The joy of Jesus, Baby! And you can have it, too, if you picks Him."

"Raymond! Raymond!" Lottie exclaimed breathlessly, bursting onto the porch. "Come inside! You've got to see this for yourself!"

CHAPTER 25.
▲▲▲▲▲▲▲▲▲▲▲▲

Happy to be torn away from Miss Charity's piercing eyes, Raymond leapt from his chair and followed Lottie into the house. "What? What is it?" He called.

At the kitchen table, Lottie showed him a section of the local newspaper. He read with great interest a recent interview with Senator Jarrett Poteet by a New York reporter.

"Pretty girl." Raymond pointed to her picture in the byline. "Cindi Fraiser. If my visit with the senator is any indication, he spilled his guts to this gorgeous blonde. He drinks too much, and he always talks too much."

"Look here." Lottie said. "You won't believe some of Poteet's answers to the questions she posed. He really stubbed his toe this time. Sounds like the Neanderthal bigot he really is."

Wednesday, October 27 - *Politics on the Hill* by Cindi Fraiser:

Q (reporter) "Senator Poteet were you aware that your fellow alum, John R. Clayburn, is a front-runner in the race for New York's governor that goes to the voters next Tuesday?"

A (Senator Poteet) "Yes, I sure am, Miss. That ole' Son-of-a-Gun may make something of himself, yet. Seriously, Honey, we're very proud of him down here."

Q (reporter) "Well, Senator, you seem to know John R. very well?"

A (Senator Poteet) "Sure thing, Little Lady, we were members of the same fraternity in our college days at dear old Judson U [wink]."

Q (reporter) "Then Senator, are you aware that John R.'s chauffeur was recently hauled in for questioning for the murder of New York attorney, Terrence Long?"

A (Senator Poteet) "Who? No, ma'am. That's the first I've heard of it, but I'm sure it in no way reflects on my upstanding friend, John R. Anyway, it better not hinder him from getting down here to my New Year's Eve shindig, governor or no governor [wink]. And Miss, you're mighty welcome to come to our bash, too. I throw one whale-of-a-party, if I do say so myself."

Q (reporter) "Oh, I see. A party to celebrate Mr. Clayburn's election victory?"

A (Senator Poteet) "No, Honey [hic], a party to celebrate my victory when I best him once and for all in our little bet. Sh-hh. I don't say this to many people, but we made a little wager back in school, and it's coming to a head as we approach our 30th Anniversary. If he comes up short in the election, the last silver dollar in our little wager is all mine, and he'll get to crown me *King* at my party.

Q (reporter) "So you feel there's a chance John R. may lose this election, even though he's the man to beat?"

A (Senator Poteet) "The tally ain't in yet, Sugar, and it could be closer than you think [hic]. But John R.'s a worthy adversary. That's what's made our game interesting all these years. He won't go down without a fight. You can bank on that. And I know he'll do everything in his power to win . . . at all cost.

Q (reporter) "'At all cost?' Well, after all Senator, who would know him better than you? Thank you, sir."

A (Senator Poteet) "My pleasure, Little Lady. Like I said, come on down to the party. I'll show you a real good time [wink]."

Lottie was hanging on Raymond's shirtsleeve. She could hardly wait for his reaction. "You think all this madness centers around some asinine wager over one silver coin?" She blurted. "Could such a thing drive a man to murder?"

"Depends on the man," Raymond said. He remembered the five, framed coins in Poteet's study and the empty slot where the sixth one belonged. "Maybe these two old Farts are willing to do anything to get that last coin."

The screen door squeaked when Miss Charity came inside and locked up. "Raymond," she said, "it's getting pretty late. You're welcomed to use the back bedroom if you want it. Lottie can sleep with me."

"I am rather tired. Thank you," he said. "Not to worry, Lottie. We'll hear more tomorrow. We'll talk to Thrush if we have to, and maybe see Charley, too. Goodnight, ladies."

When Raymond awoke the next morning in Lottie's twin bed, the telephone was blaring in the hallway. He hid under the mound of warm quilts; hoping one of the Garrett women would answer it. He was tired. His conversation with Miss Charity on the porch had played through his mind most of the night. Sleep came when he found closure, just before day.

When the ringing telephone persisted, he swaddled a quilt around him and stumbled out to catch it. "Hello. Hello." He shouted.

"Well, well," Thrush said on the other end. "It's about time you woke up, Sleeping Beauty. What're you doing back in Alabama? I thought you were going to call me as soon as you got situated." Thrush's thick South Bronx accent made Raymond homesick.

"We've tried calling you lots of times," Raymond said. "But you're never in."

"Aah, my dear Watson, and glad you should be. I couldn't have solved this case sitting around on my keester."

"You solved the case?"

"All but the loose ends, my Boy. All but the loose ends." Thrush boasted. "Where've you been? On Mars? Haven't you read this morning's *Times*?"

"Nope. We're in the boonies. Haven't made it to town yet."

"Well, get your butt in gear, because they nailed the story pretty good this time."

"I did see an interview in the local paper with Senator Poteet and a New York reporter. It was pretty damning if you ask me," Raymond said. "The Lush."

"Yeah, I know." Thrush crowed. "I sent Cindi to get that story. After what you told me about Poteet, I knew he'd be a loose cannon around a looker like Cindi; and sure thing, he was. He gave me the last piece in this squirrelly case. Motive."

"You mean that silver coin jazz?"

"Yup. Seems John R. thought if it ever got out that his son raped Ramona Clark, it would give his campaign a black eye. And he wasn't about to let that happen, because it could prevent him from becoming the next governor; and ruin his chances to win *The Bet*. But more importantly, I found out from Jessup that the mob got wind of the rape mess, and they weren't about to let their investment in Clayburn go down the tubes so close to the election. Even if it meant getting rid of the Kid."

"Kid? What Kid?"

"Clayburn's kid. Bradley." Thrush blared. "Jessup did a little talking off the record. Hopes I'll cut him some slack in his plea bargain. He'd settle for anything short of lethal injection, or spending the rest of his life in prison. He gladly gave up John R. to save his own skin."

"He told you about John R.?"

"I told you when I squeezed him he'd sing. In fact I think Jessup rather enjoyed ratting out ole' John R. There's no love loss between those two crumbs. But there's no way Jessup is gonna spill his guts on the witness stand about the mob's involvement. It wouldn't be healthy for him, not even in a prison cell."

"Who cares about his health?"

Jessup said it had to be Bradley or Ramona, and the mob didn't care which."

"For what?"

"Keep up, Raymond. Somebody had to get whacked to make the rape thing go away. Get it? The big bosses called the shots; and according to Jessup, John R. went along with getting rid of Ramona to save Bradley's hide. But more important, he wanted to get his grubby hands on that last silver dollar. I guess nobody considered the rape thing might be bogus."

"I got the feeling John R. doesn't know his son very well, or care."

"Between me and you, Raymond, I don't think Jessup really intended to do our lawyer friend in. Although Terry should've been more selective in choosing his cases, I think he was simply a victim of a bad heart put under too much stress over this Ramona thing--"

"Where is Ramona?"

"Safe. But I see what you mean about that girl." Thrush groaned. "She's a real piece of work, but I think her lying days are over." He chuckled wickedly. "She's been scared-straight. It'll save her years of therapy and loads of money."

"How's Dr. Cooper?"

"Fine." Thrush clipped his laughter. "Time to get back to work. Tie up the loose ends. I'm gonna take Clayburn down. He's a low-life scumbag, and I'm taking him down."

Raymond stopped at the bathroom in the hall and pounded on the closed door. "You in there, Lottie?"

"Yes-s." She whined sleepily.

"Get dressed! We're going into town!"

Raymond and Lottie drew the same waitress at the Old South Restaurant they had on their first visit. However, this time she appeared eminently more pleased with their seating choice in the back of the dining room. A battered emblem of the defunct White Citizen's Council presided over their booth.

Raymond paged through the morning edition of the *Times*. "Lottie, look at this!" **Thursday, October 28 -** *Clayburn Accused in Murder-Kidnapping.* The headline sprawled across the front page, with the sub-title, *Clayburn Charged.* The story was an interview with Geoffrey Jessup. Ramona Clark had picked him out of a line-up as the man who drugged and kidnapped her from her apartment. Her statement, along with the evidence in the Long murder case, had apparently loosened Jessup's tongue.

"I ain't going down as no three-time loser for something I didn't do." Jessup was quoted as saying. "Yeah, I roughed up that attorney just to let him know we meant business, but I didn't kill him. When he wouldn't open up, John R. Clayburn sent over a nurse. Never seen her before. Don't remember her name. She had a badge with a flower on it. She brought a machine with her and gave the lawyer shock treatments to make him talk. I didn't shock Long, and I didn't help that nurse do it neither. I'm not going down for Clayburn on this bum rap."

Lottie's mouth fell ajar. "Flower? I bet it was a white lily."

"Nurse Jamison?" Raymond said. "This case is getting wackier and wackier. Look."

The news account went on to quote Jessup's statement. "That lawyer fellow told Clayburn that the Clark woman had accused his son of rape, and it was Clayburn who wanted the thing hushed up until after the election. Long had some kind of file with her statement in it, and all I wanted was that file. I don't know why Long told Clayburn about the file in the first place; you know, attorney-client privilege and all. But Long and Clayburn had dealings before, and I guess Long wanted to play up to the next governor."

Jessup was further quoted as saying, "I only drugged that Clark woman to keep her quiet, but I didn't remove her from her apartment, so you can't get me on no kidnapping beef. John R. paid for the ambulance to take her somewhere. I don't even know where. He never told me. I just called John R. from her apartment, and like always, he took care of the rest."

The reporter also interviewed Ramona Clark and asked if Clayburn's son had raped her. "Of course not." Miss Clark protested. "I don't know how anyone could think such a thing. He's a nice young man. A perfect gentleman." When the reporter asked her about Long's alleged file that contained her rape charge, she said, "Whatever do you mean? File? What file? Terry Long, did you say? I don't recall knowing anyone by that name."

Lottie snickered at Ramona's latest lie. "She's good. Can anyone refute her statement?"

"I'm sure she's thought of that." Raymond smirked. "We've got the only other file. And I don't think Thrush will allow his copy to surface and hurt her any more, or bring us into it."

"Whew!" Lottie gulped. That's a relief. I didn't relish being the prosecution's star witness."

"As far as anybody knows that file never existed. Anyhow, Thrush's got enough on John R. to hang him without it, or us."

The reporter also recorded John R. Clayburn's comments for the article. "I took that man Jessup in out of the cold," Clayburn was quoted as saying. "Of course I knew about his criminal record, but I believe everyone deserves a second chance. Don't you? I believed it then, and I believe it now. Maybe someone is paying him to sabotage my campaign. But I ask you; can you believe the word of a convicted felon over mine? His allegations are totally unfounded and too ridiculous for the intelligent voters of this fine state to believe."

"Hurry," Lottie said. "Turn to page three." The story continued there alongside a reprint of the Poteet interview with Cindi Fraiser.

"Side-by-side," Raymond said, "these stories are very damaging. They magnify the idiocy of *The Bet*, and the reckless ambition of the two scoundrels that cooked it up. The press is drawing a noose around Clayburn's neck, and maybe Poteet's, too."

"Sure thing." Lottie contentedly sipped her hot tea. "Check the editorials. That's where it gets juicy."

The lead editorial read, "High ranking members of the Clayburn campaign staff are resigning amid allegations of Clayburn's firsthand knowledge and involvement in the murder of Attorney Terrence Long, and the kidnapping of young coed, Ramona Clark." A poll showed that only 47% of the voters surveyed believed that Clayburn was directly involved in the murder, but over 85% were repulsed by the arrogance of *The Bet*, and 68% indicated he should withdraw from the race." The editor ended by saying, "The facts are in. The only question remains is whether the informed voters of the State of New York will allow this man to become their governor in Tuesday's election?"

"Absolutely not!" Lottie shook her raised fist in victory. "Absolutely not!"

CHAPTER 26.
▲▲▲▲▲▲▲▲▲▲▲

Raymond and Lottie weren't the only couple reading the headlines that morning. Back in Manhattan, Bradley and his wife read the account of his father's troubles with heavy hearts. His wife convinced him to go to John R., despite their differences. Bradley didn't agree, but he could refuse his bride nothing.

When he arrived at his father's posh townhouse on the Upper West Side, Lars, the butler, showed him into the study. The drapes were drawn, and John R. was slumped into a chair in the center of the room like a broken toy. Bradley's heart was moved, and he set aside the lecture he'd rehearsed in the cab. Instead he wrapped his arms around his daddy and kissed his neck. For the first time in weeks John R.'s eyes showed signs of life, and father and son sat together in the darkened room.

Bradley drew in his breath. "John R, I didn't rape that girl. How could you think I'd do such a thing?"

"You were wild." His daddy defended. "I didn't know what you would do. You're my son --chip off the old block--sowing your wild oats, like me in my college days." He rubbed his red-rimmed eyes and tried to focus. "You must believe me, Brad. I only wanted to protect you. I love you, Son. It's just been hard for me since your Mother--"

"Stop right there!" Bradley snapped. "Don't you dare drag my Mother into this mess. My Mother's death had nothing to do with your greedy ambition, or your wretched pride. Anyhow, John R., was it me you were trying to protect, or yourself?"

"My concern was for you." He dangled his head. "Always for you."

"Sure, sure," Bradley said. "I didn't come here to fight. I didn't want to come at all . . .but my wife made me."

John R. crumbled in surprise. "Wha--What? Your wife?"

"Yup." He wielded the news like a club. "And on the night I was supposed to have raped Ramona Clark, I was at home with my beautiful bride. Furthermore, my wife wanted you to know . . . because she's sweet and forgiving like that . . . she wanted you to know you're going to be a grandfather--"

"Aagh!" John R. clutched his heart.

"And we're having a boy." Bradley slugged away. "If you do the math, you'd realize I don't take advantage of women; not even my wife was pregnant before I married her over a year ago."

"Over a year--?" John R. gasped for air. "You've been married all this time? No Ramona Clark?"

"No Ramona Clark."

"A grandson? My grandson? Oh, no!" John R. sobbed bitterly. What have I done? What have I--?"

Bradley pushed aside the massive doors to the study, and sent Lars in to tend to his daddy. In the back seat of the taxicab on his ride home, Bradley wept, able at last to turn his back on his disappointing childhood and the father who caused it. He vowed to nurture his unborn son with truth and love--at all cost.

▲▲▲▲

Meanwhile, back at the Old South Restaurant, Lottie ordered more hot water for her tea. "We got him this time!" She clucked delightedly. "We got him!"

"I'm enjoying this, too," Raymond said, checking his watch. "But it's getting late. We don't want to miss Charley this morning."

They stretched themselves to cross the square to the younger Poteet's office. Mrs. Nobels peered over her glasses, looking at them like a bad case of recurring fleas. "Mr. Poteet has a busy schedule today." She scowled. "If y'all don't have an appointment, I'm sure he can't fit you in."

"Well, Madam," Raymond said loudly, launching into his *Mr.-Big-Shot* routine. "I'm a busy man, too. And I've come all this way at Mr. Poteet's request, only to be informed that he's too busy to see me." He strutted around her desk like a spurned banter rooster. "Madam, I demand immediate consideration--"

His noisy tirade served its purpose. Charley poked his head from behind closed doors to investigate the commotion. "Something wrong, Mrs. Nobels?"

"Not really, Charley." Raymond grinned cheekily. "We just need to see you. If you could spare us a minute, we'll be out of your hair. Just a minute, I promise."

Charley raised his hands in disgust and retreated into his office, soundly closing the door behind him. Mrs. Nobels glowered at them victoriously, and they slunk to the exit. Before they could reach the door, however, a gaggle of gentlemen dressed in dark suits and rep ties streamed out of Charley's office, muttering their concerted displeasure at the interruption.

Charley shadowed his doorway, arms folded across his pin-stripped vest. He brandished an agitated nod for Raymond and Lottie to join him. "Sit down," he said curtly, "and I'll do you one better than you did my previous guests." He signaled Mrs. Nobels. "Hold my calls. We're not to be disturbed."

"We hate to bother you like this, Charley," Raymond said, "but we didn't have a choice. Have you seen this morning's *Times*?"

"Of course I've seen it." He grunted irritably. "I've had the thing read to me several times over the phone, by enemies and friends alike. The friends call to offer condolences, and the enemies call to gloat. This whole thing is like one big . . . funeral. The death of my Daddy's 30-year political career."

"How can that newspaper report cause your father so much damage?" Raymond said. "I'll grant you *The Bet* was brazen and stupid, but not lethal."

The leather in Charley's chair squeaked as he squirmed uncomfortably. "If this were a one-time occurrence," he said, "maybe it could be explained away. But my father, as you can imagine, has some very powerful enemies and he's been under investigation off and on for several years--allegations of influence peddling, drunken misconduct, sexual and racial harassment. You name it. The things my Daddy was able to sweep under the rug in the old days, even the Good-Ole-Boys at the Capitol can't condone today. The pressures for economic reform, not to mention the rights of women and minorities, are too strong down here right now."

"So this was like the last straw?" Raymond crossed.

"Nothing's been able to stick on him in the past, but when people keep asking the same questions, over and over, folks start to believe there's some truth to it. You know, 'Where there's smoke, there's fire.'"

"Unfortunate," Raymond said.

"My Daddy's love affair with the bottle has increased over the years, and it has made him inattentive to detail. And there have been occasional hints of sordid affairs, even with some of the wives of his colleagues. And sometimes, he just forgets to show up for important votes on the floor of the Senate that could benefit the special interest groups that keep him in office."

"Slipping power base?" Raymond flashed a glance at Lottie. "I know what that's like."

"It's been going down hill for my Daddy for sometime," Charley said grudgingly. "And the idea that Senator Poteet could be involved in a crime engineered on the basis of something as petty as a thirty-year-old bet, won't set well with the conservatives in this state, not even the few strong supporters he's got left. I've been told the Senate Ethics Committee is being convened for a special session this afternoon to take up that very subject, and folks are choosing up sides."

"Too bad," Raymond said. "I know how it feels to see your hard work go up in smoke. Too bad."

"I guess it sounds pretty good to you, huh, Lottie?" Charley sniped. "I guess I can count you in the enemy camp."

"Hold on there." Raymond jumped in. "What's Lottie got to do with this?"

Lottie trained her sights on Charley. "He's right, Raymond," she said. "Rightfully, I belong in the enemy camp where the Poteets are concerned, but I'm not."

"You expect me to believe that?" Charley steamed.

"Believe what you like," she said, "but you've got me all wrong. It gives me no pleasure whatsoever to see a man fall from grace, not even Jarrett Poteet."

"What's with you two?" Raymond set himself between them.

Charley poked his finger at Lottie. "Surely she's told you about our family ties?"

"I know Miss Charity worked for your family," Raymond said, "if that's what you mean?"

"Why, she hasn't told you the real reason she left our little hamlet? And why it is her mother, who hasn't worked for my family since my Granddaddy died, is still on the Poteet payroll?"

"No, Charley!" Lottie stormed to her feet. "I haven't told him a thing. You want him to know? You tell him!" She tore out of the office before her burning tears broke free. Mrs. Nobels took critical note of her bizarre behavior.

"What was that all about?" Raymond fumed.

"Sit." Charley motioned. "I guess you deserve an explanation," he said drolly. "Once upon a time . . . long, long, ago, I knew a little girl named Lottie Garrett because her mother worked for my family. Miss Charity lovingly tended my Grandfather until his death. Hasn't Lottie told you any of this?"

"No. We're in business together. Period." He failed to mention his real fear that prying into her past would open him up to her unwelcome inquiries.

"Since her mother worked on the estate, Lottie and I played together as kids." Charley continued. "She was somewhat reserved as a child, some said shy, but I knew better. She could look straight through you with those dark eyes of hers and peer into your very soul. If she chose to be your friend, she was unshakable; and if your enemy, relentless. She was on the side of the underdog, trying to right every wrong."

"That's our Little Lottie, all right."

Shades of scarlet crept from Charley's chin to his forehead. "As I grew older," he said, "I grew mean and cold to her. We were no longer playmates, no longer friends. I guess you could say it was peer pressure of sorts, because she wasn't quite . . . welcome in my social circles back then. Even though she and I graduated in the same high school class."

"That's hard to believe."

"Don't interrupt." Charley hissed. "This is tough enough as it is. I've never talked about this with anyone, not even my wife of ten years. But I think Lottie wants you to know why she hates me and my family, and I need to get this off my chest." He swiveled his chair sideways to avoid Raymond's eyes. He gulped a sip of water from the glass on his desk.

"Like I was saying." Charley went on. "Lottie transferred to the high school on my side of town her senior year. I'd see her on the estate when she'd come by to catch a ride with her mother, but I avoided her. Things were tense between us. On campus I didn't admit I knew her; so she and I never talked, on campus or off."

Charley rubbed his sticky palms together and shifted self-consciously. "One day I went out to the barn to check on my new pony. I'd gotten him for my 18th birthday the week before. He was the horse I'd always wanted. I just wanted to pet him and give him some sugar cubes," he said, raising his head to the ceiling. "I opened the barn door, and the sunlight streamed in brightly behind me. It took a minute for my eyes to adjust, but I could hear something rustling in the corner. My horse was kicking wildly in his stall."

Charley brushed the sweat beads from his brow. "I stepped inside the barn," he said. "I thought maybe a snake had coiled up in the hay pile and was spooking my horse. But as my eyes grew accustomed to the light . . . I saw it wasn't a snake after all—but two people.

Charley swallowed tightly. "I recognized them immediately. The man jumped up and staggered past me without a word. I smelled the booze on his breath. The girl was crumpled into a tight ball, whimpering on the barn floor--clothes torn, face tortured--she was a mess. I didn't try to help her. I just turned tail and ran. That sight has haunted me ever since."

He looked up to the ceiling and fought back the hot tears lining his eyelids. "If you haven't figured it out by now, Raymond." He rubbed his nose fitfully. "That girl was Lottie. And that hellish drunk . . . that was my Daddy, the illustrious Senator Jarrett Poteet."

"What? Your daddy . . . and Lottie?" He gaped. "Aw, Man. Aw, Man."

Charley lowered his voice that had risen an octave, and his words tumbled fast. "That's why over the years, I haven't had much feeling or respect for my Daddy. I did get the nerve to face him down once when this thing first happened. But he swore to me nothing happened, and I believed him. He told me he was only trying to scare Lottie for being in the barn without permission. That, I didn't believe. If I hadn't come along when I did, and if Lottie hadn't put up the fight she did, something most certainly would have happened."

Charley dropped his head. "During my heart-to-heart with my Daddy, he said he'd do anything to make amends. I translated that to mean he'd pay any price not to be brought up on rape charges. As it turned out, I was right." He sniffed. "Lottie took to wielding a knife at me at school, but I was finally able to talk some sense into her. We made a deal. She would keep quiet if we would pension off her mother for the rest of her life after Granddaddy died." Charley laughed lamely. "But as it turned out, we were obliged to do that anyway, seeing as how my Granddaddy had left that self-same provision for her in his will. But none of us knew it at the time."

"Aw, Man."

Charley sagged under Raymond's pity. "Of course my Daddy jumped at Lottie's terms-- cash for her silence; a transaction he could understand. And when she went for the deal, she was no longer a threat to him. In fact, I shudder to think what would've happened if she hadn't taken it." He halted thoughtfully. "For the most part, Raymond, that's our dirty little family secret. Except for graduation day, I never saw Lottie again until she showed up here with you."

"Wow!" Raymond gaped. "Never in a million years would I've imagined Lottie even being remotely tied to something like this. She's always so in control."

"Maybe, she can't let go." Charley rolled his shoulders. "And as awful as it was for her, that horrible incident was a turning point for me. Contrary to many of my contemporaries, it helped me see people as people, whatever their race, color, or creed. When we're cut, we bleed; and when we're hurt, we need help. My commitment to the poor and the powerless has made me unpopular at times, and my law firm has suffered financially because of it. But unlike my Daddy, I can hold my head up in this town."

"So I've noticed."

"Besides, after that day in the barn, the talks I'd had with Miss Charity started to kick in. I began to see things her way, and I've never regretted it." He glowed. "Has she had *The Talk* with you, Raymond?" He winked. "If not, she will."

"Yes. I think I've had the pleasure."

"Miss Charity's pretty amazing, isn't she? She's solved the riddle of life—*why are we here*? And she wants everyone else to know the answer, too."

"She's awfully perceptive. I'll give her that. Every time I'm around her, I spill my guts about things I haven't told another living soul."

"That's our Miss Charity, all right. She certainly helped me see the light. In fact, this guilt thing with Lottie is the only loose end between me and blessed peace."

"Is that so?" Raymond raised his brow and prepared to leave. "Maybe I can help you out on that score. Tying up loose ends today would probably be good for us all."

Charley piqued hopefully. "Do you think you could persuade her to talk to me? I'd like that--the sooner the better. I don't want to go another day carrying this old baggage."

CHAPTER 27.
▲▲▲▲▲▲▲▲▲▲▲▲

When Raymond caught up with Lottie, she was sitting on the county's famed slave auction block under an aging oak tree. She seemed oblivious to the acorns pelting her in the breeze.

"Sorry for the scene back there," she said foggily. "I was just trying to figure out why this old town tugs on my heart so?"

"Maybe, because it's home." Raymond said quietly.

"He told you, didn't he?"

"And I'm glad he did. Hope it doesn't make you feel uncomfortable. You're a brave woman, Lottie Garrett, and I've been acting like a flaming idiot. But I want you to know, I couldn't have made it all these years without you. Can you ever forgive me?"

"I already have." She smiled faintly. "So why can't Charley believe me?"

"Because he can't let go of it himself. The two of you need to talk, one-on-one."

"Maybe. Sometime."

"This is a good day for coming clean." Raymond spoke quietly. "Go see him, Lottie. Talk to him. He's waiting. I'll go back to your mother's and wait for your call."

▲▲▲▲

Back in Miss Charity's kitchen, Raymond found her enjoying a tasty lunch. "My, that even looks good the second time around," he said."

"Join me. There's plenty more where this came from. Sit down. I'll fix your plate." She hobbled to the stove. "Where's Lottie?"

"Uhh . . . she stayed in town to do a little shopping. I'll pick her up later."

Miss Charity set a plate in front of him and eased herself into her chair. "Jest so you know, Raymond," she said, "I ain't no out-o-touch old relic. I keeps up with things. Like I know you and Lottie is mixed up with that no-count Jarrett Poteet somehow. Hmph. But whatever it is, it's bout to come to a close. While y'all been out gallivanting, I got myself a phone call from Ms. Madge."

"Who's Ms. Madge?"

"Madge Tarkenton. She's the one gonna bring a halt to Jarrett's mischief. I hadn't heard from that Gal since she went to college down here with Jarrett and his pals, but she called this morning to ask my opinion." She ruminated. "Ms. Madge say she some kind o' hot-shot--ain't married, ain't got no children, and don't want no man."

"Oh, you mean Dr. Madge Tarkenton, university professor turned political activist." Raymond recalled. The media had dubbed her, Mouthy Madge, for her extreme feminist position on nearly every topic.

"She say she's got a national voice, or something like that." Miss Charity rambled. "And she gonna pull the plug on them two jokers if they don't step down outta politics--"

"What two jokers?"

"Clayburn and Poteet."

"What's she got to do with them?"

"She say she been keeping an eye on 'em all these years. She hadn't said nothing 'cause they didn't appear to be hurting nobody. She figures if the voters is stupid enough to keep putting Jarrett in office, then that's they little red wagon. But now, she say, it's different. John R. done hurt somebody else, and maybe Jarrett, too. She say they like two peas in a pod."

"But how can she run them out of politics?"

"'Magine that." Miss Charity digressed. "Ms. Madge asking my advice. Well, she always was pretty fond of old man Frank, and she knew we was close. Maybe that's why she remembered me. Should she blow the whistle on 'em or not? That's what she wanted to know."

"Blow the whistle on what?"

"Forgive me, Son." Miss Charity snickered. "I know it sounds like rambling, but I'm going somewhere with this. I ain't *always* been old, and I ain't *never* been no fool. I know'd what that low-down Jarrett Poteet done to my little Lottie back yonder."

"Huh?" Raymond gulped.

"So they told you bout that?" She nodded; her suspicions satisfied. "The day it happened, you see, Charley told his granddaddy what he saw in the barn cause he had no one else to tell. But what little Charley didn't know was, I was the only one his granddaddy had to unload on, too; so he told me everything." Her face pinched. "In that particular case, Mr. Frank was a little reluctant, but I think he went on and told me cause that fool Jarrett didn't get a chance to go through with . . . violating my Baby."

"You've known all this time, Miss Charity?" Raymond flushed. "How? Wh--"

"I kept a real close watch on my Baby, that's what I did; but I didn't want to go upsetting her all over again by letting on I knew. I must admit, though," she said uneasily, "I was real scared when I first found out--scared of what I might do to that high-and-mighty Jarrett Poteet. I didn't know if I'd poison his food or put a scorpion in his bed, but all them kind o' thoughts went running through my head."

"So what did you do?"

She twinkled mischievously. "It took a lot of praying, but finally I decided to let the Lord handle it. It sho' was a blessing, though, that Lottie's Daddy was dead. Ain't no telling what he'd o' done. But, then again, it was Lottie's Daddy being dead what gave that rascal Jarrett the nerve to do what he did." She clutched at her chest. "Using po' womenfolk with no men around."

"You okay?"

"It's nothing. Nothing." She fanned briskly. "It just gets to me every time I think about it. You see, old man Frank had already told me how he got Jarrett and his buddy out of the same kind o' trouble once before, back when they was in college--"

"His buddy?"
"It was John R. Clayburn, all right. Ms. Madge reminded me of that on the phone. They had probably done it more than once, but Mr. Frank had to pay off the girl's mamma that particular time. There would have been a baby, you see, but the mother agreed to get her daughter fixed since the girl didn't know which one of the fool boys it was no how. They drugged her up, you see. And both Jarrett and his buddy had their way with that po' girl."
"Absolutely amazing!" Raymond gaped. "Clayburn and Poteet. I wonder how much stuff the Poteets have paid to sweep under the rug over the years?"
"More than you'd like to know, I 'magine," Miss Charity said. "Them Poteet's is used to spreading they money around. Now that I think of it, it must be why Frank Poteet put me in his will. He knew me and my family deserved it for what I know'd about his 'flicted family tree, and for what his son did to my Baby in that barn."
"Will you ever tell Lottie you know?" Raymond said, realizing he'd stumbled upon a secret of his own. Needlessly, the Garrett women were protecting each other with their silence.

"I'll tell her," she said. "When I feel the time is right."

Raymond glinted mischievously. "I'd certainly like to be there when you do."

Miss Charity leaned against the table to catch her breath. "Unfortunately, it all came flooding back when Ms. Madge called for my advice."

"And what advice did you give Mouthy--I mean Madge."

"I told her she might ought to give them two codgers one last chance before she did anything to 'xpose herself like that."

"Expose herself? Like what?"

"With all the hot water those jokers is in, I told her to call 'em up and just let 'em know what she'll do if they don't step down, and see if that don't do the trick. That way, everybody in the world wouldn't have to know."

" Know what?"

Miss Charity squirmed. "Not wanting to break her confidence, or nothing; but since Ms. Madge is willing to tell the whole world, I guess I can tell you. You see, Raymond, Ms. Madge, she the young girl what Mr. Frank had to pay off her mamma."

"What?" Raymond's jaw dropped. "Clayburn and Poteet raped Mouthy Madge

Tarkenton? Man!" He gagged. "That'll be the bombshell of the century if the press gets hold of it. With Madge's credibility, everyone'll believe her."

"Anyway, like I told Ms. Madge, she shouldn't have to tell her story to the world like that. Specially not now; not since she's a national figure and all. I told her to just put them two scoundrels on notice, and then watch what they do." Miss Charity twinkled craftily. "It's been my 'xperience roaches run when the lights is turned on."

"Yeah! Hee-hee-hee!" The two of them roared with laughter.

▲▲▲▲

In the meantime, Lottie reluctantly returned to the Law Offices of Poteet and Brunson. More than the heart-to-heart with Charley, she feared having to face Mrs. Nobels again. From their first encounter, she'd recognized their common bond. They were both strong women who demanded as much from themselves as others, especially other women. Emotional outbursts, like she had recently displayed, were considered bad form for women of their caliber, totally unacceptable.

Lottie shrank back to her desk, like a visit to the principal's office. "I'm here to see Mr. Poteet." She squeaked.

"Welcome back, Ms. Garrett," Mrs. Nobels drawled pleasantly, doubtlessly under boss' orders. "Mr. Poteet is expecting you; however, he's on the phone at the moment. He asked that I make you comfortable. Please, have a seat. May I get you some refreshment?"

"No. Thank you," Lottie shook her head, grateful for the reprieve. She paced and waited.

Charley looked drawn when he emerged from his inner office, but he perked up when he saw Lottie standing there. "Come in. Come in." He smiled. "I'm so glad you agreed to see me."

Lottie sat on the edge of her chair. Mrs. Nobels brought in coffee and cream and sat it on the table between them.

"Lottie." Charley opened. "I have to be honest with you. I've both looked forward to and dreaded this meeting for some time." He paused to allow her to contribute, but she focused on the distant wall. "Is it possible," he said, "for us to have a candid discussion about our past relationship and try to find some common ground?"

Lottie was disarmed by his statesmanlike approach, and she accorded him her full attention. "Charley," she said, "I'm here because you seem to feel we have some unfinished business. If that's true, we may need to revisit some things, but before we start I want to set the record straight. I have no ill feelings toward you or your daddy. I wouldn't invite you to dinner. But by the same token, I wouldn't wish you to choke on your food, either. I hold no grudge."

Charley loosened his tie and stared at her confoundedly. "If I could sincerely believe that," he said, "I'd sleep sweeter at night. But how can you say you hold no grudge after what we did to you?"

"Let me see how I can explain this." She considered carefully. "The day your daddy attacked me, I was scared for my life. I won't lie. And I hated him with a passion. I wanted revenge. I hated you too, Charley, for leaving me laying there like a rag doll nobody wanted." She held her chin back and discouraged the tears. "But that Sunday, I went to Mt. Zion."

She sniffed stoically. "It was there I realized, I couldn't have it both ways. I couldn't have the peace I wanted, on the one hand, and keep a private stash of hate against you Poteets, on the other. It was an all or nothing proposition, and I decided hatred was far too high a price; and y'all weren't worth it."

"I see." Charley nodded evenly, spellbound by the fire in her mahogany eyes.

Lottie analyzed the worry lines etched into his forehead. "I'm over it, Charley. Why can't you let it go and get that good night's sleep you're after? I know he's your daddy, and he probably was a big disappointment to you, but he's a man like any other. He's no more or less capable of indulging in the meanness of this world than anyone else."

Charley brushed his brow with the heel of his hand and sagged gloomily. "It's not what you think, Lottie," he said. "I'm not hung up on Jarrett Poteet. I'll admit, as a child I looked up to my father with great pride. Sure, he was aloof and showed me very little affection, but that's what drew me to him. He seemed so powerful and in charge. I thought for the longest time something was wrong with me, but over the years I've made a valuable discovery." His face lightened. "I'm not my Daddy, and my Daddy's not me. I see him for who he is--incapable of deep commitment, lacking strong conviction, self-indulgent--weak. I've acknowledged his faults, and I've let him off the hook. I don't need him to validate who I am. Miss Charity taught me that."

"So what's left?"

Charley avoided her eyes. "What gnaws at me is . . . I never asked your forgiveness for that day in the barn . . . or all the days that led up to it." He stabbed his tongue into his cheek and tried to prevent his tears. "You were like a sister to me, and Miss Charity as much a mother as I've ever known; and I reneged on our friendship. When push came to shove . . . I denied you . . . to my white friends--"

His tears broke loose and he wept bitterly, dropping down on one knee beside her chair. "Lottie Mae Garrett." He held her trembling hand. "Will you please forgive me for turning my back on you . . . and being such a stubborn fool? I have truly missed our friendship."

Lottie's tears flowed like spring rain, watering the drought in their relationship. "Charles Wesley Poteet," she cried, "my long lost friend. Yes, I do. I do forgive you." They clung to each other, like when they were kids under the pecan trees.

CHAPTER 28.
▲▲▲▲▲▲▲▲▲▲▲▲

Charley was annoyed when the intercom buzzed. He moved from Lottie's side and his heels clicked across the hardwood floor. "Mrs. Nobels, I said no interruptions!"

"Pardon me, sir. It's . . . it's the call you've been waiting for all morning."

"Lottie, I have to take this." He swiveled his chair away from her.

She sipped her coffee and tried not to eavesdrop, but couldn't help overhearing Charley's clipped responses.

"Of course, I understand," he said, "and you know my feelings on the matter, too. Yes. Yes. I know. I will. I have no choice." He dribbled the phone back onto the hook.

He returned to Lottie's side. "Now, where were we?" He sputtered.

"I'll go now." She offered. "It's obvious you need to get back to your business."

"No. Please, don't go. Just give me a minute to collect myself. It's been a real tough day."

"Charley, friends are honest with each other." She prepared to leave. "If you want to share this with me, fine. Otherwise, I'll go and leave you to it. We can talk another time."

"No. Please." He motioned for her to sit, drying the moisture from his hands with his handkerchief. "My Daddy stepped down from office this afternoon at a special session of the Senate Ethics Committee," he said quietly. "The Committee was convened to consider sanctions for his involvement in the infamous *Bet*, and his embarrassing behavior with Cindi Frasier."

"Oh, my."

Charley drooped wearily. "The caller said the Committee was never called to order. Before the session began, Senator Poteet stumbled in, three sheets to the wind, and bellowed out his resignation."

"Drunk on the floor of the Senate?"

Charley shrugged his broad shoulders. "Yup. Gave no explanation, just said it would be better for the State of Alabama if he stepped down. And that was that--the end of an era."

"I am so sorry, Charley."

"I've already been approached by some of my Daddy's staunchest supporters." He confided. "They want me to serve out his term."

"Will you?"

"Whew! There's strong party sentiment for it. They don't want to see the Poteet name drug through the mud--more in deference to Granddaddy Frank than Jarrett. Besides, if I serve out Jarrett's term, it'll keep down the scandal and probably keep his big mouth shut. His cronies are scared to death he'll tell tales out of school, but he can't very well do it with me sitting in his seat."

"I see. Best for all involved."

Charley stretched his neck and rotated his shoulders. "Don't know about that. It's a major decision for my wife and me. I swore to her I'd never follow in my father's footsteps. No politics for me, but I do have a responsibility to my family. She'll have to respect that. I'll do it, but it'll cost 'em."

"How so?"

"Ever since they approached me, I've been hatching up a little scheme of my own. I want you to be the first to try it on for size."

"Okay. Shoot."

"Since you've been home, Lottie, have you noticed how dramatically this county has changed over the last ten years?"

"I've noticed."

"The demographics have shifted. A few wealthy families no longer dictate the economy or the politics."

"Yup."

"Our educational stats are lagging behind national norms. We're unable to attract high-tech jobs, and farming and lumber just can't drive the economic engines anymore. But the powers-that-be refuse to accept it."

"So what else is new?"

"We have the land; we have the infrastructure; we have the people. But despite all our natural resources, our economy has shrunk to the size of a pea. Why?" He hammered. "Because we lack the concerted political muscle to push for change. The rich and powerful aren't interested; they have their wealth to keep them warm. The ground swell for change has got to come from grass-roots people . . . your people."

"*Your people?*" Lottie blared. "So all this is about *my people* supporting your political ambitions?"

"No, Lottie. Simmer down." He backstroked. "I didn't mean anything by that, no matter how it sounded. I have the highest respect for black . . . African-American people. And maybe I don't know the politically correct way to say it, but y'all are in the majority in this senatorial district, and that can make all the difference when it comes time to vote."

"Keep talking." She gestured, encouraged by the sincerity in his piercing blue eyes.

"It's time to break the stranglehold of Good-Ole-Boy politics. In an effort to cut-off black folk, white folk around here have suffered, too. The rule of the heavy-fisted land baron and the white business establishment is over. It's time for consensus building to take full advantage of the strength of our diversity in this district--your district. What do you say?"

Lottie's excitement was growing in proportion to Charley's impassioned plea. "I think you're right," she said. "Getting black folk in this district to take their rightful stand could get you re-elected. Is that your idea?"

"No. Not quite," he said cunningly. "What I'm suggesting is that you come back home and run for my Daddy's senate seat when my term is up in two years."

"Do what?" She gaped.

"I'll serve out Jarrett's term, and when the next election rolls around I want you to be in line to claim the senatorial seat for this district. And know this, Lottie, I can make it happen."

"Whoa!" She choked dizzily. "Me? An Alabama state senator?"

"Yes, you. Why not you? You're a native daughter. You have the know-how, the spunk, and the commitment. Besides, you love these people and they love you and your family, and you're not carrying any political baggage. In my book, that's the total package for a change agent."

"Change agent? Me?"

"Sure. The old-line politicians won't go for it at first, but my job over the next two years at the Capitol will be to pave the way for your success. Believe me, they'll come around. They realize they've got to bend or be broken under the weight of the new democracy."

"But, why me? Why would you do this for me?"

"Because the folks in Dunston Quarter need you to bring them into the 21st Century; to break the cycle of poverty; to tear down the Good-Ole-Boy machine and take its choke-hold off our economy. There's never been a female or an African-American senator in our district in the history of Alabama, and its high time."

"But--"

Charley locked eyes with Lottie. "When we played together in the pecan orchard, didn't you say, 'What goes around comes around?' Well, the tables have turned, and my Daddy owes you this. Besides, I didn't help you in the barn that day, but I can certainly help you now. Won't you give me the chance?"

"But—"

"Don't give me your answer now. Think it over, and then say, Yes!"

Lottie was speechless. She had growing reservations about returning to New York. The closure of Wallace Community College, the talk of drug busts and drug buys, idle men in front of the Piggly Wiggly--not to mention the fatherless babies--had not escaped her notice.

As a girl, she'd been faced with limited options, too, but not with the sense of hopelessness that blanketed the area now. She'd been toying with the idea of staying home to help--help her mother, help her community, help herself. But never in a million years did she expect the offer to come from Charley Poteet!

Finally, she regained the ability to speak. "Charley, I am genuinely honored by your offer."

She glowed. "And at the moment, totally flabbergasted. But let's not close the door on this discussion, okay?"

"That's good enough for me." He grinned. "I'll drive you home."

▲▲▲▲

While Raymond shared a lunch of leftovers in Miss Charity's kitchen, he was overwhelmed with the urge to unburden himself. "I've been thinking about our little talk on the porch last night." He tested the waters. "You were right. I do need to change. I'm making plans to get my life in order--give up strong drink, get some counseling about my Daddy, and move on with my life—"

"Hmph." Miss Charity cleared her throat noisily. "Sounds real good, Raymond," she drawled, "but it ain't gonna work. We try all kind o' schemes to make things come out right, but try as we might we don't ever seem to get there. Some people try evil things--like chance, strong drink, lustful relations--to gloss over the pain. Other folk try good things--like charity work, hard work, even self-denial. But sooner or later, all these things fail, cause we have a tendency to revert right back to our old ways. Now, ain't that right?"

"But don't we have to keep trying?"

"Evil deeds. Good deeds. Round and round we go, like pinwheels in the breeze. And still, somehow, we keep coming up short. You wanna know why?" She glared. "Cause we can't save ourselves by ourselves, no matter how hard we try. That's why."

Raymond rolled his eyes to the ceiling. "I think this is where I came in last night."

"That might be so, Sugar, but looks like you need another dose to make it stick. Life ain't about gritting yo' teeth and making yo'self better. God ain't mad at us no more. He loves us. Jesus already settled that on the cross when He died for the sins of the whole world. And when Jesus rose from the grave, it proved God accepted His payment. We're forgiven, Raymond! All we have to do is accept it."

"So why do we keep messing up, Miss Charity?"

"Cause we keep looking at ourselves. Look up! Life ain't about fixing yo'self. Life is about pickin'!" She beamed brightly. "The way I sees it, the earth is one big pickin' ground. The Lord gives us just so much time, and just two crops to pick from." She balanced her hands side-by-side. "And this is them: Will I believe what God has said about His Son and pick Him and live? Or will I call God a bald-faced liar in

His own creation and pick my own deeds to save me and die? There ain't but two crops, and He let's us pick. He's too much of a gentleman to force His way in on us. Ask Adam and Eve."

Miss Charity didn't wait for Raymond's response. She struggled up from the table and made her way to the back yard to feed the dogs, leaving him alone to ponder his choice when the telephone rang.

Raymond snatched up the ringing telephone. "Miss Charity's residence."

"Hey, Raymond!" Lt. Thrush shouted over the cheering in the background. "Have you seen the latest news bulletin, Buddy? It's probably down there, too. It's on every channel!"

"Hold on." Raymond called out to the backyard. "Miss Charity! Where's your TV?"

"Hold your horses jest a minute, Baby." She answered as she climbed the back steps with some difficulty. "I'll get it for ya." She rolled in the black-and-white set on its wobbly stand from her bedroom.

"You see?" Thrush hounded. "You see?"

"Hold on," Raymond said, plugging it into the hall outlet. "I'm looking."

"John R. dropped out of the race!" Thrush exclaimed, too excited to wait. "You see it? You see? It's over!"

Raymond strained to see the picture on the 13-inch set. "What happened?"

"Clayburn called a press conference," Thrush jabbered in a steady stream over the background noise at the precinct. "Says his campaign has been 'irreparably tarnished,' and 'he's stepping down from seeking the Governor's office to spare the citizens of New York any further embarrassment.' What do you know? He's stepping down for the good of the people of New York." He spouted cantankerously. "Yeah, and I'm Little Bo Peep. Your man down there pulled out, too."

"Who?"

"You know." Thrush scolded. "That senator fellow, Jarrett Poteet. They're broadcasting both their pictures. They look like a pair of convicts on the lam."

"That's truer than you think," Raymond said. "I've figured out why Clayburn was so out of control. Why he didn't check with Bradley about the rape charge. Why he took matters into his own hands like some maniac."

"Why? Why?"

"Because as it turns out, Clayburn and Poteet raped at least one girl together while they were in college. I guess he thought Bradley was capable of the same thing."

"Wow-wee!" Thrush shouted over the noise. "Guilty consciences breed abominable acts," he said. "Got to go, now, but I called to tell you something you won't see on the news."

"What now?" Raymond soured.

"Jessup is dead."

"The chauffeur guy? Dead? How?"

"Sad to say." Thrush groaned. "Killed in his cell at Rikers in his sleep. Somebody stuck a homemade shive in his neck, and nobody knows who or how. He was under constant surveillance, but I suspect either John R., or the mob, or both, had something to do with Jessup's untimely demise. We're keeping it under wraps for 24 hours while we investigate."

"Man!" Raymond's mouth snapped shut.

"You remember me telling you how I never forget a face?" Thrush bragged. "Well, it bugged me I couldn't put my finger on where I'd seen Jessup before. I beat my brain until I remembered a guy who was hauled in here some years back on felonious assault charges. The eyewitness wouldn't I.D. him in the line up, so we had to spring him. His name was Big George." He chuckled lewdly. "Well, with the help of my crack assistant, the one with the legs, we played computer pin-the-tail-on-the-donkey, and guess what we came up with?" He crowed over the background noises. "Geoffrey Jessup is the alias of one, Big George Jamison. It's not widely known, but--"

"Big George is Nurse Jamison's brother."

"Bingo! You're a smart Boy, Raymond. You get a cigar!"

"Not really. It's just that nothing about this screwy case surprises me anymore."

"I don't know about that," Thrush said. Don't you find it ironic John R. comes up for arraignment on kidnapping and murder on Monday, one day before the election? And if that doesn't move you, I'll bet this one'll knock your socks off. Senator Poteet's been bankrolling John R.'s opponent in the election, Chad Dunlevy." He laughed loudly. "I guess that was his insurance policy to keep Clayburn from winning the election and *The Bet*. Looks like Dunlevy's going to win all the marbles."

"Go figure." Raymond rumbled. "Mary's candidate . . . our next governor."

"What's that?" Thrush hurried.

"Oh, nothing. I was just wondering what're the chances of Clayburn doing any serious time without Jessup's testimony?"

"Yeah. Jessup was the prosecution's ace in the hole."

"What a shame." Raymond sighed. "I'll lay you odds he gets off with a slap on the wrist. I'll bet he's got a good lawyer, too."

"The very best money can--"

"What's wrong?"

"Shush! I'm on the phone!" Thrush tried once again to quiet the revelers around him, but without much success. "Sorry, Raymond. This place is a veritable party zone since we busted Clayburn. I told you I was going to bring that Sleaze-Bag down, and I did it! It's put me and my precinct on the map," he yelled over the roar, "but I might have to take your money on that wager about John R. getting off. It might not be quite that easy. How do you think Joyce Jamison's going to react when she finds out what they did to her brother? Hmm?"

"Oh. I hadn't thought of that angle."

"She's up to her neck in this, but we promised Nurse Jamison immunity and a new identity under the Witness Protection Program for her testimony. We've got her stashed away under protective custody. She can put Clayburn away, and who's to say he'll fair any better than Jessup when he's behind bars?"

"Who's to say?"

Failing another attempt to restore order, Thrush surrendered. "I'll let you get back to watching the broadcast," he shrilled. "Ain't it a blast! You and Lottie can come home, now, just in time to vote for the candidate of your choice. Ain't democracy grand? It's all over, Buddy! See you when you get home!"

As Raymond and Miss Charity watched the newsbreak, Lottie squeaked through the front screen. Raymond sprang to his feet. "Have we got news for you!" he said. "Why didn't you call me to pick you up?"

"Charley brought me home." She admitted quietly, and Miss Charity raised her brow.

"Shush!" Raymond pointed, turning Lottie's attention to the latest news bulletin.

"It's over?" Lottie stared incredulously at the screen. "It's over! Wow!"

She and Raymond hugged and jumped round and round in the ritualistic dance reserved for men and boys. They slowed their victory jig just long enough to pull Miss Charity into the circle. "Let go of me, young'uns," she protested. "If y'all gonna keep this up, I've gotta go change my shoes."

"John R.'s going to get off, isn't he?" Lottie deduced soberly when Raymond recounted Thrush's story about Jessup's murder while Miss Charity was out of the room.

"I don't know, but--"

The discussion was cut short when Miss Charity returned, and he and Lottie flooded her with a blow-by-blow account of their ordeal, leaving out only the attack on Lottie's life and Jessup's murder. Momentarily, Raymond excused himself, and Miss Charity led Lottie to the front porch.

"I'm glad you and Mr. Charley are getting along so famously," she teased cagily. "Maybe, when the time is right, you can help me break another little piece of news to him. Something Ms. Madge told me when she called me this morning."

"Who?" Lottie frowned.

"Ms. Madge." Her mother repeated. "I met her back when she went to college with Jarrett and John R. They've got a long history, but that's not important now," she said. "What's important is that Charley's mamma was her best friend, and Ms. Madge say . . . Charley's mamma ain't dead after all. Jarrett's been lying to everybody all this time."

"What?" Lottie gasped. "Not dead? How could Senator Poteet hide a thing like that from his son for thirty years? What a cruel trick!"

"Ms. Madge say Jarrett got Charley's mamma pregnant, and Granddaddy Frank found out. Since the old man was trying to put a stop to

Jarrett's philandering ways, he made him marry the Gal. When he was a baby, Charley's mamma fell out of favor with Jarrett. Behind Mr. Frank's back, he ran her off to Europe and told everybody she died in an accident when they was away on vacation. Jarrett threatened to kill her if she ever set foot back here, and he's been paying her off ever since."

"This is just too much." Lottie gulped.

"Ms. Madge say Charley's mamma wants to come home. Maybe now, with Jarrett out o' power, she can."

"Poor Charley." Lottie lamented. "I wonder what this'll do to him? First his daddy, and now his mother."

"When the time is right, Chile, you should be the one to break the news. He may be able to bear it coming from you . . . and the fact of the matter is, I need to tell you some things, too--"

Raymond snapped on the porch light. "I have something to show you Garrett ladies," he said proudly. "Here, Miss Charity. Take a look at this. I picked it up in town today."

"Tee-hee-hee." She snickered gaily when she examined the contents of the envelope and passed it on to Lottie. "So you're gonna do it?"

"Yes, ma'am. I planned to see my Daddy after our visit on the porch last night," he said, "but after our talk today, I'm going to do it for all the right reasons. I've made my pick, Miss Charity, and it's the right one." He confessed happily. Your faith lighted my way." He embraced her tightly. "After all I've been forgiven, surely I can forgive my Daddy. I only hope he can forgive me, too."

"Don't worry, Son." Miss Charity rocked lightheartedly. "You're in God's family now. He'll make a way."

"I'm so happy for you, Raymond." Lottie bubbled. "When do you leave?"

"Lord willing, I'll be in Tucson with my Daddy by this time tomorrow," he said, "and on Tuesday I'll be voting at the polls in Manhattan.

"I'll meet you at the office on Tuesday." Lottie promised. "We need to talk about some choices I've made, too." She jumped onto her favorite step and called out the challenge of her enduring game, "I see something you don't see!"

"Whatever may it be?" Miss Charity and Raymond chimed in happily.

▲▲▲▲